CONTEN'

SIMEON

SARAH SEARIGHT

CLARET PRESS

ISBN paperback: 978-1-3999-8774-5
ISBN eBook: 978-1-3999-8775-2

Watercolour illustration by Judith Eagle
Interior Design by Petya Tsankova

www.claretpress.com

*“Dedicated to a much-loved and inspirational friend,
Judith Eagle”*

1.

PROLOGUE

The first time I visited Simeon Stylites on his pillar was in 1970, just when Hafez al-Assad had become President of Syria. The pillar – in northern Syria – was the centre piece of a magnificent basilica built around it soon after Simeon's death in 459. The site is known as Qalaat Simaan, hill of Simeon. For some 40 years this holy eccentric chained himself to the top of a high pillar beside a major East-West Road that crossed northern Syria between the worlds of the Mediterranean and the Orient. His shrine has subsequently been visited by passers-by from all over the region.

That link, that Road, explains so much of Syria's history. I travelled on it whenever I visited Simeon – the Jinn as he was known locally – and his shrine. That is set some thirty kilometres west of the great mercantile city of Aleppo. Much further to the west is city of Antioch – Antakya in today's Turkey. The Road was traversed by armies, merchants, churchmen, and pilgrims. A small patch of the ancient road still remains beside the modern road.

The pillar also came to symbolise for me the history of this tragic, beautiful country. My 'timetable' for this story starts in 1970, three years after the 1967 war in which the Arabs were roundly defeated by Israel and which led to Assad's rise to the Syrian presidency.

It is over fifty years since that first visit, years that have been marked by the chronic instability of the region in contrast with the immobility. I was fascinated by the immobility (and logistics!) of this man compared with the mobility of those who crowded to, past, by, near him, moving on that axial Road between East and West. In this fictional account I saw Simeon as a symbol of stability in the maelstrom of the Middle East. Many of his visitors were seeking comfort, consolation for the tragedies of their lives. Many also came to give thanks for happy moments.

I was fascinated by the locality of his pillar – where it stood beside a road passed by caravans, armies, tourists, above all pilgrims – Christian and Muslim – travelling through what? – the Middle East after all. Everyone now as then on the move.

Not forgetting in all this the anguish of Syria, much of the latest instalment taking place while I have been writing. Qalaat Simaan – Simeon's citadel, the hill on which he stood – used to symbolise for me the one point of stability in the turmoil of the Middle East.

But now? Where is Simeon now? Where is the Jinn?

2.

HOW IT ALL BEGAN

Syria has long been a favourite country of mine, despite so many visits being triggered by its bloodthirsty upheavals. It is the most beautiful country, its beauty enhanced by an almost spiritual quality. Yet it's also so tragic. As a novice journalist based in Beirut, I was occasionally ordered to Syria when all others had been forbidden entry; later, as a bit of a specialist in the Middle East, I've been back regularly.

The compensations have been countless. The Syrians themselves for one (despite the often-horrendous bloodletting). Archaeologists digging ever deeper into its bowels – temples, palaces, roads, churches, castles, mosques. Sumerians, Assyrians, Greek, Roman, Arab, Mongol armies, each deposited their cultures.

And cities – Hama with its creaking water wheels, destroyed in 1982 by Hafiz al-Assad, Homs destroyed by the son in 2012. And now, under that glassy cock-eyed Bashar, now Aleppo, destroyed even more devastatingly than Hama and Homs. Handsome Aleppo, once the commercial heart of the country, populated by a diverse population that for me reflected the true diversity of the Middle East. Where are my beloved friends, the hosts with whom I so often stayed?

I am in love with this savage country. And in particular with one man, the most eccentric of all, one whose spirit inspired the crowds that trooped across the centuries to where he stood on his pillar for forty years: Simeon Stylites. I have been *magnetised* by Simeon Stylites. The stability of his rock, base of his pillar. Rock of ages, that's what he was, in this country of crumbling rocks. No wonder the magnificent church built after his death around his pillar has attracted generations of the curious, admirers, and above all, supplicants.

I first met Simeon at the end of a flowery spring excursion from Aleppo in 1970. I had been in Damascus as a budding reporter to cover the latest Syrian upheaval and the rise to power of the thirty-one year-old soldier and politician, Hafiz al-Assad. Tribalism and heterodoxy, which are so often at the heart of the battle in Syria, were evident in the most recent upheaval: the loss of the Golan heights to Israel.

This moment was just after Hafiz al-Assad, a powerful air force pilot, had become President. Assad was born in 1930 in the small village of Qurdaha in the mountains above Lattakia in north-west Syria. These mountains are the core of the Alawi community, a heterodox offshoot of Shia Islam that seems to have emerged in this area around the thirteenth century, possibly having originated in northern Iran. Islam is not as monolithic as mainstream Sunnis would like and the Alawis have retained their religious refuge despite divergencies. Tribal affiliations are still strong despite pressure from Damascus to conform to modern ideas of citizenship. Assad spent his early years in the heart of these Alawi mountains. For his first schooling he walked down the hill to Lattakia on the coast, then duly graduated to the air force academy. The steep climb to presidency had been accelerated by the 'Six days' walkover,' as Seale described the 1967 war with Israel. Egyptian and Jordanian forces had already been decimated in the opening stages of that war, as had the Syrian air force.

I wasn't even sure on that first Syrian visit that I would get to Aleppo what with all the political changes being carried out at Assad's command, mostly installing his fellow Alawis in positions of power in both government and military. I decided I needed a break and took a service taxi from Damascus to Aleppo. The road was packed with anxious Syrians aiming for home after all the upheavals, inevitably endless nerve-wracking holdups on the road although good practice for my fledgling Arabic. Aleppo was the timeless merchant city between east and west and, war or no war, the bazaar was stuffed with produce from furthest east and furthest west.

In Aleppo I made my way to that landmark hostelry Baron's Hotel, established by Armenians at the end of the nineteenth century. *Not* refugee Armenians, the owners stressed, but attracted by the commercial potential of a city about to be drawn into a wider world by the development of railways. Baron's had seen better days, but I revelled in its sagging armchairs, its dusty dining room and even the noisy, fluctuating plumbing of its bathrooms. I had a warm welcome from the porter (ancient) and a smile from a young woman with babe in arms who took me up in the most veteran of lifts to a room overlooking the main street. Not Mrs Mallowan (alias Agatha Christie), I was assured, nor D.E. Lawrence's, nor this or that statesman. 'Not to worry,' I reassured my guide, 'as long as it has a bed.'

Today, so I'm told, it's dustier than ever: holes in the roof, windows blown in; though it is in the relatively safe western part of the city, nothing was unscathed.

Baron's was owned and run by generations of the Mazloumian family. Amazingly one member of the family married into that utterly English family celebrated in Arthur Ransom's Lake District fantasy, *We didn't mean to go to sea*. And it was elderly Armand Mazloumian ('I'm too old to care what happens to me, and I love my hotel'; he died there in 2016) who directed me one Friday that spring in 1970 to the site of Simeon's pillar north-west of Aleppo.

'Not difficult to get to,' he said over breakfast, 'and use the bus – takes its time but gives you the chance to see something of the countryside. Stay as long as you can. One of the locals might put you up. A very strange person that Simeon must have been – sat up a twelve-metre pillar for around thirty years. But handsome church they built later round the pillar. Finest in Syria. Raised him above all the religious and political mayhem of this country.'

I was easily persuaded.

'And look out for my old friend Ibrahim al-Mazrui,' he added. 'One of Aleppo's top merchants, used to have major operation in the *suq* but now spends most of his time on his property near Qalaat Simaan. Give him my greetings if you see him.' I promised to do so.

I found the bus station and the bus, as ancient as they come, packed top to bottom with families laden with picnics. 'Plenty coming back in the evening,' I was assured, leaving me free to spend as much or as little time as I liked. I equipped myself from stalls at the bus station – falafel (delicious deep-fried balls of mashed beans) and fruit

– fresh oranges! – and in due course we rumbled out and across the plain from Aleppo. 'Bi ism Allah,' everyone muttered just as Spaniards cross themselves at the start of a journey, 'in the name of God'. A useful precaution.

I was familiar with stories of early Christian ascetics, mainly the 'desert fathers' who lived as hermits in the Egyptian desert. It was a time that took the extreme of ascetism, such as self-discipline, denial and contemplation of the holy, however eccentric, as integral to the establishment of Christianity. It gave the fledgling faith a gravitas, a visible proof that it took itself seriously.

I had already visited some of the monasteries near Damascus that had been developed by their imitators as well as by pilgrims. But I had never had time to explore the famous 'Dead Cities' of northern Syria, let alone the site where Simeon had stood on his pillar. This consisted of the hilltop with its great basilica known as Qalaat Simaan, Simeon's fortress, built in the fifth century round his pillar, and the area below known as Deir Simaan, monastery of Simeon, because of the ruins of monasteries, hostels, chapels that had accommodated the thousands who flocked to him out of misery, curiosity, devotion – who knows?

Just as colleagues talked endlessly about the religious and political crossroads when trying to explain Syria's turbulent present, so Simeon perched himself beside a real crossroads. Thoroughly unorthodox, some would say of Simeon now, when heterodoxy can be such a death knell. Why would anyone in their right mind want to sit, stand, lie – whatever – on a twelve-meter-high pillar for forty years: about a quarter the height of the column they stuck poor Nelson on. Right mind? Who knows. How did he do it, let alone why? What did he eat? What happened to the crap? (That's what they all ask, when they hear of my eccentric quest.) And what about the audience? Simeon was no recluse. No hermit he, but ascetic yes.

These were the sort of queries I relished after weeks of the body politic. I am not much of a Christian myself but neither am I an atheist, and working in foreign parts I have always been intrigued by other peoples' gods, out of envy, I suspect.

Simeon lived in a time of conflict too. It seemed to me, anyone who had lived in Syria at any time lived in a period of conflict. Greeks, Persians, Romans, Arabs, Turks, finally French – not much peace and quiet in his time, nor did he ultimately seek it. In Simeon's day Christian orthodoxy (what orthodoxy?) was bitterly contested, striving to establish an official faith – hence my fascination.

Some thirty miles west of Aleppo, on the main east-west road, he ordered a pillar. Not for him the desert solitudes favoured by Egyptian ascetics, nor indeed by many so-called stylites who subsequently emulated his lifestyle. Up he went on his pillar, practised all sorts of self-torments, revered by all and sundry, exerting influence even on emperors and bishops. Huge crowds gathered at the foot.

It was no coincidence that Simeon triggered my imagination when Syria was once again the battlefield between orthodoxy – this time Islamic militants facing the heterodox, the Islamic sect of Alawis to which the Assad clan and their henchmen belonged. Most of the members of his inner circle belonged to this small sect with vaguely Messianic tendencies, delimited by tribalism within the mountainous backbone of the country, a sect that orthodox Muslims detested as heretical. Who's orthodox, I ask?

A grim reflection: the passage of warriors through Syria, shedding blood, the slaughtered outnumbering the blood-red poppies on the springing hillside. Too many tyrants, too many faiths.

Syrians certainly need religion, whether facing up to living forces or to that unbeatable foe, death. And they need their local gods too, not just a distant Mecca or Jerusalem. You have only to see the crowds round Muslim saints' tombs in Damascus and elsewhere throughout the Middle East. Muslims, like Christians, need intercessors between God and them. God is too terrifying to contemplate directly. Everyone needs saints.

The landscape of northern Syria is moody, as I discovered bumping out of Aleppo that spring morning, as changeable as its history. One moment you are in a gentle valley, gradual green slopes either side of the road, flowery verges, springing crops, blossoming orchards of apricots, olives, almonds. The benign beauty of spring in Syria. Only round the corner and it's an angry limestone desert, grey slabs interspersed with craggy lumps like the face of an old man, alleviated from time to time by a glorious clump of poppies. North and west the road headed towards Turkey. The bus drove slowly, grinding up little hills, twisting across the track, still paved with massive slabs of stone, of a Roman road. The driver even paused to point it out: 'They knew how to build roads then,' was his surly comment as he waved a hand in its direction. Along the way the land is dotted with gaunt ruins of churches, houses, public buildings that once rang with hundreds of busy farming communities, the churches ringing with healthy Christian voices – Syrian voices I should say. According to Warwick Ball the remains of some 1,200 churches have been noted.

Certainly, in the fourth to sixth centuries this was a prosperous well-populated region, decimated over the subsequent centuries by invasion or tribal warfare. In the wayside villages where we stopped for yet more passengers, I glimpsed sturdily built stone houses with ancient and modern stones jumbled together in their walls. The houses were like history books. Scattered among them were small stone buildings roofed with pyramids of thatch. I shall never forget one particular treat of that ride. The man recently appointed president of Syria, Hafiz al-Assad, was due to progress over part of the route I was travelling, presumably to bolster the party's power with local demonstrations of loyalty. We had reached a village (Tel Aqibrin) where the villagers, maybe hoping for fleeting benevolence or – more likely – playing safe, had erected outside their settlement a triumphal arch with a picture of the new president suspended beneath it, another longstanding tradition dating back at least to Roman times. Under the picture they had laid – and this was the treat – a thick-piled carpet of local herbs: thyme, marjoram, mint, maybe others. These were crushed by the wheels of the bus as it entered the village, releasing a heavenly aroma that I can still recall today. I hoped there was enough left for whichever grandee was supposed to come that way. I was interested to note that the arch had been erected just beside what looked like a stretch of ancient road; I resolved to stop by it on my way back. You can see the ruins of the great church built round Simeon's pillar from quite a distance, crowning the summit of a hill. Nearing the foot of the hill, on the other side of the road from what had all too clearly become a car park, is Deir Simaan; I noted substantial remains of what might once have been a thriving hospitality business for the locals (maybe for me later), as well as a more recent village of the domed houses of today's inhabitants. So great were the crowds who were drawn to this spot by Simeon's reputation, both during his lifetime and after, that a whole town developed on this spot, below the hill on which Simeon had erected his pillar: hostels, churches, monasteries and, no doubt, resting places of lesser repute. And on the rich pasture just beyond the village a picturesque group of black tents – I was not the only nomad. They represented an unexpected continuity, so it seemed, with a past marked by people on the move. The driver offloaded his cargo of picnickers at the foot of the hill. *Have a good day* I shouted after him as he sputtered off. I followed the crowd along a track up the side of the hill; a handsome stone arch marks the start of the pilgrim way, trod by thousands both in Simeon's lifetime and after. Stones littered the hillside, on either side of the track, coatings of lichen blotting out the past. A corbel here, a gable there, keystones, cornerstones, foundation stones, half buried in the scrub of acanthus, oak and pine. All the way stall-holders were tempting us with sweetmeats and falafel, popcorn and balloons. And when I reached the summit a few minutes later there they all were, today's pilgrims, families and all, carpeting a wide expanse of grass between the various groups of ruins. Escaping from the politics of the day. No doubt they too had crushed the carpet of herbs laid out for the President. Muslim, Christian – all revering this symbol of God-worshipping eccentricity.

There were two main groups of ruins. The larger was the magnificent basilica, erected one supposed around the pillar. At the other end of the plateau were the remains of a little baptistery. On this particular day the space between the two buildings was entirely carpeted with picnicking families. Garish rugs covered the ground; it was difficult to walk between them. I was not the only one escaping the tensions of Aleppo. Large women were presiding over huge hampers of food. Some families had small stoves and were grilling – oh, that mouth-watering smell. Men were standing around with glasses of arak, that sweet Pernod-style alcohol made from almost any vegetable matter, most often dates, getting merrier by the minute. Boys were kicking the inevitable football to the rage of their mothers; little girls were skipping. Was it thus in Simeon's day, or indeed post Simeon? The basilica was clearly built for a multitude of pilgrims, surely not all of them victims of misfortune.

I saw myself on that sunny day as one of the happy ones, like the picnickers, and of course I was immediately summoned to join in. Arab women can have a way of welcoming the stranger – especially a lone woman – that is far less wary than their western sisters: half flirtatiously they held out hands to shake the stranger on that spring day and in no time at all I was being passed from rug to rug, arak pressed into one hand (one sip goes a long way), kebabs of chicken or mutton into the other, the children flocking round with their tedious but friendly litany of 'what's-your-name?', 'where-are-you-from?', 'how-old-are-you?' yelled at the top of their voices. Overall a sense of bonhomie that is such a feature of Arab hospitality.

The summit had clearly been flattened to accommodate the buildings as well as worshippers in Simeon's day – church, baptistery, monastery, all built in the sixth century after Simeon's death in 459. The basilica, so-called because of its wide, single aisle established by the pre-Christian Roman need for a place of secular assembly, was large enough to accommodate a vast crowd of pilgrims. It stands at the northern end of the hilltop, much ruined nowadays but the entrance still stands, a magnificent triple archway through which to glimpse the rest.

An American visitor to the site wrote in 1900 that the church was the most important and beautiful existing monument of architecture of that period in Syria. It was commissioned in 477, nearly twenty years after Simeon's death, by the Emperor Zeno, who had just returned to the imperial throne from a year's deposition and saw its construction as a gesture of legitimacy. Even in its ruined old age – roof gone (was there ever a roof over the pillar?), walls collapsed, that pillar now chipped to a gigantic ball by seekers of souvenirs – the church was an impressive size. The colossal scale, the lavish decoration signalled an imperial desire to shelter as demonstratively as possible a saint whose secular advice, to emperors no less, had been as admired as his holy homilies.

The church was built as a Greek cross, the four great arms meeting at a magnificent octagon, itself centred on the holy Simeon's pillar. Each of the four arms was roofed but the huge central octagon must have remained appropriately open to the sky, Simeon's pillar had been in the middle, soaring to the heavens. The building was justifiably famous throughout Syria and further afield;

no other church could rival its size nor its splendour. A massive arch, lavishly decorated with the windswept acanthus, marked the entrance to the building. A vulture awaiting the picnic left-overs perched on top looked every bit as scraggy as Simeon must have looked. It gazed hungrily at the children with their half-eaten buns then decided to flap laboriously away, heading off over the distant valley.

Follow the southern arm of the Greek cross you come to the vast octagon that centres on the pillar. To your left, to the west, that arm of the cross is built out away from the hillside on a dramatic series of arcades, invisible from above of course; you have to clamber down to see the true scale of the building. The western wall has crumbled away, leaving the view unimpeded, the direction the vulture flew, across green fields and the silver streak of a river to the faded blue hills leading to Antakya. To the east monks shifted from saint to that most ancient of symbols, the sun, and insisted on gathering in the eastern arm of the cross, their congregations of frightened villagers, calling for holy protection as invader followed invader: 'O Lord make speed to save us, O Lord make haste to help us!' Below that southern wall are the remains of monastic buildings that housed the deacons and archdeacons who held the services, nursed the sick, kept intruders from climbing up to Simeon, baptised the heathen. Filled with ghosts from ages past.

Then in the middle of the sanctuary of the basilica is a massive lump of rock, set on a wide shallow plinth. This is revered as the remains of Simeon's pillar, which is estimated to have been about twelve metres high. It sits in what would have been centre of the plinth, the sanctuary of the church. The 'lump' is much reduced by generations of chipping, nevertheless is still much revered. Many were around it that day – men, women, children kissing it, praying to it – no mullahs to get in their way. I joined them, slowly circling it amidst a gaggle of children imitating their elders who were stroking the huge boulder. Small boys were trying to lift each other on top of the rock. One had triumphed and was waving a diminutive arm, clearly trying with a penknife to hack off a bit of the rock as no doubt generations of predecessors had also done. A mother was angrily ordering him to 'get down!' A man came to her rescue and dragged the child off, to the cheers of his playmates.

I propped myself against a bit of wall in the western arm of the sanctuary to contemplate Simeon atop his pillar. It was difficult to imagine this as the remnant of a pillar. How had 'they' raised it? Who tended to his needs? What about the lifestyle of the saint: how, what he ate, how he defecated, slept, who kept an eye on him? Knew when he was dead. Etc etc. And then what had happened over the centuries since? Present-day political upheavals were maybe as nothing compared with the invading hordes that must have swept past: Romans, Persians – I tried to recall the history books – Arabs, Crusaders (did they get this far east?), Mongols, Turks and then the French in World Wars I and II. Had anyone spotted the ghost of this eccentric pillar squatter? I'd rather like to meet the ghost.

Sitting against my bit of wall I looked out of the sanctuary eastwards to the expanse of ruins below, the remains of monasteries, chapels and hostels built to accommodate passing pilgrims. Who were they, I wondered. I let imagination wander (crucial to any sort of understanding of this extraordinary ascetic), seeing them occupied maybe by Simeon's attendants (he must surely have had them) or the builder of this magnificent basilica or by later generations of worshippers. Or by the generations of invaders – newly Islamised Arabs en route for Byzantium, Frankish Crusaders, their conqueror Saladin (alias Salah al-Din), then Mongols battling those slave warriors, the Mamluks, who were led by the extraordinary Baybars. He began life in the steppes north of the Black Sea, was sold again and again (unpopular because of a cast in an eye) and was the most supreme horseman of a people notable for its horsemanship, the Turks. And finally the French.

What a succession of potential pillagers but also respectful of the man on the hill above whose ghost still haunted the basilica. It was the sort of moment when the imagination takes over from history. As Simeon and his pillar did for me that day.

From the western sanctuary I spotted a path and scrambled down a few yards. I could see it led under the building. I supposed it a good shelter for shepherds and their flocks. No doubt over the centuries locals might have made it a useful shelter from marauders and those invading armies I'd contemplated from above.

At the southern end of the plateau, some two hundred metres away, was a much smaller building – at one time a baptistery. Baptism in early Christianity was an elaborate dunking affair, involving total immersion and therefore a free-standing building encircling a pool of some sort, which must have been fed by streams from further up the hill.

I was accosted as I strolled along what I liked to think was the equivalent of an aisle, that large open place where I was greeted from all sides by picnicking families: 'Come on! Come on! Have some falafel, some cake, a sandwich! Here – some *qamr al-din* ('apricot slab' as foreigners called it: stewed fruit spread out in slabs to dry in the sun).' Impossible to resist. Loaded with all manner of delicacies I made my way to the baptistery where children were jumping in and out of the empty pool – no water nowadays but maybe it was sometimes filled by spring rains. Little did they realise the dunking they would have suffered in Simeon's day.

I watched for a while then wandered a little way down the hill and sat down under an olive tree to eat the delicacies pushed into my receptive hands. I could see Qalaat Simaan as meeting the needs in earlier crises in Syria's history – invasions by aliens from south, east, west and north – the need for an intercessor with an Almighty who all too often seemed more cruel than kind. How did this scraggy seer (I had developed a clear picture of him, coming along in the bus), help them? Rather pleased with himself, I reckoned, but what did his chosen lifestyle do for them? Fantasising about him was a pleasant release from contemporary politics, just as visiting him in the fifth century must have been a welcome refuge from contemporary torments. Anyway I was free to fantasise for a day. I lay back, later, in that bed of thyme beside the great monument, stones still warm from the midday heat, larks overhead, doves in love on the architraves, a buzzard screaming high in the heavens. A hoopoe swooped between the pillars. Who had brought the pillar down? Who? Whoo, whoo, cooed the pigeon on the battered architrave.

The drive had been long and I was tired. Why not spend a couple of days in these hills, hence the relaxation in the bed of thyme? The place, the breeze sighing in the pines like waves on a distant seashore, the aromatic herbs cajoled my imagination. Simeon is said to have lived from around 390 to 459 AD. Plenty of the weary and dispossessed of the Roman Empire, mainly from the west fleeing from a mixture of Goths, Vandals, Huns, from the high and mighty to the very low, from orthodox to heretic. Then there were the pilgrims, thousands of them over the centuries, helping to fund these buildings, then keeping them intact. Later came Muslim warriors, perhaps the forefathers of the owners of the black tents out there on the plain, nomadic herdsmen passing to and fro across these rich pastures to establish their creed, their orthodoxy. Crusaders: I envisaged a rendezvous between some dastardly Frank and Saladin himself. At dead of night perhaps? Avoiding an assassin's knife? Other warriors of course, sons of Genghiz Khan, perhaps Tamberlane himself, Ottoman Turks. And finally Europa, represented by commerce, antiquarianism (picking up stones hither and yon to dot a northern landscape), literary and artistic fashions (imagine Byron's Childe Harold gazing up at the column. Or indeed the mournful Tennyson). Politics: I came back to the politics of empire. What a panorama.

I must have dozed, at peace with the world, banishing its upheavals, for I never saw or heard the approach of the scraggy old man who was suddenly stooping over me. Rather to my annoyance (he reeked to high heaven) he squatted down beside me, a hoopoe on his shoulder (wisest of birds, spiritual leader of all other birds and chief adviser to Solomon). His head was wrapped in an old rag and indeed rags clothed the rest of him – barely. He was filthy, like a goat that had been caught for days in a briar thicket; stank of wine, goat dung, even sweat, though I cannot conceive now how so desiccated a creature could manage to sweat. The smell is in my nostrils now. He looked and smelled as if he belonged to the place. His feet were horny, looked like the rocks around. I greeted him and got a sort of growled response. We sat in silence for a while. Then he stood up, looked me up and down and offered me his hand as if to pull me to my feet. I spurned the hand but rose, recognising that he expected me to follow him. He growled in a nutter-mutter voice as if giving me a guided tour; perhaps he is the guide, I thought. He had a sort of skipping gait despite legs bowed with age, nimble compared with my awkward ill-shod stumble, but would stop from time to time and stand still, raising withered arms to the sky. I felt myself spell-bound, literally. But oh the stink.

My mountain, my ruins, where I once lorded it over them all. (Could I really understand a word he was saying? yet I seemed to think I did.) '*Up there,*' – he pointed heavenward – '*for forty years! Thanks be to God!*' He shook his head from side to side. '*I know it well, I've had the run of the place long enough. Run? Don't go away, wait a minute, wait.*' He turned and seemed to be pleading. '*I whisper to visitors: have you come far? They don't hear, they aren't listening yet. Grey-brown like the hills, between the stones. Plants in every cranny; the goats like them, tug them out. Yes, it blends well with God's handiwork, this handiwork of man, where once it attracted attention for miles around.*' He spoke in a kind of croak, as one might after addressing multitudes. I'd heard the same dryness of throat in a hundred demagogues. '*Some came to build, others to destroy, some to worship, others to desecrate.*' He cackled. '*One army thought they would erect a temple for their own god inside mine. I soon made them change their minds. Some were offended by the pillar, tried to destroy it, thought they could suffocate the spirit. Fools! Faith's in hearts not stones.*' Was I putting words into his foul-smelling mouth? He frisked away from me, then picked a stem of budding thistle and rubbed his face in it. He grabbed another stem, leaned over and bit off the head with seemingly toothless gums, continuing to giggle as he masticated. '*I reached the Almighty through pain, found him and now no pain.*' And he sort of gambolled into a clump of the stuff like a child showing off. He beckoned – I had no intention of following but I did – and he led me back towards the church. '*Listen,*' he pleaded in a high singsong chant, '*how the wind whistles its song of desolation, tosses that thorn bush against the walls, laughs as it skims the hillside. Come over here, croaks a carrion crow. I know those crows, a pair of them used to tease me year in year out. Demons! Get off! I shouted at them. But they only laughed, souls of my desecrators. Through these arches came men from India, men from Persia and Mesopotamia, men from Constantinople and Rome. Not women. Not them. Keep them out! Out! They arouse men's eager lusts, yes even mine – you wouldn't believe it, would you, this shrivelled cock! Oh he was the devil. Look! I spent my life fighting them off, they were my pain, so how can ordinary mortals expect anything but defeat? Women! Keep your distance! Mind you, there was plenty to keep them busy. Best brothels in Syria down at Telnessin, they used to say.*' I could almost believe it. '*Note the nave, once covered with great timbers from mountain forests. They tried roofing the pillar.*

That made me laugh. Why bother, I shouted at them from the top of the walls, why shut me in after all these years? I haunted the architect, breathed down his back as he and the masons drew and re-drew the problem as they saw it. Until one day the architect saw me, yes he finally saw me and listened, chucked out the drawings, sang out loud. No roof! he sang to the masons. Who needs a roof?

As for the column, the nub of the matter.' The scraggy creature had led me back into the sanctuary. Squatting down beside the remaining rock, he ran his hand over it. *'This great stone was its base and this carpet of rocks'* – he gestured around – *'its crumbled height. Eight men on each other's shoulders and the top one might just have had a chat. Quite a circus act and firmly discouraged; approach strictly controlled and only by way of a ladder. Jacob hated that ladder. Army after army pulled the pillar to earth, stone by stone. I ran away, hid in the acanthus.'*

He picked at the stones with a horny nail. *'That's what the pilgrims used to cry up to me. "Speak to us, holy father," they used to wail. "Speak to us that we may live. Men say you know the path. Show us the way, holy one!"'* He had his arm round my shoulder, his foul breath on my cheek. *'Hush,'* he whispered, *'can you hear, can you see? Feel that breath on your cheek? How it sighs in the pines? See the wisp of sun dancing on the stone leaf? Hear their sighs over the hillside? Come closer'* – he was almost hugging me – *'I'll sing you a song, a song of great holiness, of a spirit broke free: I'll sing you a song, you can hear it in the wind, oh, a difficult song, of a difficult path.'* Suddenly he broke away. *'Go! The dying sun's calling. Watch out for thistles and thorns. I revel in the agony, roll myself in them every night. But you, my friend, take care.'* He seemed almost to dance off, then came to rest on an upturned capital; I stood beside him. *'Ha! On a column? Thirty years? No sleep? Two thousand prostrations a day! You don't believe me? A myth inscribed by the centuries. No one could or would. Could you? More to the point: would you?'* He snapped at me; I had to jerk myself to answer. 'Most certainly not,' I said, my voice sounding as hoarse as his. And then he broke into song, a surprisingly strong voice. *'Tell me, O thou whom my soul loveth, where thou feedest, where thou makest thy flock to rest at night?'*

And away he skipped, singing as he went. *'The voice of my beloved! Behold he comes, leaping upon the mountains, skipping upon the hills!'* Then he was gone, like the past, leaving me feeling strange-ly alone in the present. The arrogant old ghost. *Aywah! Aywah!* He croaked as he disappeared amongst the whispering jungle of acanthus.

Hurrah for dreams. Where indeed would I rest?

The day was beginning to fade; the picnickers were heading home, leaving their debris behind. The phantom had abandoned me amongst the stones. I decided to come back for a longer look next day and meanwhile see if someone in the village could provide a bed. Slowly I started back along the great south aisle, past the baptistery and down a rough patch to the 'propylaeum' ceremonial path up which the pilgrims would have clambered, hoping – alternatively to the village – to find a lift back to Aleppo. Maybe even old Mazloumian's friend could help. The sky was filled with whistling swifts, swooping over the evening's feast as I reached the track down. At the bottom of the hill a man stood up from a stone wall and waved at me. Rather better dressed than the one I had just been with up the hill, he wore the local baggy black pants and a black-and-white chequered scarf round his neck. A couple of salukis, the slim hunting dogs of the desert world, sat alert at his feet, one of them rising to sniff me over. 'Welcome,' he said, rising from a rock and extending a hand. 'Ahlan wa sahlan! I saw you coming down the hill, too late in the day to return to Aleppo. My friend Mr Mazloumian sent me a message. You need to eat and sleep. Please come to my home. My name is Ibrahim al-Mazrui.'

The salukis stared at me with suspicion. One

growled, its ears laid back. 'She's just had pups,' their owner explained and cuffed her gently over the nose. 'Follow me', which I most gratefully did. 'I think you have met the Jinn?' I wasn't quite sure what to answer so gave a polite shrug. 'He likes strangers,' added my new friend who luckily seemed solid enough. He became a very dear friend. A crowd of dishevelled children emerged from the stone-walled compound towards which Ibrahim led me. 'Welcome! I am Ibrahim.' He spoke excellent English. He led me firmly by the elbow to a battered steel door. 'My children! Mahmud, Ali, Salih' and he paused to put his other arm round a small girl, 'Sabrina, my princess, the most beautiful! Come all of you and meet – what is your name, my friend?'

I told him, and each one of them came up and very nervously shook my hand. As the little girl led me through the door I noticed some fine well-dressed stones in the wall, no doubt the residue of a useful hostelry in Simeon's day. The tallest struggled to open the door and we all entered. A large courtyard, scraggy goats in one corner, better looking sheep in another. I could hear women's voices inside the house. 'My wife is inside with her friends. You will meet them.' Ibrahim led me to a wall of the house and pointed to a shallow cross carved into a stone. 'Christians were here,' he said almost proudly. 'Now all Muslim.'

He shouted to a small boy. 'Please. My home is your home.' Mahmud reappeared with a sloshing bucket of water and his father directed me to a cubicle on the far side of the courtyard. 'Please refresh yourself as you like', and I followed the boy to the curtained area. Thankfully I splashed all over, the water clearing my head of my mysterious hillside traverse. I came out to find Mahmud nervously holding a tray of tea and his father demonstrating to a most promising pile of cushions against a wall of the house where I collapsed without demur. My host rose to his feet. 'Now I must wash and pray. Otherwise the Jinn will be after me!' It was spring chilly. One of the children brought me a finely embroidered shawl. The evening closed in. I speculated about Simeon, cold on his pillar. Ibrahim reappeared well-shawled himself.

'You are interested in Saint Simeon?'

'Saint?' I queried. 'You call him a saint?'

Ibrahim smiled. 'Oh yes, everyone knows him as a saint. He has guarded us for hundreds of years. Muslims and Christians though not many Christians in these parts today.' He shrugged and grinned. 'He brings good business.' Mahmud poured us small cups of sweet tea (how I relish that sweet tea of the eastern world).

We talked about his world here and in Aleppo, the state of his flocks, his hunting with his salukis (an English friend of mine had made a special study of this breed of hound), the state of the spring weather and, briefly, current politics. ‘Today it is difficult for me to make the hajj,’ he said at one point. ‘Either too expensive. Or too dangerous. The government says it will help. But what government? These Alawis are not interested in hajj.’ I sympathised. This offshoot of Shia Islam was regarded as dangerously heretical by orthodox Sunnis, though I suspect Hafiz al-Assad has long since shrugged off his adherence and paid his respects to the Kaaba, the sacred stone at the heart of the pilgrimage. ‘I do not like these people – pretending to be Muslims. They drink alcohol in the precincts of the church. They have no mosques in their villages.’

‘Do they go to Mecca?’ I asked.

‘They do,’ he frowned, ‘but they should be kept away.’ We sipped in silence. Then he asked, ‘How is Aleppo now?’

I shrugged. ‘Not happy.’

‘My brother is there, tells me the market is shut much of the time. But Aleppo is like that. The shutters rattle down but up as well. We have survived many upheavals.’

I hoped he was right. ‘Tell me,’ I asked, ‘what do you make of the old ghost, the Jinn as you call him?’

He smiled. ‘The locals make a lot of money

out of him, much as they always have. I'll walk you round the village in the morning, you'll see how useful he's been. New gates, new roofs, cars. All thanks to the Jinn, so they say. It must have been the same in his day – visitors, all types, from every direction. This was once on a major route between east and west, after all.'

'Plenty making money today,' I commented. 'Souvenir-sellers all the way up the hill.'

'Just so. And we surely need all the help we can get in these difficult days. If the old Jinn can help, I'm all for it. The satisfied to give thanks, the needy to call for help – they've been coming for hundreds of years – my forebears from Arabia for instance ...' he tailed off leaving me briefly with thoughts of generations of conquerors, invaders, even down to the last lot, the French. The boy Mahmud appeared beneath a huge tray which his father helped him put on the ground in front of us. 'Eat!' he ordered. 'The Jinn will have made you hungry.' And I was happy to obey. Ibrahim's wife came and sat beside me as if to accept my presence as both woman and man within the family. After we had eaten she took my hand and gently pulled me to my feet. 'Come,' she said. 'You will sleep with me.'

Next morning Ibrahim led me among the lanes between the well-built stone houses, children playing hopscotch, boys kicking footballs.

'Many visitors stayed here and still do,' he explained as we walked. 'Praying to the holy Simeon – I suppose it helps. Like you they need and needed places to stay. Not always in monasteries though there were one or two of them. Some visitors liked their comforts I think.' A bell clanged from somewhere in the village and the children slowly, reluctantly drifted towards the sound, presumably a school. Sabrina ran up, shook her father's hand and followed the crowd. Goats wandered on the scrounge, a flock of skinny sheep led by a skinny child. A smell of cooking drifted out from the walls. We came across the remains of a more substantial building, rooms now unroofed, arranged around a sort of hardened mud courtyard – could this have been a monastery? Opposite another small building had a mini minaret – the village mosque; it looked new. 'Built last year,' commented my guide. 'From the proceeds of the Jinn.' I had heard the call to prayer before dawn as well as the previous evening. Ancient stones had been used in the walls of the mosque as in the village houses – I could see them in the walls we wandered past. I glimpsed one with a well-worn cross carved into it in the wall of the little mosque, similar to that in Ibrahim's courtyard. 'God is one to all men,' said Ibrahim piously. And how about the Alawis? I wanted to ask but decided against.

Christianity has had its ups and downs in Syria but on the whole survived amongst the moderate Islam of most of the population. Bearing in mind also the ups and downs generally of the monastic appeal: periodically standards of austerity doubtless wavered as they did all over Europe. 'Let us eat meat', I hear a ghostly voice complain. 'Let's invite the nuns,' calls another. We should all go to Jerusalem, says one. Antioch's pleasures entice, calls another. Poor harvests, marauding soldiery, plague, not enough hands for maintenance – all these were challenges to the monastic life and over the centuries contributed to the sad desolation of the so-called Dead Cities of this part of the north Syrian plain. The survival – albeit scarred – of Simeon's magnificent abode is all the more remarkable.

The buildings we walked past were roofed with skilful pyramid-like roofs of thatch to shelter their occupants from the bitter winter of northern Syria as from summer's blistering heat. 'My ancestors belonged to Arabia,' said Ibrahim 'but they came here in the spring for the pasture. And then they stayed – despite the winter. That can be cruel; in winter I stay in my house in the city. We wonder how the creature on his pillar survived it.' I wondered too. Again, imagination took hold as I saw Simeon a long way now from Antioch, looking for shelter for the night. I discussed this with Ibrahim. 'I doubt they would have been as well fed and comfortable as I've been.' He grinned. 'Maybe some wise merchants catered for those who could afford it,' he said. 'We've always looked after visitors.'

In the distance I could see a bus approaching the foot of Simeon's hill. 'That's the bus from the border,' said Ibrahim, 'heading for Aleppo.'

'I'd better catch it,' I grimaced. 'Time to get back to work.'

We embraced wholeheartedly. 'Please thank your mother and your wife for looking after me so well.'

'You must visit us again,' he said. 'And in Aleppo make sure to visit my brother in the *suq* – you should find him easily – ask anyone: Muhammad Mazrui'

'Don't worry,' I shouted from the bus. 'I shall.' I clambered on board. It was full so I squatted on the floor beside the driver.

'Where you from?' he asked me in somewhat broken English.

I told him. 'Where did you learn English?' I asked in turn.

'In church school,' he replied. 'I Armenian. My grandfather from Armenia.' I thought of the Mazloumian family and their generosity and care of the desperate straggling flock of Armenian refugees that arrived in this part of Syria in 1915 and

1916, and wondered if any had taken shelter in Simeon's church.

On the way back to Aleppo I noted the triumphal arch still in place, though the photograph of Hafiz Assad had tilted to one side and there was no carpet of sweet-smelling herbs underneath him. 'Did the President pass this way?' I asked the driver. 'Not him,' he growled back. 'Far too busy deciding what to do with enemies in Damascus.' I didn't pursue the conversation.

In Aleppo, I dropped my bag at Baron's and headed for the *suq*, hoping to find one of the Mazruis in operation. Such a variety of faces and costumes topped by exotic headgear in the crowded lanes, taking me back to some of the thoughts I had beside Simeon's rock. It was evening, the best shopping time, especially for women. The mixture of faces – Turkish, Kurdish, Arabian – was as good as a busload of Londoners these days. After asking the way again and again I eventually found what had once in the 16th century been the Venetian caravanserai, the Khan al-Nahasin, the copper warehouse. There I found a brother of Ibrahim's busily totting up a consignment of Indian silk that had just arrived. 'Shoddy stuff nowadays,' he growled as he ran a hand over a bale, 'but what can you expect? Sit, please, and I shall call for some tea.' This was Mahmoud al-Mazrui.

We sipped the sugary brew. I told him about

my interest in Simeon Stylites. 'The old pillar squatter?' he commented. 'Good for business out there, I suppose. How is my brother? He is wise to leave the city.' In response to my question as to the state of affairs in Aleppo, he shrugged. 'Calm at the moment,' he said, settling down on one of his bales. 'But you never know. The authorities in Damascus do not like Aleppo. And here in Aleppo we have too many guns and too many calling themselves Muslim, who do not like the Alawis. Not good for business, that's for sure.' He held up a handful of gaudy scarves. 'Even the tourists stay away, though they'll be back. Here, have one,' and he pulled one from the bunch. 'And here's some of our famous olive oil soap – no one wants our olive oil these days but they still like our soap.' I remembered visiting a village factory where they made it. He made a grimace. 'Don't stay too long in Aleppo, my friend, though you should be safe with old Mazloumian.'

I walked back along what had once been part of a Roman road through the *suq* to Baron's, calling on the way on one of the Armenian churches. It was dark and cold inside, a few elderly citizens on their knees while a priest chanted prayers in the gloom

Once, Syria had been not just a way station for the marauding hordes but also a sanctuary for those fleeing violence, like the Armenians. Once diverse peoples had fought and killed, rubbed shoulders and mingled, survived and thrived. More spiritual than doctrinal in their religiosity, they all appreciated Simeon, the pillar sitter turned stinky Jinn. In 1970 with an ascendent Israel and a new dictator in power in Damascus, I was not so confident that the old tolerances would hold and instead feared the recrudescence of ancient animosities.

3.

THE BOY

My saga is an exercise in imagination: how Simeon came to be in fifth century Syria.

Simeon was born into an empire ruled from Constantinople by the Emperor Theodosius whose wily forebear, Constantine, had recognised the binding power of this resilient but still prohibited faith, Christianity. In 312, Constantine claimed that he had ensured his victory in a key battle by declaring – the night before – religious freedom for all adherents of the already popular Jesus Christ the Saviour. A year later he was signifying a change of his personal allegiance from the Sun god to the Christian god, and then used that change to strengthen his control of the eastern empire from his new headquarters on the Bosphorus, that swiftly running channel linking eastern and western worlds. He renamed the settlement after himself – Constantinople – and had himself baptised on his death bed in 326.

The faith already had strong roots in that eastern empire, not so strong however that from time to time a new gardener with new convictions might try to redirect a root, a shoot in this flourishing amalgam of Mediterranean and oriental discourse. To ensure the unity of Christendom the Emperor Constantine in 325 summoned a congress at Nicaea on the Asian side of the Bosporus, in what is now modern Turkey. The most significant issue was the nature of Christ: was he god or man? Was he subordinate to God the Father, therefore not of the same substance as the Father? The argument threatened the universal nature of Christianity and the assembled patriarchs confirmed what became known as the substantiality of Christ – of the same substance as the Father. It was not the end of the issue, which continues to this day.

Simeon was born about 390, the youngest son of a family of maybe many children. A contented family with a small but adequate farm in the Cilician foothills in today's Turkey. Cilicia is a region of rocky forested hillsides, to the north the frowning peaks of the Taurus, to the south the mellow waters of the Mediterranean. The foothills of the Taurus have seen generations of intruders – some invaders, some crusaders, some passers-by. Hittites, Babylonians, Persians, Greeks, Romans in one form or another. A melange of Eastern peoples. Simeon's village was many weeks' journey from that magnificent metropolis Antioch where he found himself later, but not so far from the city of Tarsus, birthplace of the holy Paul. Rolling hills, a narrow shining river edged by fields of wheat, terraces of olives and vines, leading through pungent pine forests to the stony crests where Simeon as a boy took the family's sheep and goats to pasture. Hard work but they had all they needed, including the Lord who cared for them even more tenderly than they tended their flocks.

Something of the atmosphere that surrounded Simeon as he grew up – smells, sounds, glimpsed patterns – one can feel now, round the village of Telnessin, Deir Simaan, where he eventually came to rest, carried on swifts' wings. Sounds of hens cackling, women chatting at the well, screeching for children, children squabbling, men gossiping – a background of clatter and bustle and occasional peace. And smells – acrid wood smoke, softer charcoal – animals' bodies, stale dusty sweat in rough clothes hanging on the back of the door. Warmth, lying at night on the mud floor, softened by years of goat droppings, sour ammoniac smell released by the heat of the body, warm cocooning of the spirit. Simeon grew up with the animals: first as a child helping the women check through the sheep every morning, weed out the sick, milk the ewes, cherish the lambs; then, a little older, shepherding them up the hill with James his brother and the other boys, past the terraced orchards (snatching at a peach, a pomegranate, a bunch of grapes, the fruit tasting all the better for being snatched), over the dark carpet of pine needles to the tops of the hills where the sheep and goats roamed and munched to their hearts' content, and Simeon too could roam, in body and soul.

A small world. Grey hills speckled with green that merged into distant blue-grey ridges, snow-capped in winter. In spring Simeon picked bunches of wild irises for his mother Miriam, in summer herbs to be dried on the roof, in autumn baskets of berries and mushrooms. When he was old enough to take the animals up the mountain, he and his friends practised slings on the birds, putting their skills to good effect to bring down plump pigeons. Serious harvesting was in the apricot orchards, the boys happy to help when it came to spreading out the cooked fruit to dry like blankets in the sun, nicking mouthfuls when the women weren't looking.

Other events marked the seasons. The village was baptised, wedded and buried by the Presbyter. It celebrated the sacraments. But people also marked the solstices and equinoxes, discreetly conciliated the pagan gods, the local gods. The village still followed the pagan year. At harvest time they trooped up the hill to the old temple. Not so long ago they would have been welcomed by its ancient priest, who seemed to emerge from the very rocks. But he had returned to them, invisible now since imperial prohibition of pagan gods though some did say they saw him from time to time and infertile women would leave him propitiating baskets of food. In an unpredictable world you need to propitiate everyone.

The Presbyter was a strong-voiced man who increasingly commanded their loyalty; he taught them the life of Christ. He baptised them. Simeon had been handed over to him at an early age, dunked with his friends in an icy stream; and he gave them the body and blood of Christ, a sacrificial meal familiar from rival faiths. Some he buried. The declaration of faith, the creed with its differing versions and arguments, he left well alone; he was not sure he understood what it was all about. The villagers recognised the Lord, the Lord who loved them, who had walked among them. Like the spirits who sang in the streams, dangled from the branches of the forest. Like the sun, the great god sun, the inhuman god Baal. But the Almighty God had sent his son (of one substance with his Father, they said, they being distant patriarchs whom nobody knew) to live amongst them, suffer with them and by them and love them.

Whoever he was, the Lord was close to them and they loved him. He was everywhere around them. How they danced and sang and wept in his honour. But they were also wary, hedged their bets, listened to the Presbyter, conciliated the spirits, just occasionally – but no longer sacrificing to the great sun god. But maybe to the goddess of fertility, now called Mary.

As for Simeon, he saw the holy spirit in the clouds, heard it in the wind, felt it in the sun and rain, smelt it in the fragrant gums the boys collected and in the wet wool of the sheep. Called it all the spirit holy, breath from God the Father Almighty and God his son, as he'd been taught.

He also felt the stirring of the Lord in his loins. He listened to the coupling of his parents, watched the sheep on the hillside, touched the hands and skirts of the village girls who laughed and teased his young lust. He danced and sang and wept with them on the spring feast of the Lord, chose his favourite, yearned for her when he lay down at night. 'Like a lily in a field of thistles, such is my love among the young women.' He felt the exquisite pain in his groin, finer than the stab of a needle, came to love the surge, how it raised his spirits.

Then one day running over the hillside after the goats, one of the rocks came alive and turned into a hermit huddled in a cloak. Plenty of them in those days, claiming they knew the Lord, wandering the hills and valleys, some driven by persecution but others by evil spirits, full of the fire of the Lord, no time for anyone but the Lord. They were inspired by rumours of distant holy men, abandoning the sown for the desert, flaying themselves by deprivation for the love of the Lord, famous for their fortitude, like Christ in the wilderness. Everyone had heard of the holy Antony of course, Antony in the Egyptian desert, and many others who had followed his example. To detach oneself from vanity was already an ambition for many Christians – nothing new in this, men and women had done it for hundreds of years in the east. Some withdrew individually, totally, others into communities. The individual sought for a union with the Lord in his passion; the soul should be elevated to the bliss of such union. The endurance of suffering became the power of endurance. Such men fled into the Egyptian desert, some found caves, others wandered as haunted spirits.

The village was vague about its hermit and Simeon on this first encounter was terrified: the man stank whenever he moved, a raw smell, worse than the goats. And his legs! His raggedy tunic left them fully displayed, like branches of a dead tree. Hair uncut, as tangled as a bramble thicket. He pounced on Simeon as the boy lay dozing in the grass, staring contentedly at the sky and gently caressing a yearning erection.

'That's not the spirit of the Lord in your loins,

boy! That's demons!' shouted this dishevelled creature.

Demons? Demons?

Yes, demons, boy!

Demons, in this exquisite world? God's all around me, in the grass, that butterfly (that girl, though he kept her to himself). Sun, cloud, rain, stars – you've only to look and you'll see him. Temptations, said the scraggy creature, sent to lead you astray from the true path. Rubbish! said the arrogant boy, furious at being disturbed in his arousal; how can beauty be a temptation? It leads me to love and praise the Lord. 'I sleep but my heart wakes,' he sang loudly. 'It's the voice of my beloved that knocks saying, Open to me, my sister, my love, my dove, my undefiled, for my head is filled with dew and my locks with the drops of the night.' Simeon was pleased with his voice; he'd been told it was very fine.

But the hermit, profiting by the strength of the boy's spirit, insisted on spoiling the afternoon with stories of sorrow and sacrifice; he must erase, obliterate, exile the demons; he must be hungry, thirsty, frozen, burned; he must groan and cry and mould his spirit with vigils. Suffer, in order to overcome suffering.

Simeon laughed. 'Buzz off, old man! All this talk of demons!' What a prospect, what a life. 'My beloved is white and ruddy, the chief among ten thousand!' he sang after him. 'You should have a try!'

There you have it. Peace for one person is turmoil for another.

Simeon lived in a world in which life-denying forces were in constant battle with life-giving forces, a world beset by demons despite that vaunted love of the Lord, for the Lord. Demons now jumped out from behind every haystack, they followed him up the hill, in the little stone church, by the river. They flattered his vanity, comforted his puzzlement at the transience and hopeless insecurity of human happiness; they haunted him night and day, wild-eyed, roaming as a mountain goat. They danced, night after night, in his dreams, turning themselves into village maidens. One girl in particular taunted him, pushed forward by her friends, twitching a scarlet scarf across her face, her delicate hands and feet still unblemished by too much toil, decorated with fiery henna. Susannah, he learned, was her name. 'O God,' yelled Simeon, passing her as she washed clothes in the stream. 'Kiss me, make me drunk with your kisses!' Nightly he dreamt he held her, nightly he talked to her, gently pulled aside her veil; in the daytime he lay in wait near the well, hoping for a glimpse, getting a glimpse too when she came down with her water jar in the evening. I am my beloved's and she is mine, so he dreamed, and casually walked out with his own jar, pushing through the babbling women, his member proud before him. He relished the surge in his guts when he saw her.

He sought out again the hermit in his cave a mile away. 'Sin, Simeon, sin!' he cackled; man must control his lust. What did the holy Paul say to the followers of Christ in Rome? 'I see another law in my members, warring against the law of my mind and bringing me into captivity to the law of sin which is in my members.'

Simeon buried his face and howled.

Legions passed by on the road past the village. They were heading east to garrison the frontier against the Persians, pagan worshippers of Ahura Mazda, sun god, forever pressing on the imperial frontier. They were loaded with weapons, helmets and scanty packs of food on their backs, goat skins to be filled with water at the village well. Simeon noted the young men's eyes swivelling to the young women who flicked their scarves as they returned the flasks. Pilgrims were also on the road. 'Off to Jerusalem!' they sang. Months away but who cares. Others were on their way home. Either way the Lord was with them. Did no one fall by the wayside? Some did; the Lord obviously looked the other way.

And traders. A caravan of donkeys belonging

to a large well-to-do merchant on horseback on his way home from Antioch stopped at the well. 'Good business there,' he declared to the men coming in from the fields. 'The city's bursting with gold. People eat off gold plates – well some do. They wear gold! Full of schools – very learned place, Antioch. Palaces galore. And you should see the markets – all the goodies of the east.' The boys' eyes sparkled. Mouths hung open. They whispered over their games of dice. 'Come on!' urged Simeon, 'Let's go!' Not quite so simple but one autumn when the harvest was in, 'I'll be back in the spring,' he told his mother, 'with some of that gold!' But he stayed, the local temptations seemingly more accessible.

The family's security proved precarious. One autumn a party of raiders from Isauria to the north of Simeon's country swept down from their hard mountains and carried off the village's winter supplies. Simeon's father never recovered and died soon after. One by one three sisters also died, one barely a year old. Talk about the hand of God. Then his brother went off to fight for Emperor Theodosius against the barbarians. 'At least I'll make a better fortune than staying here,' he said as he strode away, 'and one mouth less to feed.' Simeon was left to look after his mother and his remaining sister. He was young to take on the farm but not too young, and his mother and sister were there to share the burden. They could manage well enough.

'How can God treat us like this?' Simeon furiously asked the Presbyter. 'He's supposed to love us, isn't he? You said that was why Christ walked among us. What's the answer? Come on, tell us!'

'Ah,' the Presbyter fumbled defensively, 'who was it who went up the mountain last month, who was seen in that abode of demons, sacrificing to the monstrous Baal? Wasn't that your brother? I tell you, the wrath of God is revealed from heaven against all ungodliness, all darkness, all blasphemy, all heathen practices. What can you expect?'

Was that really so, wondered Simeon.

The villagers lowered eyes to the ground as they listened to the Presbyter's sermonising. What has this good woman Miriam done to deserve such cruelty? Simeon, in the crowd around his sorrowing mother, watched the girls, their eyes slipping sideways inside their scarves. The Presbyter rattled on: 'Wherefore God gives them up to uncleanliness through the lusts of their own hearts, that's what the holy Paul told the Romans.' Boy nudged boy.

Simeon forgot the dead, his father, his sister and his grieving mother, and thought only of the girls. He had grown tall and gangly, his hair flourished in tangled curls and he swore at his mother when she cut it. Indeed, he swore: at home he was foul-tempered and was frequently ordered out of the house. 'Go fetch the water!' Miriam screamed at him. 'Get out from under my feet! And no ogling the girls at the well!'

One day, taking sheep to market, Simeon saw some outlandish visitors sitting on the ground in the market place. People were bringing them food. 'Who are they?' he asked fearfully. 'Where are they from? Why are they here?' Everyone was asking the same questions.

A man looked up from his bowl of curds. 'We're pilgrims.' He wiped his mouth. 'We're from Rome on our way to Jerusalem.' Rome, city of sin, Rome beset by barbarians. No wonder they were heading for the City of God. Everyone talked of doing it. What an adventure; the market was a-buzz. 'We're not doing it for fun,' said the curds man sternly. 'We're doing it for the love of the Lord, for the forgiveness of our sins.'

'Come off it,' muttered the older men. 'If you are Romans, we've heard all about you.'

'The mother of the holy Emperor Constantine, God rest both their souls, showed the way to Jerusalem. We are following her footsteps. We shall pray with the holy Jerome in his cave.' The visitors frowned back at the crowd.

Not a bad idea, mocked the men on their way home, provided you can walk out of house and home for months, maybe years on end, shedding care as well as sin. Simeon, bowed down by a sin he could not shake off, thought about it more and more. The more he thought the more he hung around the well, one day even touching Susannah with the red veil. How he burned, with a fire as red as her scarf! He watched her house, watched her washing clothes. One day he captured a fragment of her scarf he found caught on the thorn hedge round her family's animal pen, wrapped it round his little finger, sucked it in the night to create that sharpness.

And how he gazed one day when the village trooped up the hill to mark the spring equinox (the Presbyter stayed behind of course; not for him these pagan rites). What a day. The hills burst with life. Simeon felt the same. Poppies everywhere, blood-red. After the sacrifice and the feast, the women danced opposite the men, Susannah with the red veil opposite Simeon. They touched hands, they held hands.

'Go to the Presbyter,' said Miriam maddened by her son's moodiness, 'he'll tell you what to do.' But the Presbyter was busy, told him to pray to the Lord.

'I can't,' said Simeon, 'it doesn't work. This thing goes hard, even when I'm asleep. The demons are all over me, crawling under my skin. I have to get rid of them. Help me.'

'Not a lot I can do.' The Presbyter was preoccupied; he had the rest of his flock to look after, not just overheated youths. 'I can give you some work here' – he was building a new chapel for the village, men chipping stones all over the place – but Simeon could see the girl out of the corner of his eye, he heard her friends singing by the well.

'I'm leaving,' he told Miriam. 'One day I shall come back but now I need to go away. To shed my sins.'

'That's what your brother said. And he hasn't come back. And where on earth will you go? Who will look after us? We need a man.'

Simeon scowled, then grinned. 'To Jerusalem!' he shouted to the world. 'I'm off to Jerusalem!' No one could object to that, not even his mother.

'Young fool!' said the village elders. 'It's years away. You do not even know the way. You have no business abandoning your mother like that.'

Simeon paid no attention. He knew best. 'For the Lord's sake,' he told them. 'To shed my sins.'

'Sins! Come off it, boy, you have not been that bad, no worse than the other boys.'

'You'd be surprised,' he frowned at them. 'The demons are all over me. Those are my sins.'

'Everyone's got demons; you learn to cope.'

'I cannot! And I will not!' he yelled at them. 'Not here anyway. I shall go to Jerusalem.'

'Let the boy be,' said the Presbyter fed up with

the boy's posturing. 'He'll be back. He'll come to his senses. I can give you one or two addresses for Antioch,' he told Simeon, handing him a few dinars. 'Syria is full of monasteries, especially Antioch. They will feed you at least, if you give them a hand.' Teach him a thing or two as well.

His mother wept but saw it as a way to get on in the world. The boy might talk about demons but she recognised a possible path to progress, prosperity even. And Simeon was resolute now: if the demons were to go, so, for the time being, must the women in his life, the singing girls and weeping mothers. She consoled herself half-proud; after all it wasn't everyone who planned to walk to Jerusalem. 'Do you want the donkey?' she asked apprehensively; they only had the one.

'Mother!' His voice was full of scorn.

'Take your father's sandals then,' sobbing as he tried them on.

He found a friend, one Ephraim, who was also disenchanted with village life and yearned for enchantment elsewhere. One more night they together lay with the goats. Sleep softly, hooted the night-jar from its rocky nest. Sleep as soft as Simeon slept that last warm cradled night, putting his body tenderly into the arms of his love, such a rest, ah, such a rest, relaxing each young muscle from his little toe to his little finger, such a rest. In the arms of his henna'ed princess for the last time. Pliable limbs, pliable soul. 'O my dove, that art in the clefts of the rock, in the secret places of the stars, let me see your countenance, let me hear your voice; for sweet is your voice, and your face is comely.'

So off the boys set, sandalled and shaven, a few loaves of bread pressed into their arms by the weeping Miriam, and a small skin of water. Ephraim, who came with him, was also followed by his mother's wails. Courage, boys, courage!

In the early morning in spring the Creator is in glorious evidence. The air is heavy with the certain knowledge of later heat but still leavened with the delicacy of the night's dew lending its transient sparkle to the plain. A land where the gifts and the punishments are so lavish, so extreme as to be accountable only by some heavenly power. The boys passed beneath trees whose branches were decked with rags and ribbons, acknowledging that power, propitiating the gods, seeking the good in the world. Little shrines at intervals, witnesses to the religious expectations of the countryside, built to guard against devils such as tormented Simeon. Nameless cohorts of them, lying in wait for the unwary.

Once they had left the village and its lands, they became respected pilgrims. 'We're going to Jerusalem!' they told one village after another. 'Ah, the ways of the Lord are miraculous,' someone would sigh, to be echoed again and again. 'Brave boys. So young. Go safely in the love of the Lord,' sending them on their way after a night's hospitality, bread, lentils, a bit of whatever they had. And Simeon and Ephraim would skip off in the cool of the early morning. This was the life! Not a moment to think about demons.

The road was crowded. Some only as far as the bustling city of Tarsus, a week from the village, birthplace of the Holy Paul. They saw his house, drank from his well. His companions taunted Simeon to divert to the sea, a few miles off. Sea? They even saw the sea. A fisherman took Simeon by the hand, led him over the rocks, made him put his feet in – the sea! 'Aow!' he screamed, scrambling up the rocks, then tried again, dipped an arm, a leg, washed his face. 'It's salty!' 'What do you expect?' the fisherman growled. 'It's the sea! But watch out for pirates. They're keen on young lads like you – good slave material.' They joined a party of pilgrims. 'Antioch's far enough,' they said, 'a city of great holiness, thanks to the most holy Peter who came there. Forget about Jerusalem, you'll never make it in a thousand years. You need money for that.' In a barn one night shared with soldiers heading east, 'Come with us,' one of them urged, 'see some action.' Maybe, thought Simeon, but let's get to Antioch first, greatest city in the world.

Along the way, they met sorts of people. The boys loved the company, the variety, the stories. And hairy ascetics, matted and foul, who appeared neither to eat nor to drink; their clothes were rags, their feet as horny as a goat's, their eyes glazed. Some were hounded by sobbing women who saw in them men inspired by the word of God. 'Speak to us, father, that we may live,' the women would cry, rolling in the dust. Others he watched being chased by villagers and deacons. 'Off with you. Claiming to be close to the Lord. Public nuisances, that's what you are.' Simeon loved them all.

Months later, in the cooler days of autumn, they reached the rich plain of Amuk, lay by its great lake, then eagerly pressed on to Antioch. Antioch was one of the three great cities of the Empire, alongside Rome and Alexandria (Constantinople still had to catch up). Founded by Alexander's general, Seleucus, on the east, left bank of the River Orontes, Antioch was sheltered from eastern winds by Mount Silpius and watered by the Orontes, itself fed from Amuk lake to the north.

The word of the Lord brought by the holy Peter, fostered by Paul. Colonnaded streets, palaces, villas, the greatest church ever built, its golden dome seen from all around. Churches galore, as the merchants had said.

This was a Christian empire through which Simeon was walking. The faith had strong roots, spread by faithful disciples; it had survived persecution (including by the builder of Antioch's grandest palace, Diocletian). The city was renowned for its tolerance of the orthodox and the unorthodox. There was a large Jewish community maintaining links all over the empire. There were shrines to pagan gods, especially in the popular suburb of Daphne. And there were conflicting views among the Christians: who and what was Christ? And how ferocious the adherents of either side could become! Loud and long discussions at Nicaea with the patriarchs eventually and wearily agreeing: of course the son is of one substance with the father, two in one. Thus the glory of the Christian mystery: God becomes not just man but the very bread for man to eat! Clergy in Antioch were not convinced.

But this was a pleasure-loving city, its pleasure-loving citizenry revealed by the magnificent mosaic pavements and floors commissioned by its plutocratic merchants, despite being battered by severe earthquakes as well as conquering armies.

The boys were nearly suffocated in the crowd of people and animals milling around the great northern gate. Workers, tourists, travellers, traders. Simeon found himself almost under the belly of an animal with the longest legs ever seen, reeking unbearably, grunting and puking as its owner pulled it and its fellows through the crowd, carrying the biggest load Simeon had ever seen. 'Watch out!' someone pulled him out from under the animal. 'Camels have a vicious kick. And they bite!' The noise of the crowd was overwhelming; strange voices, all shouting at top pitch. 'Make way! Make way!' Overpowering smells. Dust. Big feet. Sharp elbows. At the gate soldiers swung spears over the heads of the crowd, pushing them apart, trying unsuccessfully to impose order. The boys linked arms to keep together and suddenly were through and found themselves looking down a magnificent colonnaded street, still full of people but now more orderly, calmer, even relaxed. The camels plodded softly down the middle.

Oh Simeon – it was the biggest city he had ever even imagined! Some had told him to avoid it. 'City of sin, don't go near it, whores and heretics, everyone arguing.' While others extolled its elegance, its architecture. Away in the distance Simeon's eye was caught by the vast golden dome of the Great Church built by Emperor Constantias, crowned with a huge gilded wooden dome, the finest church in the Empire. The boys sat exhausted on the steps of one of the stalls tucked behind the colonnade. 'Up you get, you pair of thieves!'

yelled the stall holder. 'Don't you dare nick anything from here! Go on! Before I hand you over – the police will know what to do with you!'

Pulled and pushed by the crowd the boys eventually found themselves in a vast market place. Later he tiptoed inside the great building, gleaming inside and out with gold, silver, marble. This was one of the great centres of the faith, its monks, priests, patriarchs repeatedly stimulated to dispute in its precincts the roots of the new theology, to dig its foundations deeper in the minds as well as the hearts of the faithfull. Also to eradicate the grip of pagan gods, pagan pleasures. He listened to them singing in the dark entrails of the building and leapt outside – oh, the din, the smell, the crowds knocking him around, pinching his skin of water and one of his precious dinars. Everyone shouting, gabbling in strange tongues he couldn't understand. A smattering of Greek picked up from the Presbyter didn't go far in Antioch. Most people were incomprehensible. He sat on the pavement outside, worn out. 'What to do next?' he moaned to his companion from the road, Ephraim.

'I tell you what,' pondered Ephraim, 'that church is stupendous, I agree. But what we should really see is the shrine of Daphne. Now that's a lot more fun. Special. So I've heard. You won't believe what they worship up there! Let's give up on Jerusalem for the moment.' They joined a jolly crowd heading out of the city up a long narrow street lined with stalls selling all manner of temptations. The boys resisted. The road led through an aromatic grove of tall dark cypresses that opened out into a huge space, a sort of fair ground. 'This is where they have the Games.' Ephraim pointed to a knot of young men furiously exercising along one side of the space. 'You'll see the fastest, the strongest, the tallest men in the world at the Games!' On the crown of the hill, above the city, was the great accumulation of shrines, dedicated to Apollo. 'They hold the Games every fourth year. They used to think the Games represented the great god Apollo's chase of the maiden Daphne who changed into a tree to escape him. Let's tie something on. You never know – might change your life.'

Simeon, bemused, did as he was told. They found scraps of rag on the ground. 'Wish, as you tie it on,' instructed Ephraim. 'What for?' 'Whatever.' Jerusalem, thought Simeon. 'An exquisite maiden,' whispered Ephraim. Good idea, thought Simeon, and did the same.

'Hey, what's up, young man?' A woman's voice. Simeon looked up, saw a chair being carried by a couple of black boys (black as night: he'd never seen people like that before) and in the chair, a goddess. A young woman, draped like the little statues he'd once found in the bushes behind the old temple above the village. Orange hair, red lips, clean white skin.

'Cheer up,' said the goddess. 'You can't sit on the pavement all day. Someone'll spit on you if you're not careful.' Her voice as clear as a bell.

Simeon, revolted, rose to run away.

'Don't be silly.' The goddess again. 'You look exhausted, in need of a good meal. Put me down,' she commanded. 'What's your name? I can't go on calling you boy, as if you were one of these.' She gestured dismissively at the slaves.

'Simeon,' he said, keeping his distance. 'I'm on my way to Jerusalem.'

'Not another! Everyone's on their way to Jerusalem these days. Mighty ambitious, if I may say so. Well, I could do with some credit in the eyes of the Lord. Come on, handsome one. Let's get another chair.' She clicked her fingers at one of her men. 'I'll make sure you leave this sinful city with a good meal inside you. And maybe one or two other things!' She giggled. Two more blacks pulled up alongside Simeon. 'Climb in,' she ordered and Simeon, confused, tired and extremely hungry, did as he was told. 'Home!' she ordered, and off they set, bounced in and out of crowds, past churches with deacons yelling on their steps, past desecrated temples, past markets with voluble preachers waving their arms and addressing small crowds, big crowds until eventually they turned off the main street, down side streets garlanded with orange blossom, jasmine, red roses, and in due course came to a halt outside a gate in a high wall.

In they went, Simeon in a trance filled with flowers and fountains, his head empty, dizzy from hunger, from the movement of the chair. They were in a courtyard. The goddess was laughing at him. 'You really must be more cheerful,' she said. 'And clean. I'm going to order you a bath. You can't eat in the state you're in. Take him away,' she ordered a slave who'd appeared in the yard. 'Give him to Maria, she'll know what to do.' And helplessly Simeon followed the man through rooms and down steps to a clammy inner chamber. The man indicated he should take off his clothes. Take off his clothes? Simeon hadn't stood naked since he was a child. All of them? Well, there weren't many. The man indicated a pair of wooden sandals. Simeon slipped his feet into them and clattered after him into an even clammier room, hot too, steam everywhere, he couldn't see a thing. The man pushed him down on to a raised marble slab.

And then, out of the mist, appeared a girl, naked from the waist up.

Simeon screamed, terrified, his voice bouncing back at him from the marble walls, he himself bouncing off the slab. The slave pushed him back down; the girl, grinning, bent over him, her nipples brushing his lips as she began slowly to scrub. And what a scrub: laughing she showed him the scrubber, covered with specks of his very own grey skin. Then back to work again, front and back, top to toe, until she sloshed a bucket of water over him and then the oil, at which point Simeon gave himself up to the pleasure of the whole process, resistance finally yielding to the senses. He longed to cup his hands round those breasts, bury his face in them, feel her body yield to his, as his had yielded to her.

'That's better, Simeon,' said the goddess when he appeared before her. 'How beautiful you are, dear boy.' She was draped in a gorgeous gown. 'Maria's done a good job. I'm glad she found you some clean clothes too,' and she took his hand and led him to a couch beside a low table, a table laden with steaming meat, with every kind of salad, with jugs of amber liquid ('You'll have to try our famous Antioch wine.'), glass bowls piled high with fruit. 'Sit,' she said, pushing him down and lounging beside him. 'And eat. And drink.' He hardly knew where to begin. But hunger overcame reticence. His hands plunged into the feast again and again until finally he paused replete. 'My name's Susannah,' said his hostess smiling over him.

The name sank in only slowly. Simeon paused,

a slice of melon halfway to his mouth, and stared at her. Suddenly he saw the scarlet scarf of the village girl, his dream, reflected in this Susannah's scarlet mouth. The mouth smiled as she stroked his clean curls. 'Don't look so worried, Simeon. Now we can begin our fun.' It wasn't difficult to obey.

Sated and dizzy with food and the strong sweet wine, he lent back into the cushions of the couch. 'It's my turn now, my friend,' whispered the goddess. 'It's not often I can have a go at a novice. And that, I feel sure, you are.'

For a moment, his Greek too limited, Simeon didn't understand. Not for long. Her hand slipped up his thigh under his tunic, she took his member – oh! – she caressed him, slipped an arm out of her own tunic so that her breasts fell over him, smothered him as she shifted over him. 'Oh boy, oh boy,' she whispered so softly in his ear, 'take it slowly, my little friend,' as she bent down and put his member in her mouth, licking it, nibbling it, filling him with exquisite agony. Yes, exquisite! How the agony swelled inside him.

'No, no!' he shouted. She was astride him; the demons were back; the pain was delicious, unbearable. No! He wrenched himself away, leapt off the couch. 'Don't touch me. I'm a pilgrim!' At which point the goddess lay back, white, exquisite, more beautiful than any woman he had ever seen, even than the first Susannah, and laughed and laughed and laughed.

'Oh my pretty, pulsating pilgrim,' but Simeon was off, running into the alley, through the street, along the road, out of breath, chased through the sinful city by a legion of demons, each and every one of them laughing like the goddess, their laughter ringing in his ears, Satan, the stinking whisperer who whispers in the breasts of women until he collapsed on the steps of the most sacred Cave Church of St Peter.

4.

THE ROAD

That Road! In trying to understand the magnetism of the craggy man on his pillar I became deeply attached to the great east-west Road that brought the people to him. Most importantly it was a major link between two empires - Byzantine and Persian - and two trading worlds - Mediterranean and Asian with Antioch and Aleppo major staging cities on the route. In Simeon's day it climbed steeply out of Antioch up the slopes of Mount Silpius. Simeon and his companion followed a long line of heavily laden mules and camels. My next visit to the world of Simeon Stylites was also on the Road but starting the other end, from Aleppo.

Now in the spring, the year 1974, just a few months after the disastrous October War - also known as Yom Kippur - between Israel and its Egyptian, Jordan and Syrian neighbours. The major disaster of the allies' defeat included Israel's invasion and effective annexation of Syria's Golan Heights. In attempting to deny Israel a presence on the Heights, Syria suffered an immense loss of life and weaponry, and Israel remained in occupation of the district, able from there to threaten even Damascus. Thousands of Syrians were displaced from their towns and villages.

In Aleppo there were refugees everywhere, huddling in doorways, desperately trying to feed tired children on scraps thrown out by restaurants. From that now familiar bus station on the edge of the city I made my way to my favourite haven, Baron's Hotel. The city was quiet; there were very few people on the streets and not surprisingly the hotel was empty. 'This is not a happy country to visit these days,' muttered Armand Mazloumian over our tea. 'But welcome, Madam Sara.' The *suq* was silent and shuttered, the silence broken only by the evening call to prayer. I sensed that crowds of the destitute would be pushing into the courtyard of the Great Mosque.

Simeon was on my mind. There must have been similar crises in his day. But also refugees fleeing periodic outbursts of war. I decided to return to the small stretch of ancient road between Aleppo (Beroia in ancient times) and Antioch, beside the village of Tel Aqibrin that I had spotted on my previous visit. Its tarmacked successor would be busy.

Not surprisingly thoughts of ancient invaders were on my mind. Central Aleppo is dominated by the small hill once capped with its ancient citadel. To the left of the bridge leading up and across the glacis to the main entrance was a way into the market area that led directly to the Bab Antaki, the Gate of Antioch that leads to the wider world much travelled by the great caravans trundling goods between east and west. An earlier 'gate' might have been the starting point for Cyrus the Great's army heading west in the sixth century BC, or the Greek army of Seleucus, successor of Alexander, driving the Persians back to the Land of Two Rivers in the fourth century BC. Or or or: I felt in battle mode, affected by Israel's capture of Syria's Golan Heights. For thousands of years northern Syria has been at a much-travelled crossroads.

So this seemed an appropriate moment to investigate the little bit of paved 'street' I had noticed on my first visit to Simeon. It would have been much used by similar crowds of mourners in past centuries. Sure enough the bus was packed with mourners heading to Simeon for consolation. One of the women, shrouded in black, told me she had lost two sons in the Golan fighting. 'All of us have lost sons, husbands,' she nodded towards our fellow passengers. 'The holy man will console us.' She stopped in Tel Aqibrin. Not surprisingly, there was no welcoming arch with a picture of the president, let alone that delicious carpet of herbs he was supposed to crush. I jumped off the bus.

That day I gave The Road a life contemporary with Simeon. But it was surely already there, perhaps laid on the orders of Roman commanders in the long strife between eastern and western empires. What about the tragic Emperor Julian who saw himself as a second Alexander marching himself and his army of over 60,000 to their deaths at Parthian hands near Ctesiphon in 361. I supposed the locals had been dragooned into laying the Road, more easily to reinforce Roman generals and legions on the eastern frontier and the better for the emperor *et al* back in Constantinople to communicate with the front. Then my mind wandered more widely. All sorts would have passed this way. Roman soldiery of course (or should I call them Byzantine?), those legions of armoured warriors defending the borders of the Roman empire drafted from every corner of that empire. Romans and Iranians (as I like to call those from the great Iranian plateau: more relevant for the world today) – Parthians, then Sasanians sometimes at war but in Simeon's time, mostly at peace.

Why not that imagined brother of Simeon's, drawn to military adventures in the east? There may have been peace at the time of Simeon's childhood but the eastern border of what had become the Byzantine empire still needed to be guarded, hence (I imagined) Simeon's brother succumbing to the temptation of frontier glory (and loot) and joining the army in the east. Maybe he marched along this very stretch of road. And hence over the hundreds of years the feet not just of armies but also of merchants, pilgrims, refugees too, who flocked to the holy Simeon or post-Simeon to his church and the remains of the pillar inside. Maybe speculating about the magnificent church built around his pillar, the pillar still intact inside the church. Some paying their respects to its occupant. There must have also been local farmers, their produce especially for nearby Aleppo or the great metropolis of Antioch, thanking Simeon for a good harvest or bewailing a bad one.

The piece of ancient paved road is impressive, albeit short. It branches off from the modern road for about two hundred metres at Tel Aqibrin, following a gentle upward slope before disappearing into the hillside. It was laid with hefty slabs of the local limestone – surely laid to last. It is part of a network of roads remnants which appear all over northern Syria: bits of arches, cisterns, hostelries, old, tumbled walls demonstrating the range of communication between east and west, commercial, cultural, as well as military. Of course, one wonders who the road builders were. I walked up to its end and sat on one of the boulders which it was made of, slightly dislodged from the main track. It was a reminder of the interplay between east and west in the empires of Simeon's day. And ever since.

From my vantage point on top, I looked out across a treeless plain marked by the skeletons of ruined churches, the so-called Dead Cities of what in Simeon's time had been a scene of prosperous farming communities worshipping within those now collapsed walls. The prosperity had melted away, not so much with the arrival of Islam in the seventh century AD but more with the devastation of 'crusader' warfare from the eleventh century followed by Asiatic and Turkic warriors and so on. (How had my raggedy Jinn survived that, I wondered.) No need for Roman roads but instead riding rough-shod across the fields, burning a village, a church or two *en passant* no doubt.

Stiff from daydreaming about the luckless legionaries and Asian hordes – perhaps they halted as I did now to ask for water. Round a corner was a sheepfold where an elderly baggy-trousered farmer was milking his flock. A skimpy hound barked at me. Seeing me approaching, the shepherd abandoned his sheep and took me off to a nearby well and drew a bucket of water. I dipped and drank a cupful. Then he left me to wander round the small stone houses looking for ancient stones. It was easy to let my imagination carry me on – the succession of passers-by drew me to the survival of Simeon and his basilica. And the Pillar. It wasn't until the French in the 1920s – awarded governance of Syria in the aftermath of World War One – that 'my' old road was cast aside by the new.

The farmer returned to where I had perched beside the 'French' road, with a mug of sheep's milk that I drank (not quite my taste) while noting the old stones built into the walls of the houses: were they recent additions, post-dating the French-built road? 'No,' he replied, 'my father, grandfather, great great great father....' My imagination again filled in the blanks. 'They built these houses.'

'You've still got your triumphal arch' – I pointed – 'but no presidential picture?' Maybe the president had turned around earlier, done his bit and headed back to the comforts of Aleppo. 'Did you see the president a few years ago when he came through?'

He looked me up and down, shrugged his shoulders and spat on the ground. I took that for a negative – indigenous disdain for the outsider, as the Alawi Assad family certainly were in this part of the country. 'He never came,' was the growled response.

I wandered off among the lanes, the smell of cooking whetting my appetite. I came across the remains of what was once a more substantial building, now unroofed, arranged around a sort of hardened mud courtyard – could this have been a monastery? This region, I knew, was famous for its churches and monasteries now dismantled, their stones used in village houses.

Christianity has had its ups and downs in Syria but on the whole has survived alongside the moderate Islam of the population. Bear in mind also the ups and downs generally of the monastic appeal; periodically standards of austerity doubtless wavered as they did all over Europe. 'Let us eat meat,' I hear someone complain. 'We should all go to Jerusalem,' says another. 'Antioch's pleasures entice,' calls a third and fourth. Poor harvests, marauding soldiery, plague, not enough monastic hands for maintenance – all these were challenges to both village and monastic life: and over the centuries contributed to the sad desolation of the so-called Dead Cities. The survival – albeit scarred – of Simeon's magnificent abode was all the more remarkable.

The houses I walked amongst had been roofed with skilful pyramid-like roofs of thatch to shelter their occupants – sheep, goats grunting over their meal – especially from the bitter winter of northern Syria. Again imagination took hold as I saw Simeon a long way now from Antioch, looking for shelter for the night.

However Baron's in Aleppo was beckoning. I

heard the coughing and spluttering of the bus in the distance and soon it came round the corner, grinding to a halt as the driver spotted me by the wayside. I clambered on board.

5.

MONK

Simeon stumbled out of the city in the wake of the monk, on to the road to Jerusalem. Or so he thought. They set off before daylight, following a crowd of travellers. Many were leading lines of donkeys laden with huge sacks heading for the markets of Beroea (Aleppo) and on further east, on maybe to the 'land of the two rivers' (Iraq), to the Persian capital at Ctesiphon and maybe even further east. Some were leading camels, their soft tread a contrast to the clitter-clatter of the donkeys' hooves on the rough track. This led up and over the shoulder of Mount Silpius. At the top Simeon turned to look back at the sinful city from which he was fleeing, just visible as it emerged from the night. He shook himself to shrug off the vile memories that still haunted him. They walked all day, sharing the bread and water his companion thoughtfully provided, and finding a farmer's pile of hay beside the road when it came to dossing down for the night.

Next night, long after dark, after walking all day, they knocked at a door set into a high stone wall, the door marked with a cross. 'They will take us in,' said his companion. The door opened and they were ushered inside by a man dressed in a short hairy tunic. 'I am on my way to Jerusalem,' said Simeon. 'Come in and rest,' replied the man at the door.

It opened on to a courtyard surrounded by low buildings. Sheep grunted in a corner. We have just finished building,' the doorman explained. 'I am Elias.' There was a well in the middle of the yard but little else visible in the feeble light of the man's torch. The place was wrapped in sleep. 'Follow me and we will find you food,' said Elias and led them into a long dark room that ran along one side of the yard. 'Wait here,' he said and a minute later reappeared with bread and curds. 'Eat,' he said curtly which they quickly and silently did. 'Follow me,' the man said again when they had finished, and this time led the boy through the yard to a tiny room with a roll of bedding in one corner. 'Sleep here,' he said, 'and we will talk in the morning. God bless you with sleep.' Simeon did as he was told but felt he had hardly slept when he woke to the sound of feet outside his room and low voices. Still dark but through the tiny slit of a window he could see the lightening of the sky. The door of his room opened. 'Come with us,' called a shadowy figure. 'Come and pray with us.' Once again Simeon did as he was told, following the figures into a small chapel. Candles cast shadows; incense sputtered. Men already knelt in prayer. Simeon knelt too. Some distance away he spotted his Antioch companion. 'Teach us, O Lord, the way of thy statutes,' the man at the far end chanted.

'Give us understanding, and we shall keep the law, yea with our whole hearts,' sang Simeon's companions, the man beside him in a reedy falsetto. Understand? wondered Simeon at the strange language: how can I survive this jumble of languages, let alone understand?

'Make us walk in the path of thy commandments, for therein is our desire,' sang the leader.

'O turn away our eyes, lest they behold vanity.' Poor Simeon and his Antioch adventure.

'Take away the rebuke that we are afraid of.' His mother's.

'Let thy loving mercy come also unto us.' Hers again.

The chanting resounded round him; Simeon's confusion was overwhelming; he longed to be home. Yet the words were familiar.

'Behold, our delight is in thy commandments. O quicken us in thy righteousness.'

'Let us sing as the holy Ephrem taught us: However great our wonder for you is, O Lord, your glory exceeds what our tongues can express. Glory be to Father.' His companions gathered him up and took him to the long room where he had eaten the night before. They wore hooded sleeveless tunics that came to their knees, scraggy shins below. Girdles held them in place. All knelt for ages it seemed, then rose to dip bread in bowls of olive oil and sipped their curds. They ate ravenously in silence, hoods over heads. Simeon felt exposed but among friends. He glimpsed his companion at the far end of the room.

'I am Elias,' muttered one of the men. 'We met last night.' Simeon, eating, stared at him, silent as the rest. 'We are servants of the Lord,' Elias spoke again. Simeon was introduced to an older man at the head of the table. 'This is our Superior,' whispered Elias.

Afterwards the Superior took him to one side. 'Welcome.' He patted the bench beside him. 'You have come a long way. I hear you are heading for Jerusalem, the best so to speak. But this is not the road to that holy city. Why not stay closer to here?' Simeon wished he could explain his need to put as much distance as possible between himself and the demons. They were still after him, he tried to explain.

'I favour pilgrimages,' said the Superior. 'Not sure how good they are at expelling demons though. I dare say you are right to head for the top, the best so to speak. I would be happy to give you an introduction to the holy Jerome. But if it is a question, as you say, of banishing demons, might

I make a suggestion? Ask anyone here if they have ever had demons and you will find we have all had problems. One reason we do not admit women. Except our sisters in holiness of course; there is a household of them next door and from time to time we worship together. But outside the community they can give rise to all sorts of problems. Rise is about the right word!' He smiled. 'Don't blush, boy,' said Superior Mikhail. 'We are all the same. "Some for marriage, others for virginity," ordered the holy Basil, he was born not so far from your part of the world in the Taurus. Stay here a while amongst friends and banish these damned spirits. "Do not be anxious about tomorrow," the blessed Antony told us. When you have the measure of them, then's the time to continue to Jerusalem.'

Simeon sighed, drained of the spirit of adventure. The goddess had knocked that out of him. The bowls of curds, the fresh bread.

'Stay,' said the Superior.

So he stayed, to be taught. And to work.

For the holy Basil, work was an integral part of a communal, monastic life. Basil had no time for hermits such as he had seen during extensive travels in Egypt. Prayer *and* work – both strengthened the community and its dedication to the Almighty. In Egypt Basil had visited communities established earlier by the Egyptian Pachomius, who was said to have prayed with his arms stretched out (difficult, thought Basil), stressed obedience (crucial), allowed individual cells especially for the disabled or feeble but that led to a more relaxed communal life. The able-bodied cultivating gardens and tending the sick, at least as important as prayer and fasting. And the most holy Egyptian Antony? Even he cultivated a garden and had his followers weaving mats. No godliness without toil.

The monastery that Simeon now entered was new, one of many in that part of the world inspired by the teaching and the organisation laid by Bishop Basil. Neither Basil nor the Superior who followed his rule had any time for histrionics: obedience lay at the core of the monastic discipline. Talking was kept to a minimum; meals were silent. A dozen men sworn to a life of devotion, prayer and hard work according to Basil's precepts.

The Superior was greatly respected by the village; he adjudicated their interminable disputes over water, boundaries, threshing rights, while also striving to rid them of the evil spirits that haunted their lives. As for the men (the brethren as they referred to themselves), Simeon's companions had had their fair share of misery and misfortune and were the reason many were there: one had lost his farm through fire, another a wife in childbirth, another a leg to bandits, another orphaned and destitute. Some had been soldiers on the eastern frontier. They spent their day praying and ploughing, harvesting their grain and the blessings of their faith.

'O all ye works of the Lord, bless ye the Lord; praise him and magnify him for ever!' How lustily they sang in the little stone chapel.

For four years Simeon learnt to read and write in Greek as well as the local Aramaic, to study the holy texts in both languages. He sang the hymns of St Ephrem, praising the Trinity: 'While we hymn Father, Son and Holy Spirit, let all creation sing amen'. He loved the music. One brother taught him the craft of the mason, how to cut the limestone from the hillside, to chisel the face of the block, to smooth its edges to a precise angle. Another taught him how to graft fruit trees: patience, Simeon, patience, as the boy hacked clumsily at the branches.

Days were long and laborious, especially in autumn. Wheat, nuts, apricots, pomegranates. Harvest festival was an ancient condoned rite. 'All things bright and beautiful,' sang the brothers, 'All creatures great and small', swotting the flies on the dates which visiting Arabians had presented for the occasion. 'All things wise and wonderful, the Lord God made them all.'

But the plenitude became too much for Simeon. He retched in his cell, disgorged his dinner, seldom stayed awake even through vespers. 'Now let your servant depart in peace,' sang the monks around him. Peace? 'For my eyes have seen thy salvation.' I can't see anything much, he thought to himself, too tired. How can I be a light to lighten anyone for that matter. Too bloody tired.

The Superior was right up to a point. The Holy Spirit was showing him how to defeat the evil spirit; he saw the world through different eyes now, no longer needed to plod on to Jerusalem; he was enveloped by this new world of the Spirit. But nor did he want the busyness of the monastery. All very well for the Superior to help the villagers, advise them, settle their quarrels, for the brothers to sweat out their sins in the fields, but he, Simeon, reckoned he wanted nothing to do with the world. He was tired after four years' toil. He no longer felt pain but longed nevertheless for agony, the agony of the Lord.

'We all go through this,' said the Superior. 'But you need the community. This is a well-grounded community, brother Simeon. Its walls properly built, its trees taking root. As the holy Basil taught us, God does not mean us to be idle. Obedience too, if you live in a community.'

But Simeon wanted to stand aside from these people, from their world, from the food they grew. Their obsession with toil. To understand the Lord, the holy spirit. Why else should he have left his family? 'All the toil of man is for his mouth, yet his appetite is not satisfied.'

And one particular evening, returning from the fields past the village and hearing the long-lost sweetness of girls' voices gossiping by a gateway he found he was still tethered to his lust. For a moment he stood still to listen to the music of girls laughing in the courtyards of their houses. Demons grinned at him across the fields, lay in wait for him to chase him home at nightfall. Instead of forgetting his body he found it hard not to dwell upon it constantly: sweat, blisters, thorns, above all hours spent growing food he did not want to eat. How can you escape the flesh when it was fed with such labour?

'But we must eat, therefore we grow food,' brother Elias protested.

'I shall do without,' said Simeon and did so, to the dismay of his colleagues who complained he wasn't pulling his weight. He had less and less weight to pull. For days he remained shut in his cell, cross-legged in the middle of the floor. Not helping on the land, not sweeping the yard or baking the bread or grinding the salt. They grumbled.

'If you cannot obey, you cannot stay,' the Superior warned wearily.

'I am leaving,' said Simeon.

'Woe unto him who lives alone,' cautioned the

Superior with a heavy heart, 'for if he falls there's no one to lift him up.'

'I don't want to live alone. The Lord God will lift me up.'

'I would not be so sure, brother. For Jerusalem?' asked the Superior.

Not for Jerusalem,' answered Simeon, 'not yet anyway.'

The Superior sighed. 'Try Telada,' he said. 'The holy Heliodorus may be able to help. It isn't far and he is a good friend of mine. Inclined to the path of the holy Pachomius.'

So one day Simeon left his retreat and walked many miles over the hills of Telada, through the forests, cornfields, olive groves and pastures that bound man to a livelihood, well endowed for some of course; for others further away, this was a year of terrible misfortune. The Western Empire had been threatened, invaded, devastated by barbarian Visigoths for several years. In the year 409, under their leader Alaric, they besieged Rome. 'Rome, the mistress of the world, shivered, crushed with fear, at the sound of the blaring trumpets,' warned Pelagius, a British moralist in Rome at the time. The following year, the year Simeon moved on, the city fell to the barbarians. In his cave near Jerusalem the holy Jerome wept when he heard the news: 'If Rome can perish what can be safe?' Well, Jerome for one, thousands of miles from the disaster experienced by Romans and their city, though the barbarians soon left it again to its own devices. But bad news travels faster than good news; the Eastern Empire trembled and that old troglodyte Jerome pointed to the heavens and told the crowds who came to call that the wrath of God had once again made itself manifest.

The village of Telada was clustered at the foot of a hill round a large monastery, Eusebona, established nearly seventy years earlier. It was under the guidance of the long-suffering Heliodorus, a man of great learning and goodness who had been dedicated to the monastic life since the age of three when his parents had left him at the door of the community, his legs being too short to carry him away. This monastery was run according to the precepts of the Egyptian monk Pachomius, a contemporary of the holy Antony, who had set up his community in the Nile valley.

Simeon arrived at the roasting end of an exhausting day, villagers returning from the fields with their tools, children driving in the sheep, a chorus of song from inside the monastery compound. A high wall surrounded the compound. Simeon knocked, a scrawny youth of twenty, shoulders broad and well developed from all that ploughing, hair sprouting in all directions, under arms, up from the groin, blackening his legs.

Proud unfortunately, despite his efforts, unable to yield to the Lord or to anyone else for that matter. No response to his knock and the singing continued. He knocked again. Still no response. He squatted dully in the shade of the wall, a mangy hound sniffing at his feet. The shadow lengthened and Simeon dozed. Suddenly the door was opened. 'Come in,' said a voice. 'We were praying.' Stiffly Simeon followed the voice, belonging to an old man, barefoot, wearing the usual sleeveless tunic. Simeon followed him across the courtyard to a room where the inhabitants of the monastery were squatting round a large dish of gruel. No one was eating because one man was reading. He stopped when he saw Simeon.

Simeon stood in the doorway swaying slightly, seemingly at the end of his tether though, as the Superior Heliodorus was later to point out, no one knew the length of his tether.

'Would you have taken him in if you had known?' asked his friend Patriarch Theodoretus. This scholarly friend of the Superior was Patriarch of the great northern see of Cyrrhus; he was used to accommodating a variety of religious experiences emanating mainly from further east.

Heliodorus smiled. 'Probably not,' he replied. 'But that evening I was stirred to great pity at the sight of the grubby youth. A most unusual boy, though even now I find it hard to define why.'

‘Father, take me in,’ Simeon whispered.

‘I was startled by the expression in his eyes,’ Heliodorus later wrote to Theodoretus, ‘an expression that belongs to those human beings who are born with an understanding of the ultimate reality, God in all his holiness. I had heard of men like this – the holy Basil describes them, men indeed like the holy Pachomius himself when a young man in the Egyptian desert, more often than not men who were unable to come to terms with their knowledge. Not Antony of course who desired to share his knowledge of and love of the Lord Almighty. Welcomed visitors to his cave as long as they stayed outside. In my presumption I thought to guide Simeon to give.’

Poor Heliodorus – there were trials and tribulations ahead.

‘Father, take me in,’ said the boy. The community stared expressionless.

‘Enter,’ said the generous Heliodorus. ‘You can wash over there.’ Simeon washed and returned to the circle, its members moving silently to make space for him. ‘We shall eat,’ said Heliodorus, and fourteen hands stretched out to the bread. Simeon held back. ‘Eat,’ his neighbour nudged, ‘before it’s all gone.’ So he obeyed. Bread, onions, oil, salt; no eggs, meat or fish. He ate with relish. Again in silence. A jug of water passed from one man to the next, voices loosened and interrogated the newcomer. Where are you from? Why are you here? Who sent you? He did not have much to say. 'The Lord God,' he mumbled, thinking suddenly of his mother.

O Father Heliodorus: what a burden you are shouldering. He was a simple man who had lived in Telada for over forty years, never beholding the things of the world or one Christian controversy from another (and there were plenty of them around). Heliodorus passed them over. There was no controversy in his life – until Simeon came along.

Here was a boy with lust in his loins, seeking God alone with undaunted and uncompromising singleness of heart. Sometimes he refused sleep, sometimes he refused food. No one dared to remonstrate. The holy Egyptian Antony had done the same, though his contemporary countryman Pachomius was more moderate. Demons rained blows on his head when he stood sleepless in his cell. Later his fellow monks would find him lifeless on the floor. Simeon assured them repeatedly how he needed their company, people around him, but his brethren found this hard to believe.

From the beginning it was the lack of compromise that bedevilled his relations with the community. The devil, muttered his fellow monks. 'We believe it is important,' Heliodorus wrote to his good friend, the scholarly bishop Theodoretus, 'to beware against the aggrandisement of self along such a rigorous path as chosen by Simeon. The Egyptian father Antony warned against this: we should heed his words. This boy is in danger of worshipping pain not God.'

'Mine is a private journey,' sang Simeon. 'The pain and the suffering are mine; only through God can I understand them. There's precious little you can do.' He must not yield to the soft importunate voices of men. If I tell them I am afraid they will take me in their arms to comfort me. If I do not tell them, I shall one day comfort them.

The community was upset. 'We break our fast every two days. He breaks his once a week. It's not fair.'

'Oh brothers, brothers. You are no less worthy just because you eat.'

But Heliodorus also had his doubts. Ecstasy and ascetism: two great forms of inspiration that may appear in one so holy, the most deeply rooted instincts of the religious heart. But they can also be sins of pride. Regulation and control are essential to avoid excess. 'Continence, brethren, and temperance,' he told them all. He wrote again to Theodoretus. 'Obedience? Fraternisation? Such concepts the blessed Simeon would have none of. I have to say, he lacked humility.'

Simeon insisted on a private journey; he denounced the well-travelled road. As a boy he had wandered freely over the mountainside; now he wanted to maintain that freedom in seeking his inner soul. 'I seek for God within, not without. I do not need instructions. God gives me my own,' he told Heliodorus. 'How can I know your instructions are correct?'

'How can you possibly know yours are wiser?' The Superior ignored the insolence.

'I shall know when I find God.'

'The Lord saw the creation as though it were asleep,' Simeon sang loudly in his cell, 'that by the distress of his servant he might arouse the world from the heaviness of its lethargy of sleep.'

'Distress!' exclaimed Heliodorus, when the brotherscametohim,evenhispatienceunderpressure. 'There are limits. One should never offend. We live, as you know very well, in an age with great respect for austerity, asceticism, solitude, contemplation. Our troubles drive us to take refuge in caves. And our community is well known for its accommodation of such inclinations. But – Lord have mercy upon us – Simeon put us to the test.'

The Telada monks indeed lived for prayer and meditation, the renunciation of all cravings, taking refuge in truth, studying the true knowledge of others. A contemplative life must be austere.

Food must be cheap, plain and scarce. Drink, weak and meagre. Sleep – brief. Clothing – coarse and shabby. Such a life must also be disciplined, or so Heliodorus believed. To Theodoretus again. 'The community imposes a discipline which the hermit may not be able to impose on himself. For instance the holy Basil stressed how important it was that we should be as self-sufficient as possible, even the Egyptians allowed for that, not to run the risk of being parasites on the larger community.'

Then Simeon refused to go to the fields.

'I point out that a certain amount of labour keeps a man fit and that is more important than some realise. It's all very well to subdue one's cravings but not at the expense of life. Toil also encourages a spirit of service and humility.' Ha!

Then in the third year or so his penances began seriously to intrude upon the sensibilities of his fellow monks.

'How often did I call on the Lord for patience, even guile, in dealing with this boy,' cried Heliodorus. 'No reason could prevail. How could I best allow him scope within our essential togetherness? The answer you know all too well, my friend: I could not.'

Fasting for instance: Simeon was always going off on private fasts of his own – all very well if he had not emerged at the end of them weak as a dying man's breath and scaring everyone that he was on his last legs. He was not of course; he had an uncanny way of knowing just how far to go. But it alarmed his fellows; they disliked being frightened and they hated being out-fasted. It upset their peace of mind. Washing too. Now they were all aware of the virtue of not washing – humbling themselves, forgetting themselves in the glorious unwashed state. But again there are limits, especially when part of a community. The stink! A bit of washing was necessary for health too and Heliodorus used to order a thorough wash once a month.

Not Simeon: he never washed. Never. Heliodorus besought the Lord God for guidance and even changed cells with the brother who was Simeon's neighbour. 'The smell – forgive my saying so, my friend – was horrific, surrounding us with a vile miasma. Certainly a penance. I could hardly pray.' And unhealthy: his dirt soon led to running sores which caused more resentment among other monks. Due to the modified operations of their bodies achieved by sleeplessness, meagre diet and other such austerities, they were more vulnerable to infections. Newer members found tolerance very hard.

'If Christ can wash his disciples' feet, the least you can do is to keep yours clean,' the Superior warned Simeon.

'I shall wash yours, holy father,' offered Simeon.

'You are more than welcome' – Heliodorus was cross – 'but that's not what I mean. The holy Basil taught us that to live together is a noble path but also a continual training. It's no good behaving as if you were the only person who counts. Obedience, brother.'

Simeon would go to any extreme.

'There is no doubt in my mind, none whatsoever, that for Simeon to survive some of the things he did to himself presupposes the divine hand of Almighty God. But mortification must be controlled by prudence, I told him again and again: we were not taught to be body-killers, only passion killers. The devil is within; there are times when a man is his own devil. I even told him he was in danger of worshipping that devil.'

Not far wrong. Sometimes Simeon dared not sleep for fear of the visions that tormented him. If he slept he woke drenched with sweat, his penis erect at right angles to his soaking body. Such lust could only be killed by wakefulness though it was himself, not his lust, that he nearly killed. Lust, the Superior advised him, is a part of life however much one might dislike admitting it. The human man remains in and of this world.

But O Lord, moaned Simeon in his cell, clutching his penis, lying in wait for it at night and the moment it stirred binding it with rags saturated with the lusts of earlier ambushes. If he closed his eyes Susannah with the scarlet scarf, Susannah with red, red lips danced between them, so he bound up his eyelids also. He revisited Antioch. The Susannahs in his life. Rise up, my love, my fair one and come away. Jumbled voices whispered in his ear: 'Kiss me with the kisses of thy mouth, for thy love is better than wine.'

The brothers watched askance when he dug a deep hole in a field and buried himself up to the neck: it can't rise, if he covered it with earth. When he thought he'd taught it a lesson he tied himself to a tree near the village well to prove it, but when the girls came down to fill their pots, oh Lord, up it popped again. 'Disgusting,' one of them informed Heliodorus, 'the way he hangs round the well. You'll have to speak to him.'

The brothers found it a great strain on their brotherly love. Up to a point asceticism symbolises the sacrifices which spirituality calls for. But it should be a battle witnessed by no one except God. Not amongst us, for heaven's sake. The annihilation of the flesh is a terrible, searing victory but it needs no witnesses. The brethren began to wonder whether demons weren't in Simeon for the rest of his life. Maybe even contagious.

'Holier than thou, that's what he is trying to be. As if it's some sort of competition.'

'Ruthless.'

'No brotherly love.'

'Come now,' remonstrated their Superior.

The boy looked ghastly, an old man barely twenty, withdrawn, eyes sunk, hair falling out, hardly able to walk. He didn't even make his basket, instead he made a rope out of palm fibre, the fibre exchanged between villagers and Arabians from the south who came each summer to pasture their flocks on the rich northern plains. Palm fibre makes the strongest rope, even in Simeon's fumbling fingers, but also the coarsest. And Simeon had tied a length of this round his waist under his tunic and was wearing it night and day. Very quickly the rope rubbed through the tender skin, burying itself in the young flesh. His tunic was so foul, so tattered and caked with mud and sweat that Heliodorus failed to spot the blood that it was also absorbing. Only the hideous smell of gangrene gave him away. Maggots swarmed, guzzled the flesh, fell on the floor of the chapel.

The brethren came in a body to the Superior. 'Our guide, the holy Pachomius, would never have allowed it. Nor the holy Basil.'

Heliodorus told Simeon to come to his hut, ordered him to undress. Simeon refused. 'For the love of God which we share, and for your own sake, do as I ask.' The boy looked him full in the face as he pulled off the rags in which he was clothed. The rope was revealed encrusted with blood and pus. The wounds crawled with worms. They stank. Heliodorus retched. A maggot popped out and fell on the floor. Heliodorus tried again not to retch. The Devil is not to be blamed for everything, wrote wise Augustine about this time, there are times when a man is his own devil.

'Why do you hide these things without seeking advice?' Heliodorus asked him ('My stomach heaved,' he confessed to Theodoretus).

'Forgive me, Father,' Simeon could do no more than whisper. 'My sins are many and my mistakes as numerous as the waves of the sea. I deserve to suffer. I repeat the words of Christ: if thou wouldst be perfect ... I am a worm and no man,' he croaked, 'a reproach of man and despised of the people.'

'At your age how have you managed to be so sinful?'

'If David was brought up in sin and conceived in iniquity, what about me?'

Heliodorus was weary. Read the works of the holy Basil, he told him, or Pachomius. Continence is not merely not eating. Continence is the avoidance, not the indulgence, of excess. He watched another maggot fall to the floor. 'I have to say, brother Simeon, those worms in your body are the demons. You are in danger of being eaten alive by the Devil himself. You are in even greater danger of worshipping your pain.'

He watched with some satisfaction as Simeon sank to the floor. A brother came with water, another with vinegar, another with herbs, another with clean cloth. 'No,' he said to one; 'no,' he said to another. 'No, no, no, NO!'

What could Heliodorus do?

'So I asked him to go. If you wish to live close to God, I told him, you can either be part of a community such as ours at Telada, but then you must be part of it and obey. The alternative is to be a solitary like the holy Antony in the desert.'

With how heavy a heart did he watch him go, this man of God. 'Go to Telnessin,' he told him. 'They cherish solitude there.'

Simeon defended himself. 'The wound is the fruit of my love.'

'Beware, beware,' Heliodorus warned him, 'beware of the dangers of ecstasy; to love the Lord through His creations can be an unholy love.'

'Oh the passion of the boy. As he went Simeon turned in the doorway of my cell. "My time here has been full to overflowing," he sang. "I am sad at the end that it's over. But I dance with joy!" Imagine, my friend! He grabbed me by the hand and tried to drag me round my cell! Too close to madness. No strength in his arm. I could have danced him off the floor with my little finger.

'That, my friend, is the limit of my personal knowledge of the holy Simeon. I have of course visited him several times. At a distance of course. To this day, though I love him for himself and for his holiness, yet as a general principle I cannot approve his austerity. It is too easy to abuse.'

Δ

The dancing did not last long. He was too weak, the hillside too rocky. Soon he was hobbling, found a patch of hyacinths in the shade of a boulder, lay down beside them and slept, their perfume drowning the foul smell of his body. Warm night caressing cheek, hair. Flying ants whispering in his ear. Millions of stars, the million eyes of God. 'I am afraid. He sees me too well. Welcome night! O welcome, wonderful night!' The blood and pus in his wound congeal.

What was it like for the holy Antony, holed up in his Egyptian cave?

When he awoke, he found himself in an abandoned temple, and stood there through the night. 'Keep still, Simeon, keep still. The demons are chasing you, keeping you on the run.' He listened, caught beside a towering acanthus, calmed his breath, his breast. 'Yes, Lord, I hear you. I can hear you. Mind confused, legs belong to someone else.' 'Hey, boy, feeling hungry? Like a drink?

A blanket?' But he didn't move. Even lust was denied an entry. On the altar steps, stained with ancient sacrifice, the demons finally moved off.

In the morning, devoured by thirst, he searched through the temple for a well. Stumbling through the thickets enveloping the ancient gods, he fell into an empty cistern. His fall was cushioned by ivy and brambles but they weren't quite strong enough to halt him. Down he went to rest on a mat of tangled vegetation, unconscious from thirst and pain. No one would find him there. Perfect solitude. And easy to keep still.

It is dark and damp of course. Frogs. 'And I saw three foul spirits coming from the mouth of the dragon, from the mouth of the beast, and from the mouth of the false prophet.' A dragon-like lizard, that ancient serpent Satan, deceiver of the whole world. He watched a frog, concentrating on its lurid spots, how its throat inflated and deflated, how it spread its webbed fingers, rolled its eyes from side and side, then stared at him. Simeon was transfixed by the frog's stare. The creature carefully shifted its weight across the couch of branches and leaves on which Simeon lay, came closer until it was nuzzling against the boy's side. Suddenly its tongue flashed out, and again. The frog had found a feast, a meal of Simeon's maggots. What a banquet. Come on, everyone, roll up. A lizard obeyed, and another. 'O worship the

Lord in the beauty of holiness,' he whispered to the lizard, who stuck out his tongue in response. Simeon was proud to be nurturing God's creatures.

Then it rained. He tilted his head back and opened his mouth; manna from heaven trickled in. The rain poured down, soaking him and his couch. Just as a stag loves to stay by springs of water, so shall my soul love to come to thee, O God. When it stopped the frogs came out; what better expression of emptiness than the chattering of bull frogs? he reminded himself and slept.

But as he slept the fever returned. Lurid temptations came and went as they did to the holy Antony. The wretched Devil himself climbed down, divinely beautiful, draped in scarlet of course, lips as well, but also in a myriad other disguises, yes, disguises: so tender sometimes, so loving, caressing the youth, running fingers through hair on top and below, that fearful stirring again but oh, the exquisite joy of it. How he yearned to be cocooned against a full breast, to suck the firm nipple, to rest on a yielding stomach. At other times the demons were more easily recognisable as the enemy; seven of them robed as rats broke down the walls of the cistern, assailed him with their cries, stamped on his toes, pulled his hair. And sometimes the hole was filled with lions, bears, leopards, serpents and asps, scorpions and wolves. Antony, he remembered, had dismissed such horrors: 'A sign of your helplessness that you ape the forms of brutes,' he had told his demons. Now he knew what the blessed Antony had endured. 'Why do you stand so far off, Lord, hiding your face in the needful time of trouble? Keep still, Simeon, keep still. Get me out.' he cried. 'I want to get out!' Looking up to the top of the cistern he saw suddenly a young girl's face. She stretched a white arm down to him, her dress slipping back as she did so to reveal a small rounded breast, so perfect that Simeon raised his own arm to her. Oh help me, he cried again, weeping. But the girl became a sheep that fell down on top of him, moaning at his feet.

Thus the Arabians' salukis found him, smelled the rotting sheep no doubt, barked for the boys who looked after the sheep. They peered over the top and giggled, made rude remarks about the smell and idiots who fall down wells. Simeon couldn't understand a word but he could see by their tousled black hair and dark skin that they came from the black tents he'd seen on the plain – herdsmen, nomads from Arabia. Pagan types, the brothers used to say. Don't trust them. Simeon had no desire to trust them as the boys stared down from the rim of the cistern. They lowered him a rope but he ignored it and they pulled it up again. They whispered together and moved away, calling their dogs to follow. That evening they threw into the cistern the remains of their lunch, a dried crust and dates. Simeon ate the dates and gave the crust to the lizards.

Next day they returned. Simeon sang to them, to keep their company, an awesome demoniacal echo from the cistern. Discarded temples are full of such ghosts. They told their families camped on the plain and in no time the ghosts were banished and crowds of Arabians gathered, sticking their heads over the edge and asking Simeon to sing prayers for them. Safe in his cistern, Simeon welcomed them all. Hallelujah! No peace; more temptation; but no more loneliness.

Women came to pray; they asked for the arms of a man, for the push of his sex, for his seed in them. The devil again, groaned Simeon, telling them to get back to work, he didn't want anything to do with their lusts. They shrieked with laughter and one of them threw her scarf down the cistern. It fluttered to his feet. 'Lord have mercy, mercy, mercy! Lord have mercy and lighten my darkness,' he called in panic.

As summer faded into autumn he prayed. 'Is it wrong to love light and dry winds and sun? Wind, rain, frost and baking heat? They're beautiful. And You made them after all. I worship them in the beauty of holiness. They are God. Some say, every time a man walks he does evil. Is that what you want me to believe? Are you ashamed, Lord, of what you have created in the world – moon and stars, hills and plains – that you must hide them from me? Oh all ye works of the Lord, bless ye the Lord, praise Him and magnify Him for ever. Don't you want us to praise your handiwork? Is it wrong to worship your creation? O Lord, lighten my darkness!' cried Simeon down in the cistern, yet nourished by the Arabians.

With autumn the Arabians came to say goodbye. They were heading south again to their sands greened now by the dews of autumn. Simeon decided to leave the cistern, to move. But he couldn't climb out. The sides of his refuge were slippery with autumnal dews, his legs and arms too weak. Seeing his dilemma one of the Arabians jumped down with a rope and took hold of his arms. He touched him. Simeon could feel rough calluses on the man's hands, scraping his skin. No! Tried to wrench himself free but the Arab misunderstand his revulsion, threw him over his shoulder, grabbed the rope and was pulled to the top. Simeon tumbled, scrawny and blinded, on the ground, slowly opening his eyes to a forest of legs. The boys were giggling, their hounds barked and jumped back afraid, but the elders were full of wonder and admiration.

'Come away with us,' they urged. 'You can live in the desert like the holy Antony.'

But Simeon was disinclined to wander; stillness had entered his soul. So they withdrew respectfully, leaving a pile of dates and a jug of water; one left a tunic to cover his nakedness.

6.

BETTER UP THAN DOWN?

Soon after he became Emperor, Constantine had alighted on the small town of Byzantium as his headquarters, guarding the passage between Asia and Europe. His descendant, Theodosius II, was proclaimed emperor there in 413 and soon after ordered the construction of massive walls round the new city to meet the growing menace from the horsemen from northern grasslands. South-east of his empire was the other potential adversary, Persia, necessitating frontier garrisons. Roads and rivers led south to Ctesiphon, seat of the Sasanian rulers – Shahs – on the right bank of the river Tigris. The ruler in Simeon's day was Shahriyar. Relations were always tricky.

In the Eastern Church patriarchs and popes were kept busy with their dissensions, not least in Alexandria. The Trinity – God the Father, the Son, the Holy Spirit – established at the Council of Nicaea in 323 was mostly recognised in both Western and Eastern Empires of Rome. But the powerful Patriarch of Alexandria, Cyril, was preoccupied with the increasingly heated row over the nature of Jesus and his mother.

The eastern Persian world also had its religious problems. There, some hundred and fifty years earlier, a wise and holy man in Mesopotamia found an answer to the vile destiny besetting man. This man believed in light and shade, in the rival energies of Good and Evil; if God made souls, then the Devil imprisoned them. All around him this man had seen the Devil's handiwork: houses ruined, crops wrecked by weather, bodies unburied – everything that weakened man's spirit, that made him lust and covet and compromise. Birth was a misfortune, death a deliverance. The Christ of the Manichaeans, as his followers were known, was the suffering Christ, 'crucified through the whole visible universe'.

Mani had been executed long ago and his followers cruelly persecuted, hounded out of the Persian empire, many of them fleeing westward along that Road. Other refugees were military, fleeing the on-off fighting between Roman and Sasanian-Persian armies, bedraggled remnants from the battlefield finding refuge in Telnessin as would many generations to come.

Crisscrossing of cultures and beliefs.

Then as now. Too many looking for consolation.

Pressurae mundi, Augustine called it, the pressure of the whole world. Writing in the shade of his luscious African olive trees, he saw pressing as an active process, extracting good oil. 'The world reels under crushing blows, the old man is shaken, the flesh is pressed, the spirit turns to clear flowing oil.' All very well for Augustine, contemplating his ripening harvests. The barbarians had not yet reached Africa – yet. His homestead was not under threat.

And the Emperor continued to buttress his walls.

So the Road was continually under the tread of armies, diplomats, holy men, messengers and merchants exchanging the riches of one world for those of another. And always refugees, tossed out of towns and villages by such as the terrifying horsemen from the wild country north and east of the civilised world: Huns appearing on the north shore of the Black Sea, Visigoths invading Italy, Vandals invading and settling in Spain. In 409 Alaric the Visigoth besieged Rome; a year later he captured but for once did not sack the city; he respected its antiquity and – amazingly – its sanctity. Yet also on the move were caravans of traders needing food and water as Simeon did with when he was led out of Antioch. Along the way were resting places. Sometimes they were great cities such as Antioch and Aleppo, famous for the exchange of goods as well as news, replete with sustenance, jollity, conversation. Other times there were simple hostelries, sometimes monasteries.

Not so far was the village of Telnessin, whither Heliodorus had directed Simeon, after he was heaved out of the well, though it took Simeon all day to get there. Again on the Road between east and west. Once again he arrived as the shadows lengthened and dogs growled in the gloaming. It was a prosperous village that benefited from its location on that main Road. It consisted of around fifty small stone houses set within courtyards and surrounded by high walls. Some were grouped around a small church.

A central space was occupied by a communal well. Beyond were fields and orchards, watered from time to time by a small river descending from the nearby hills. Courtyards contained chickens, sometimes goats, but there were also pens on the edge of the village – noisy when village boys opened up to take the animals to the hills for the day.

Travellers paused at Telnessin's solitary inn – not for long: the standard was grim. In Simeon's case the innkeeper took one look at his ragged figure, his glaring eyes, recognised the type ('UNWASHED!') and packed him off to the community established outside the village, a small huddle of buildings round a chapel. This was the monastery which Simeon had been directed to. Through the open door of the church shone a light. Simeon went in. Half a dozen figures were clustered round an altar (a rough stone), chanting a raggedy hymn. No one turned round. Simeon stumbled up the aisle to join them. Two moved over to give him space.

The community here was different from the other establishments where Simeon had stayed. Hardly a community in fact. Similar to those set up by the Egyptian monk Pachomius on the edge of the African desert where women as well as men each followed his or her own ascetic routine, some alone, some in pairs, others in groups. Such was the pattern at Telnessin. They were scattered nearby, each in his own hut or hillside cave. They assembled once a week and on holy days to sing psalms and hymns composed by the holy venerable Ephrem (wah Wah wah as far as Simeon was concerned), listen to the sermon of their Superior Bassos, pray together. Then they dispersed over the stony hillside, carrying nourishment for the next week. And uncommunicative. Buzz off, they muttered to the flies, attracted to their grouchy flesh. Buzz off to all visitors.

Their Superior Bassos was from northern Syria but had travelled widely in his youth – to Jerusalem, other parts of Palestine, Egypt, in each place spending a few months or years in monastic establishments each with distinctive disciplines. He studied at the feet of such solitaries as Hilarion in Palestine and Jerome in Bethlehem. But after a while he missed the orchards, the flowery hillsides, the rugged landscape of his beloved Syria.

Bassos was the gentlest of souls: he had little desire to interfere with the ruminations of others, who might live apart, hermits perhaps, but still have the assurance of a community. Not much conversation. Dirty. No formality. The holy Antony undiluted, you might say. Simeon was (more or less) made welcome.

No one bothered him. He spent the night on the hard floor of the church and next morning followed the silent Bassos up the hill. It was pocked with caves, many of them improved by the hand of man. Simeon was directed to an empty one and with a broom propped up outside swept out the sheep droppings, the bats, the cobwebs. He collected rocks and piled them up at the narrow mouth of the cave to shelter from wind and rain and ensure a measure of privacy. That evening he stood outside his new abode and sang loudly to the stars. Across the hill his fellow hermits joined in.

Soon winter blew in. Snow outside his cave, Simeon immobile inside. The mobility of the world hardly bothered him even when passers-by clambered up the hill to stare, to pray, even to sing along with him. Travellers heading east or west relished a bit of sanctity. A prayer or two might last as far as their next destination; no harm in climbing up to a cave to ask an inmate for his blessing. Leave a scrap of food outside cave. Some knew him from the well. Simeon discovered he did not mind obliging, discovered the gift of eloquence. A bit of a performer. And they liked his homilies, his hymns. He could always hide himself at the back of the cave if it all became too pressing. In the spring Arabians arrived. He saw their flocks first, the boys marshalling them with slings. Then he would see their women erecting long black tents. And then someone came with a bunch of well-travelled dates for him, dusty but delicious. They gave him crumbs of incense to burn at the entrance to the cave. They also liked his psalms: 'Light our lamps, O King!' he yelled from the mouth of the cave, relishing the echo spun across the hill. 'We remember that song from the well!' they grinned. And the boys gave him a heavy black cloak woven by their women over the winter. 'The Lord is my shepherd!' he yelled after them as they headed down the hill. 'Thanks to you I shan't freeze!'

To offset the world's mobility, Simeon decided to highlight immobility. 'Everyone's on the move,' he shouted to a grouchy neighbour as he strode down to the village to ask the blacksmith if he would be so kind as to find him a heavy iron chain and collar to put round his neck.

'That's crazy!' Joseph commented to Superior Bassos. 'At his age? A young man like that should have other thoughts on his mind.'

'You never know nowadays,' replied the Superior. 'That's probably why he wants to tie himself down. Look at the road – everyone on the move. Good to have someone who doesn't move. Or not much. Make the chain long enough,' he cautioned. 'He will need to move away from the cave to shit.'

'Bad as a rutting dog,' said Joseph. But he made the chain. What's more he took it up the hill himself. 'You never know, I might earn a bit of credit with the Lord above,' he muttered to his wife.

Simeon had Joseph lock it round his neck; then he hooked the other end over his shoulder, persuading the iron master to follow him back to the cave to jam the other end into the rock of the cave.

'I will love thee, O Lord my strength!' He sang as Joseph locked the chain end inside the cave. 'The Lord is my stony rock and my defence!'

The blacksmith was deeply impressed, saw his own path to the Almighty (better still, to Paradise) improved by obedience to Simeon's command. He spread the word within the village, then to travellers along the road. The crowds began to grow. Once a week a fellow monk came with a key to unlock the chain so that Simeon could descend to the church to pray and collect bread and water. And defecate further from the cave. What sanctity! The news travelled, people came to look and stare, to seek consolation. 'The Light has dawned!' Simeon was happy to comfort. 'Rejoice!' Wa wa, as the great hymn writer Ephraim sang.

Then Simeon acquired a young attendant to chase those who came too close. Jacob was his name, a refugee from Mesopotamia, alone and adrift along that great road. Jacob was a Manichaean.

The Manichaeans had taught Jacob the primeval conflict between Lightness and Darkness. In due course, they said, the darkness would be sloughed off like a snake skin. Hmm – who can be sure? There was also a pessimism that the deeds of the world seemed to confirm, even their own deeds. In Mesopotamia Mani had been hanged: the Zoroastrian priesthood would not tolerate a rival. Jacob fled the persecution, trudging fearfully through the desert in the footsteps of caravans and imperial battalions, arriving one day, after many adventures, to sit outside Simeon's cave. 'From what cause is evil done to us?' he asked from outside the cave, weeping and moaning.

As consolation, 'All things bright and beautiful, boy,' sang Simeon at the top of his voice, to the irritation of his hillside neighbours. Jacob, lanky and stooped with misfortune, was much the same age as Simeon but with none of his resolution. Simeon ill-kempt and ill-fed and distinctly smelly, radiated optimism. 'All creatures great and small', and he stroked a rat running over his leg to chew a toe. 'The Lord God will provide,' he assured Jacob although in Simeon's case his many visitors did the providing. Jacob took on the role of a faithful hound doing for Simeon all the things the limited length of the chain prevented Simeon from doing. 'Sing praises!' sang Simeon, attracting visitors from other caves, away from the other hermits much to their irritation. Jacob brought him sweet titbits and faithfully scooped up Simeon's turds, hurling them far away across the hillside.

A major event for the cave dwellers each year was Lent. No food, no water for forty days, so Simeon decreed.

'You can't,' said Superior Bassos, trying to exert a little discipline.

'He can,' Jacob replied from the mouth of Simeon's cave. 'God is his food and water.'

'This means death,' his fellow hermits murmured crossly to each other,

'God isn't ready for me yet,' shouted the young man from inside his cave.

The debate lasted several days. Eventually – compromise: the Superior agreed to allow Jacob to wall Simeon into the cave, provided he took inside ten loaves and an urn of water lugged from the nearby stream. In case of need. No one need feel guilty if he died; they had done all they could. Jacob collected stones from the hillside and walled Simeon in his cave.

In the dark, wrapped in his blanket, Simeon at first yearned for company, for sound and sight until his eyes and ears accustomed themselves to the dark and to silence. Then he found company. He came slowly to see the spiders and beetles, their webs and holes, life in the rocks and heard the chatter of that life. Not a glimmer of human life for forty days. His blanket attracted company; a family of mice came to stay, tickling his armpit. His senses dulled by hunger he ceased to be aware of silence and darkness, instead peopling it with sounds and smells and chinks of light. This was an intensely private journey; no one else could tell which way to go. 'He who sits in solitude and is quiet,' the holy Antony said, 'has escaped from three wars: hearing, speaking, seeing, yet against one thing shall he continually battle: that is, his own heart.'

'Oh Lord God,' he shouted to the walls on the twentieth day, 'I have cried day and night before you, for my soul is full of trouble. My life draws near to hell. I am so fast in prison that I cannot get out.' His feet were numb but it warmed him to rub them back to life. He scratched his flea bites. Sucked the blood that oozed from them

'O God, how my soul thirsts for you, my flesh also longs for you, in a barren and dry land where there is no water,' he croaked on the thirtieth day: 'I am no thing. I am no state. I am nothing.'

On the fortieth day, Superior Bassos shouldered the responsibility of unwalling the cave. Jacob had plastered the wall with mud. It had hardened and the Superior himself was weak enough from his own Lenten fast to find dismantling it a demanding task. Jacob gave him a feeble hand. Inside the cave Simeon lay unconscious on the floor. The food and water were untouched.

Gently they moistened his lips and the corpse came slowly to life. It responded to the sacraments. The body and blood of Christ gave body and blood to the young starving Simeon. Later Jacob fed him gruel, then garlic and onions cultivated in a little garden carved out of the hillside near the cave. Soon his ululating laughter rang out, even reaching the village. 'Miraculous!' sighed the village happily, already aware of the pecuniary value of the youth in the cave. 'Hallelujah! Hosanna in the highest!'

Thousands who felt themselves crushed with fear, looked for points of security, stability. They clustered round. Jacob bathed their wounds. The villagers patched them up and the Arabians lent them tent space. They woke Simeon who discarded the blanket and clambered up the stone. The dogs also rose and snarled at the newcomers. Simeon dimly remembered his brother from long ago: where was he? He remembered the barbarians who had raided his village. Where are you O Lord? Not everything is bright and beautiful. But the Lord God will heal your wounds, he shouted and crept back under the blanket.

With the waning of the moon came not only the end of Lent but the arrival of spring. Boys from the village led the sheep into the hills, shouting as they went, pointing rude fingers at the hermits outside their caves. Their mothers brought posies of early flowers and bits of cheese wrapped in leaves.

It was cold; there was still a touch of snow on the further hills. It rained; Simeon sheltered at the mouth of his cave. Then the Easter celebration of the risen Christ – still chilly but the hillsides springing to life.

Jewish merchants came from Aleppo on their way to Antioch. It was Passover and everyone was happy to celebrate together. The emperor published a decree allowing Jews freedom of worship in their synagogues. Simeon, hearing how all the old synagogues in Antioch were being opened up, scrubbed, given a coat of paint, was enraged. 'Here we are, worshipping the Son of

God, of one substance with the Father, and you grant freedom of worship to those who crucified the Son of God – how good a Christian are you?' he addressed the emperor by pigeon, but then remembered the Jews who were down the hill in Telnessin and how he welcomed their sweetmeats.

A caravan of Persians arrived from the Euphrates, also celebrating spring with their festival of Nawruz. Simeon could see their grumpy camels tied up outside the village. Their owners tossed bars of sticky sweets into the camel enclosure. 'O my teeth!' groaned Simeon (he had few left). Jacob the Manichaean ran off into the hills for fear of these Zoroastrians.

The Arabians saw Telnessin's potential as a useful market for their flocks. They camped below the caves, lighting their incense, pelting the holy one with dates, which Jacob gathered up for Simeon. Their children trampled Jacob's newly dug garden; the voices of their women disturbed Simeon's prayers. 'Let all my enemies be ashamed,' he shouted to the carrier pigeons briefly out of their coop. 'Let them suddenly return and be ashamed suddenly!' and he cast a bitter eye in the direction of the children. Presbyter Ezekiel from the village could hardly push through the crowds to offer Simeon the sacraments.

Simeon's arousal became an annual event as the weather warmed up, attracting God-fearing sightseers from far and wide. The crowds began to press too close. They threw coins in the cave for good luck and bruised him. 'But they come around me like water,' moaned Simeon to Presbyter Ezekiel after taking the sacrament: he was too weak to descend to the village.

The Presbyter discussed the crowds with the village elders who unanimously offered Simeon a plot of land above the village; after all, the attraction of the young hermit and his hymn singing was improving the village's fortunes. Here, when he was stronger, Simeon and Jacob built an enclosure, collecting rocks off the hillside, chipping one against another as Simeon had been taught in his childhood, piling them up to make rough encircling walls. Simeon settled down within, fenced off, he thought, against intruders. Unmoving. Movement equals distraction until the spirit has earnt the right to be free. Movement takes you from the Lord, he told the crowds peering over the wall.

Just to strengthen the point he got Joseph blacksmith to solder his iron fetter to an ankle, fixed again to another ten-foot chain, the other end embedded in the hillside. He roared with laughter, defecated in a circle, different spot each day – not a very substantial turd, it has to be said, but enough to discourage people from climbing into the enchanted circle. Always standing during the day, sometimes hands clasped above his head. Other than Jacob and kindly Bassos, only the lizards and salamanders were allowed in, sitting on his toes, flicking fly-catching tongues. And crows of course, pecking moodily at the turds. Simeon only left the enclosure for his Lenten fast.

Arabian children collected their sheep and goats and squatted still round Simeon's enclosure; saluki hounds curled at their feet. When the autumn chill came, they urged Simeon to come away with them, as they had done when he lay in the cistern. 'The desert is just the place for you,' they said. But Simeon only laughed and spurned their offer, as before. 'The desert is not for me,' he told them. 'I need to smell the apricot blossom, the thyme you crush with your feet. I need my hoopoe and my owl, the lizards and the mouse who nibbles my scraps. The people who feed on my silence. You have none of these in your desert. Besides, you move too much.'

Autumn was as popular as spring. Most visitors now came from Aleppo, several weeks away; an autumnal journey (such a beautiful season!) to this eccentric holy man before it was too cold, much to the delight of the villagers, charging exorbitantly for miserable lodgings, refreshments. 'You should not take refreshments when visiting the holy Simeon,' the villagers rebuked their critics but were only too happy to supply them. Liars and swindlers, the grumblers muttered back, sleepless from bugs in the blankets.

Δ

Up the hill, tempted by the cooler weather, ladies from Aleppo were particularly delighted to stare at Simeon doing his exercises. One even clambered over the wall to touch him but Jacob soon chased her away down the hill. 'Go!' Simeon shouted after her. Then a whole bevy of them came one day, fleshy and beautiful as ripe peaches in all their fruity finery, not quite how more sober folk might choose to deck themselves for a visit to so famous an ascetic as the young Simeon was becoming. They had a bet amongst themselves – of just such a nature as you can imagine – and flew up the slope to Simeon's enclosure like a swarm of butterflies. At the enclosure they accosted Jacob. 'Hey beauty!' they giggled, 'are you going to let us kneel before the holy Simeon?'

'No fear!' said Jacob inaccurately; he was terrified. 'No one may go in!'

'Ohhhhh?' queried one of them, more daring than the rest. 'Hey, holy one!' she yelled across the enclosure to where Simeon was standing on one leg, arms raised to the heavens. 'Look over here, my friend' and she pulled up her skirt to show a shapely plump leg. At a nudge her companions grabbed poor Jacob: 'No running away, holy boy!' And with that she hitched up her skirts, climbed over the low wall and ran towards Simeon. Disturbed in his heavenly concentration Simeon took one look at her and lost his balance, falling to all fours on the ground. 'Jacob!' he screamed.

Now everyone was cheering her on, suddenly seeing Simeon's antics as a big joke, which in a sense, they were.

'You asked for it, lovely boy! Showing off!' the crowd yelled. 'Go on, lady!'

To Jacob they seemed the ultimate torture. He tore himself free of his captors and jumped on the woman as she jumped on Simeon, frantically tearing at her dress to force her off. The crowd was howling, relishing the scrap. In no time everyone was in the enclosure. Suddenly the Arabians came to Simeon's rescue. Their dogs snapped at the heels of the intruders, getting a mouthful of the woman's dress before she took the hint and fell into the arms of her companions.

'Hey ho!' they sang as they skipped off down the hill to investigate the delicacies of Telnessin. 'Worth all the trouble we had getting here!'

Simeon moaned, remembering his adventures in Antioch.

Later, that evening, after a monastic meal of bread and milk improved with some tasty sweeteners the girls had brought with them: 'If I sat on a hillside at any season,' sighed Simeon's fruity visitor, 'I wouldn't last an hour'. She shifted her buttocks on the hard mud floor of the monastery's refectory, the only place in Telnessin to offer lodging.

'We'd none of us leave you in peace, dear lady.' A fellow guest nodded knowingly, an Aleppo merchant with extensive commercial connections with the east. 'I've seen some real oddities in Persia. You should see the tricks they get up to. Profitable business too.' His name was Sergius.

'Tricks?' giggled his drinking companion. 'I'd rather have yours any day, Sergius dear.'

The merchant, Sergius, dipped a finger in his wine and drew it across her arm. 'Only too happy to show you some of my tricks.' He crooned in her ear.

'Now now,' she giggled. 'Patience, patience, dear friend. Wait till you visit me in Aleppo!'

The next morning Presbyter Ezekiel waylaid the merchant as he was reorganising his caravan. The Presbyter was high in his own esteem, regarding himself as the guardian of Telnessin's great treasure. He sat Sergius down in his cramped cottage, pouring him a glass of apricot liqueur. 'We need a proper hostel here, honoured sir,' he began, 'for the better sort of pilgrim. People like yourself, honoured Sergius. I notice you never bring your wife – there's nowhere suitable for her to stay. The only available place is little better than a brothel. A hostel for the likes of you and your friends, there are more and more of you. Important visitors heading west from Aleppo, even from the land of two rivers, or from Antioch. Providing peace and quiet... In fact, just what the boy up the hill is trying to find, not so successfully at this time of year. A bit of an exhibitionist, don't you think?'

'A useful exhibition nevertheless. A magnet you might say. Good for the village too. So,' he asked. 'What's on your mind?'

'Just wondered, honoured sir, any chance you could help with the idea of a hostel of quality? Should be someone from the city, who knows the ways of city people. Somewhere with a bit of comfort I suggest.'

'Not a bad idea,' ruminated the merchant. 'I'll discuss it with my wife. She has always been on the lookout for a good investment. And might even be tempted to visit.'

'More wine, honoured sir?'

'Don't mind if I do .... We do like our city comforts. I might find an Antiochene to run it, they're familiar with the ways of the world.'

So Presbyter Ezekiel took the merchant on

a walk round Telnessin, taking in the lie of the land, the availability of space, of water, of grazing for donkeys etc. 'I think the villagers might welcome the investment,' murmured the merchant. 'Perhaps some gentle enquiries, dear Presbyter? See who's interested?' The merchant's faith was practical enough for him also to be filled with wonder at Simeon's explicit sanctity. Back in town he tried out his idea on colleagues. 'I'm no saint myself,' he held forth to commercially minded cronies, 'a conversion of convenience, you might say. But I know a good man when I see one. And a good opportunity. Take note. This is where the future lies: in a plethora of holiness. Don't fret about Rome.' Which was just as well.

Then came Simeon's mother Mary. A terrible day. Simeon's fame had even reached the sea, even Tarsus and his village beyond. She had travelled for many months to reach him. Shrivelled and sick, accompanied by fellow villagers, weeping and wailing though also longing to see her son. The old woman had to be carried up the hill. Poor soul, she must have thought she'd have no problem getting to him, famous as he already was for goodness as well as godliness. Jacob was guarding the enclosure. Those who had been carrying the old woman put her down by the entrance and explained who she was. Of course he let her in. She hobbled towards her son who was standing as usual, his eyes closed. Suddenly sensing the old woman's presence and opening his eyes he flung himself on the ground, on all fours (like an animal, said Jacob later), bobbing his head from side to side, shouting 'No! No! I won't see her. No women here! Take her away! Out!' He was hysterical. She was silent. Why the rejection? An earthly tie, like his chain. 'My love is only for the Lord. Mothers are no better than other women, even harder to renounce when lust for the rest has been starved out, strangled.' So the old woman's helpers gently raised her and carried her away down the hill, sobbing all the way.

'O my Beloved,' wailed Simeon, addressing his Lord, while the Lord took his mother. She was carried down to the tender care of Superior Bassos. Half of her mind was already with the Lord, while the other half struggled with her son. Placing her on his couch, Bassos fed her the herbs brought for Simeon and prayed with her through the night. 'For everything there is a time to pluck up that which is planted,' he told her, 'and an end to every purpose under the sun.' Her eyes half opened: 'a time to pluck up that which is planted,' she whispered, her final words. The Superior wondered whether she was condemning her son to be plucked up. 'Lord, now let your servant depart in peace.' he chanted quietly, 'according to your word, depart in peace, depart in peace.'

Before the next day dawned she had indeed departed though whether it was in peace after that rejection it was impossible to say. She was interred outside the village, a new Christian practice that Bassos had observed in Palestine. Disgusting, murmured certain villagers

The Arabians gave Simeon a goat's horn. 'Come and sing unto the Lord!' He blew across the hill with such fervour that even the sick on their litters joined in. 'Praise the Lord upon the harp!' he sang and a boy leaped past Jacob into the enclosure and handed one to him. 'Sing to the harp with thanksgiving,' yelled Simeon waving cheerily to the crowd. He had not a clue what to do with the harp but laid it reverently against the rock. The boy jumped again over Jacob's fence and began plucking it. Simeon raised shrunken arms to the heavens and let out a shriek of joy. 'All things bright and beautiful!' he sang, a favourite of his.

Jerome in Bethlehem, surrounded on his sick bed by devoted women and acolytes, snorted his disapproval when he heard of Simeon. 'Courting the attention of men when he should be courting the Almighty' was his verdict. But he was too near death himself, too near the Almighty, to be bothered by minor hermits. Obscure holy men in Syria remained obscure.

Soldiers also came by, looking for respite from

the distant muddy Euphrates where Roman garrisons were defending imperial frontiers from Persian incursions. Relations with the Sasanian Shah were often uneasy. In 421 Emperor Theodosius decided to avenge the decimation of an expedition led by his forebear, the pagan Emperor Julian, at the hands of the Sasanians; Julian meeting his end on the battlefield. This new Roman expedition was not a particularly useful gesture. It defeated a small Sasanian army, re-established a series of frontier garrisons and allowed the remnant to march back home. Simeon was a welcome interlude in the hardships of the road. Late one evening some wounded youths in rags arrived from that eastern frontier. Their clothes were torn and bloody. Two of them were sharing the load of a third whose head hung down over their backs. Who are these? Where have they come from? Where do they go? Simeon remembered his brother – where was he? They staggered up the hill to Simeon; Jacob gave them water and a few scraps of food; there was never much left over from Simeon's meals. The Arabians were more generous.

Pigeons were despatched between generals, patriarchs, merchants. The court in Constantinople giggled when it heard of these holy antics in Syria but the Emperor Theodosius frowned and sent missives to Telnessin to find out more.

Simeon was flattered, dictated a letter, telling the emperor to remember the Nicene Creed, to pray to the Three in One but not to exalt Mary's elevation as the mother of God. That was a tricky issue dividing the Christian world. Pigeons flew back and forth; Simeon kept a basket in the enclosure. The sympathetic Patriarch Thedoretus of Cyrrhus to the east, when passing by Simeon's enclosure, warned of the dangers of Mary's elevation. If she is declared simply as the earthly mother of Jesus then that surely splits the Trinity which the fathers of the Church had worked so hard to define over a hundred years ago at Nicaea. That could threaten to tear the Church apart.

Jacob took on the role of a faithful hound. But Simeon was singing. 'The Lord God made them all. Even these onions! Garlic too!' He radiated optimism. 'The Lord God will provide,' he reassured Jacob although in Simeon's case his many visitors did the providing. And Jacob. At sunset Jacob would unlock Simeon's chain, hand him an onion and a flask of water and help him across the hillside to his cave for the night. Peace all round. At last. Simeon scratched the night away.

But why, when you pray for freedom to reach up up up to the divine, must you chain yourself to this troubled earth so relentlessly? Surely that's not the right move. The thought stuck, made Simeon laugh out loud. Everyone on the move; they need an anchor. Angels beckoned to him from the heavens. 'Come on up, little one,' they sang. Angels trumpeted to him through the long night, their glory gilding the cave and reflecting the heavens outside. Then the angels gave way to a greater spirit that spoke to him, commanded him to set himself way above the crowd, to show them the way, not to hide his light. The voice was like an arrow of light in the darkness piercing the obscurity of his soul, his cave. He had another thought: God be merciful unto us and show us the light of his countenance. Simeon must show his countenance. He would show his face to more thousands if he rose above them all. No one could touch him but they could see, and through him see the Lord in all His glory.

One day Simeon was particularly irritable. The iron chaffed his ankle. By day and night in summer especially the hillside was overwhelmed with noise; he could hardly hear himself pray, let alone make himself heard to others. Fires flared, donkeys screamed, children babbled, men hacked and coughed, peddlers sold pipes that were then badly played from bush to bush. And women! Simeon collapsed at nightfall into the most unconscious of slumbers. Jacob and Bassos, with whom he had prayed before and after they broke the day's fast with an onion mush, had gone to their huts at the foot of the hill. 'Lift up your hearts O ye gates, and be ye lift up, ye everlasting doors.' They had sung together before departing, 'and the King of Glory shall come in.'

They still try to touch me. Trespassing ...

Rustling, squeaking. Tickling. He sat back on his stone. The iron chaffed his ankle. 'I'll go to the cave. Get a rock while I'm inside. A whopper. Get the village to help. Smooth it down. I'll live on it. Tell the men down there I'm a good investment. The women know that already, feeding my visitors.

He limped over to the wall to urinate on Jacob's vegetable patch; signs of life among the cabbages. 'Petrus used to live in the top storey of a tomb near Antioch, probably dead by now. Could only be reached by ladder. Or the barley eater: only eats barley. At least I have your vegetables. Or Eusebius, Abbot of Coryphe, who chains his neck to his girdle to keep his eyes on the ground. Or Thalelaios who bundled himself into a cage and had it suspended from gallows. Lord Jesus, what a bunch. At least I see human beings, even talk to them. As long as they keep their distance. I like my fellow men – unlike you, sour son of Mani.' Simeon, complain as he did about their din, their smell, their brats, relished the company – 'helps keep demons away' – while Jacob was soured by it. 'Damn you,' he spat hopelessly at the Arabian children.

Jacob had a an even larger fund of gruesome asceticism, a strong sense of the macabre. 'I've heard of holy men in India climbing up pillars. The righteous Mani wrote of them. Lived up there for years on end. They say they do it in Egypt too. Plenty of fresh air. And you could still have my vegetables.' Jacob was angry. He could not understand Simeon's enjoyment of the crowds. Loneliness was the condition of his life, Simeon the only man he loved.

He challenged Jacob. 'You talk to me of Abraemes, walled up in a cave for forty years. He has neither seen nor spoken, nor been seen nor spoken to by anyone. They put his food in a hole in the rock once a week and as long as it disappears, they know he is alive. Copying the holy Jerome without the wisdom.'

Raise me higher, O Lord – higher! Higher!

Suddenly a beam of light. 'Hey Jacob!' he grunted to the figure by the fence. 'I must indeed rise higher. Above them all! But still with them all!' Simeon fingered his lifeless member: he could never quite trust it however much he tried to beat it into submission. If he rose, it too would rise. He grinned at that and fingered it more fondly. The birds could perch on it, even the wise hoopoe. Particularly the wise hoopoe. 'GET ME A STONE!'

Jacob was furious. He fed this man, watered

him, grew his veg, kicked his ladies out (hey! he seemed to have recognised one). Fed his pigeons! But then he went to the village and asked Superior Bassos if some locals might be prepared to find a rock as tall as the tallest man and would they please roll it inside the Holy One's space.

They scoured the hillside for a stone, finally raided an old temple on the hill nearby. He won't know which god was worshipped here.

They opened the cave. Simeon lay on his back, eyes open, horn on the ground alongside him. Hey holy one! Time to rise. Slowly slowly they massaged him, dripped water between his lips, stroked his legs back to life. And as they pushed the boulder away Simeon broke into song, a croaky note admittedly, but song nevertheless, to the great relief of Jacob who found he could join in. 'Sing unto the Lord a great song!' Simeon had an excellent voice, gathering strength as he emerged bent and bowed from the cave. Now the whole hillside reverberated with it. 'O all the works of the Lord, bless ye the Lord!' There was the bedraggled Simeon once again in cracked voice. They all joined in. But they had to wrap a cloth over his eyes to shield them from the bright spring sun.

Then they hoisted him on Joseph blacksmith's back to carry him across to the enclosure. A cheer rose from a hundred throats, thankful to see their holy man alive. Just.

In the enclosure he saw the stone. The villagers had found it in the ruins of the old temple up the hill; Joseph had smoothed its wrinkles and hacked a few steps into a side. Simeon cackled, a sound like the seeds on the dry acanthus stalk rasping against the wall, and crawled across to it. This would infuriate the old Jerusalem cave dweller, Jerome, God rest his soul. The stone they found, big as the biggest ox, was about six feet high and took several such oxen to drag it down the hill. Nevertheless, the villagers already looked on Simeon as an asset worth pandering to and obliged with the loan of their animals. And their muscle. The steps led to a small platform just big enough for Simeon to sit or lie on. Jacob had cleared a patch of ground and sown some onions, they had pushed up just enough for Simeon to crush between his fingers and relish the strength they gave.

A sturdy stone leaving Simeon capped with a slab on which to spend the day. Upended in the middle of the enclosure, Simeon could sit with his legs dangling over the edge, chanting psalms, blowing that horn, cheering refugees, almost joking with the girls from Aleppo as long as they kept their distance, which of course they didn't despite Jacob's efforts – and how they teased him!

At least there were no Susannahs. All things bright and beautiful, he blew on the horn. He came down at night, slept curled up on the ground under the great Arabian blanket; the Arabians themselves insisted on one of their salukis watching and gently growling over him against intruders.

7.

INTERLUDE

In 1976, high up on that hill overlooking Aleppo I perched on a ruined wall in the citadel waiting for sunset. That building epitomises the antiquity of this Syrian world and also how critical a strong citadel has been over the centuries. Syria's intruders have all had their say in this 'palatial' fortification but there's enough to remind one that this was a military, administrative and show-off establishment. Aleppo had suffered a major earthquake in 1108 at the height of Frank (crusader) attempts to conquer northern Syria. It was the great Kurdish warrior Saladin who was in my mind as I sat amidst the massive fortifications. Saladin's victories over the Franks was followed by those of the Turkish warrior Baybars. Other Asiatic raiders also fought over northern Syria but over the years Aleppo's position on the main Road between East and West re-asserted itself and it became once again the great commercial metropolis, as it had been in Simeon's day.

Now in 1976 it was Muslim against Muslim, tribe against tribe. Hafiz al-Assad and his Shia regime held tightly to the reins of power and a giant portrait of the president's brother Rifaat had been hung across the cobbled approach to the lead up to the citadel. Now in neighbourly Lebanon similar problems had erupted between rival religious sects. God was certainly in trouble – or so it seemed from the citadel that day.

No doubt Simeon would have had some mourners looking for comfort in his time too.

The sun was just catching the top of the superb minaret in the city's Great Mosque below. At forty-five metres it was surely built as a rival to Simeon's pillar. Amazingly it survived the many earthquakes that had shaken the city over the centuries: good Roman mortar no doubt. The sun dipped below the horizon. A few minutes later the call to prayer rang out from the minaret; in the courtyard of the mosque a few men hurried in to wash before entering the prayer hall.

I could hear the rattle of shutters as the shops in the *suq* closed down. So it was predictably quiet when I went to look for Muhammad Mazrui. 'No life in the market these days,' Muhammad sighed. 'Why should anyone want to do business with the Assads messing about in Lebanon. How about a visit to your old friend on his pillar? Plenty of unfortunates around him I reckon. And Maryam will be delighted to see you.'

The car park at the foot of the hill was packed with cars with Lebanese number plates. 'Christian pilgrims,' Muhammad commented as we turned off on to a rough track through Deir al-Simaan village. 'They often come to the Jinn when there's trouble at home.' But I also spotted a couple of heavy military vehicles.

Muhammad drew up by military cars. A driver in army uniform sat behind the wheel of one of them. What had brought them to Qalaat Simaan? A small group of men was coming down the processional way from the basilica. One of them was in uniform; he had lots of important-looking stripes on his chest, presumably the commander of the car with uniformed driver. I nodded to them as they reached their cars and returned their 'salaam alaykum'. 'What brings you here, madam?' the medalled one asked suspiciously. 'Where are you from?'

'Curiosity,' I shrugged. It was half true after all. 'I've come from Beirut. Qalaat Simaan is better than Beirut at the moment. That's where I live. What about you?'

'Ah Beirut,' another said. 'The Lebanese make a lot of trouble for us at the moment. And the Americans. God willing, we shall sort out their problems. This old man of the mountain – he is our go between with God.' He opened his hand to show off some small stone fragments. Everyone needs such safeguards, go-betweens and intermediaries – however much orthodox Sunni Muslims disclaim them. The pillar looked shrivelled – earthquakes and warriors as well as pilgrims had their impacts. 'We need all his help. 'Another warrior spoke out. 'There were many like him in these parts. Now all gone. Except him.' I wondered aloud how much Aleppo was affected by the strife in Lebanon. 'We are thankful,' the officer continued, 'that our president protects us from such fighting.'

But for how long? On that first visit I had noted Muslims of all loyalties paying their respects to Simeon, alongside Christians. Now there must have been as many as a hundred people just visible up the hill, the latest generation of mourners. Still, I liked to think, that Simeon could ease their approach to the One God, Christian or Muslim.

Islam was never as monolithic as is sometimes assumed. Just as Christianity had developed its theological divisions so sectarian divisions arose within Islam. The path was overgrown and tall acanthus leaves waved in the breeze between baptismal chapel and basilica. The remains of the basilica seemed much as ever. Weeping visitors were heading for the path. A crowd of mourners were crouched round the pillar; one of them was hacking at the rock for his relic. Some women were howling into their shrouds but they hurried away when they saw me.

Then I spotted the Jinn leaning against the remains of the great arch over the western arm of the octagon, I joined him. War, war and more war. '*Oh yes –they all charged up my hill like summer tempests – Franks with their God, Turks with theirs. One on the blackest of chargers, bow over shoulder, arrows at the ready, howling their war cries, came to a halt just where you are now. He reared up up up – what monster beasts! Blacker even than Satan himself. Allowed his slaves to chip away at my stone. Talismans. Ha! On his victory path against those Frank invaders.*'

He gazed up at the remains of the arch. '*The Lord Almighty came to our rescue,*' he whispered, '*sent a great trembling of the earth. Smashed the city down the road which the heathens were trying to grab. But also knocked another stone off my pillar! Fell on the heads of people moaning at the bottom. And wounded this great arch.*' I looked up past the arch to the fields beyond, imagining the fears of the pillar worshippers.

What would these Franks have made of the ruins where I now sat, or indeed the Christian remains on the plain below, no doubt ravaged by them for supplies. And the pillar itself, looking the worse for wear after that quake, no doubt surrounded by those afflicted by the catastrophe: how much of that would those medieval Muslim or Frankish warriors have seen, damaged by earthquakes not just humans? I glanced across into the ruins of the monastery built – one assumed – to accommodate visiting pilgrims. People huddled round their fires, more refugees, more looking for consolation. The plain, beyond the village of Deir Simaan, was studded with fingers of ruined monasteries. Quite a concentration of sanctity, which had not however preserved it from ravaging warriors. No doubt everyone had chipped away at it, like today's military visitors.

The Jinn hopped over to the chippings that littered the ground. '*They always hope it will bring better fortune,*' he cackled. '*No wonder I wanted to be above it all.*'

I noted that someone had been digging up some mud from the foot of the rock.

He leaned against the stone. '*Their leader ordered a slave at his heels to hack a piece off the fallen stone. Off my pillar! My pillar!*' He clambered down from the pillar platform and did a sort of dance round the rock. '*Not so brave that they didn't need a talisman to help them on their barbaric way. They all call themselves crusaders, marching in the name of the lord. Which Lord, I ask them, whose Lord?*' He plucked a thistle huddling in the shade of the rock. '*They come from all directions – from south, from north, from east and west. All calling themselves holy crusaders. Savages more like. They all hack bits off my pillar. Talismans!*' He hooted at the very idea and scrunched the thistle; I remembered his liking for the spiny beasts. He rose, hitched up a ragged loin cloth (I wondered if my friend Maryam left the occasional cloth for decency's sake), touched his toes a few times and swung his arms. *'Got to keep going,'* I heard him mutter almost to himself. *'Warriors on nags. Some of them charged up my hill, drank from the baptistery pool in springtime but when they turned in my direction – O my! How I waved my arms, swished these hairs* (and he swished a threadbare chin in my direction) *and away down the hill they howled. "Jinns! Jinns! Shaitan! The Devil himself!"'* and he emitted a shriek clearly of joy at the recollection. Saladin maybe? Or Baybars, Saladin's successor in finishing off the Franks. We all need our intercessors after all.

In 1138 a catastrophic earthquake hit the not-so-distant Aleppo. It came just in time to save the city from its Frank besiegers. No wonder a bit of Simeon's home had collapsed. But now I was cold and imagination was fading. 'Time to find Ibrahim and the gentle Maryam. See you anon,' I told the Jinn, 'I'm not sure when. But I shall be back.' He made a rude thumbs up. And I slowly made my way through the darkening ruins and down the hill. Boys were kicking a ball among the remaining cars.

'You remember me? I am Mahmud,' one of them announced with the aplomb of a young teenager. 'Come,' he commanded and took my hand. 'My mother will give you tea,' and taking me by the arm he led me through the village to the compound. I recognised the ugly steel door set into the wall of Ibrahim's compound; Mahmud pushed it open shouting, 'Al ingliziyyah! ingliziyyah!' and scattering hens to left and right led me across the yard just as Ibrahim himself emerged from the house. Followed by Maryam. He opened his arms wide. 'Welcome! Welcome, oh English woman! Miss Sara!' and he led me inside the compound and sat me down on the bench. 'Tchay, ya Mahmud!' he called to his son. 'Have you come to see our Jinn? Maybe you come like the Franks from their castles?' I noticed how tired he looked. 'I am just back from Aleppo,' he said again. 'Not good.'

'Not good in Beirut either. Too many weapons, too much anger, I see your Jinn has many visitors?'

Ibrahim shrugged. 'The Qalaat has seen more than its fair share of unwelcome visitors,' he said. 'Not all of them at peace with each other. Sometimes they even fight by the pillar. The Jinn is said to have a way with them. Calms them. Now the Alawis come to pray.' I could tell from his voice they were not his favourites. 'How is Lebanon? We only hear bad news.' I did my best to brief him without being too depressing. 'I think there is no good news,' was his comment when I paused. 'I do not like these Alawis,' he said. 'They are not Muslims. They do not have mosques. They do not mark the *Eidh*. Not good.' I was not sure what to say but pondered instead on the melange of faiths in Syria as in Lebanon – what hatred lies between them these days. 'I am worried for my family in Aleppo,' he went on. 'My brother Muhammad is with my mother – she is not well – I visited her last month but I do not like to go near the city more than I have to. Aleppo has become a strange place and the *suq* is quiet, empty.'

In the early morning I wandered round the village while he was praying. As before I noted the ancient stones incorporated in the walls of the houses. There was a posy of flowers in the little roofless church. Some ancient walls had canvas stretched over them to give shelter. I could see children sleeping inside these makeshift tents. How often had these walls seen similar scenes? Refugees, I supposed. The Jinn was on the wall. 'C*ome again*,' I liked to think he said. Maryam gave me a huge hug. Come back soon,' she echoed the Jinn. 'We all need you, so does the Jinn.' I promised and Ibrahim led me to an ancient Peugeot. 'We pass through Alawi territory on the way – the President's homeland.'

The Alawi Shia sect to which the Assad family belonged diverged from mainstream Shia Islam around the eleventh century. But the greater split between Shia and Sunni ('orthodox') Islam had occurred immediately after the Prophet's death in 636. Saladin was a particularly devout Sunni Muslim with zero tolerance for any vestige of divergent Islam and he may well have been the cause of the Alawis hiding deep in Syria's mountain spine, where they are still concentrated. Access that day to any investigation of their villages was blocked by an armoured car, a sleepy driver inside. Another track by a hefty road-making machine with a young man in military fatigues leaning against it. Progress in that direction was clearly out of bounds.

To Chastel Blanc we went, so named due to the local white limestone of which it was built – and as it was known to the crusading Franks. It was the most remarkable of the many Crusader castles that dot the mountain spines of Syria and Lebanon, as well as the coast. It was originally built by the Byzantines, who needed to guard the approach to the coastal plain, as did the Templars, who developed it further in the twelfth century. It is also known as Qalaat Saladin, after the man who ousted the Franks. It was easy that day to envisage the siege and its consequences that ultimately drove the Christian infidels to their coastal enclaves. What an embattled part of the world this has been. (Has? Is?)

We munched Maryam's olives and *shwarmah* sandwich from the top of the keep, contemplating the to-ing and fro-ing of armies in this embattled world, not forgetting that at one point the Byzantines actually occupied Aleppo. Back into the car, pondering on the east-west movement of horseback 'missionaries' as we drove down a narrow twisting road, imagining the great Saladin, riding up from the coast to besiege the castle. On the way we passed several small lanes leading into the tribal base of the Assad family. Not a politic moment for a visit, nor would Ibrahim have countenanced any such thing. 'I do not like these people – not good Muslims in my opinion.' Various small lanes leading off into the bush were discouragingly guarded by military vehicles.

Later in the afternoon we reached the town of Tartus, driving past the crusader church and down to the little port. In a café at the foot of the little castle we looked across at building works where President Assad's Russian friends were hard at work developing a new 'warm water' port, always a Russian ambition. 'Good employment for many friends of mine,' muttered Ibrahim. Not exactly another invasion but certainly an 'interesting' arrival. Competition for the Americans who assumed Syria was its baby. A group of slick-suited men were drinking tea at the further end of the café. Russians, the café owner shrugged when I asked. Memories of history lessons flashed through my mind, about warm water ports.

Ibrahim headed off to do his businesses before returning to Deir al-Simaan. From a beachside hotel I treated myself to a long swim and a delicious and prolonged *mezze* and next morning a 'shared' taxi took me along the age-old coast road back to Beirut. The road continues by Byblos, most ancient of ports that thousands of years earlier had despatched goodies from Mesopotamia (including lumps of lapis lazuli). Millennia later in 1098 the Christian Franks staggered out of the Anatolian highlands, besieged and captured Antioch, and moved on to the so-called 'holy land', ultimately leading, so they determined, to Jerusalem. Just before Beirut the road passes beside the Dog River where inscriptions have been carved into the cliff wall by all these conquering 'passers-by', including the French in 1860. Foreigners again – a constant factor in Syria throughout its history. Pig in the middle. No wonder Syrians need Simeon.

8.

AND UP AGAIN – NEARER TO GOD?

Jacob was frantic with guarding the enclosure. Simeon sat disconsolately on his rock, hoopoe on shoulder. The Arabians were as always camped too close, burning their smoky incense as if someone was about to die.

Jacob enlarged the enclosure, built himself a small hut beside a stronger gate, though the children still climbed over. Inside the enclosure his garden was well watered by the holy Simeon's urine. The turds he dug into the soil. 'Not too many eggs,' Simeon instructed the villagers who with Jacob supplied his nourishment. 'Too knotty a defecation. It's up to you to keep my bowels loose.' He couldn't sleep on the rock of course; at night he clambered down and out of the enclosure across the hillside as before to his cave, trying, often in vain, to avoid the fingers, the laughter, the sobs and supplications.

That good friend of Simeon's, Patriarch Theodoretus of Cirrhus tells us the little that is known about Simeon and his pillar. Cirrhus, the city of Theodoretus' domain, was far to the east of the Empire, his congregation from a wide spectrum of religious backgrounds: Armenian, Zoroastrian, Manichaean, a panoply of Greco-Roman gods. On that Road between East and West the Patriarch who was much in demand at church councils held on the Mediterranean shore often travelled. Now Ephesus. Quite a trek. Telnissus and Simeson on the way.

Theodoretus was notable for a deeply engrained spirit of harmony. One starlit night Simeon descended from his rock to sit with the Patriarch on the platform on which his rock had been set. 'The church is divided by dissension. Let your rock be a symbol of the Church's unity,' suggested Theodoretus longing for a universal symbol. 'At least we all celebrate Pentecost. Even the Jews camping right here. And of course the Arabians. All over the place. A most thoughtful father of the Church, aware of all the stresses within its body. Empire too.'

At the end of the day, sitting below Simeon on his rock, 'O Simeon!' he sighed. 'Get away from it all. Get away from these crowds. Nearer to his God.'

Hmm.

'I've risen but must go on rising. Up, up, my friend. Above them all. I have sat in holes, lain in caves, on rocks. Still, I sin. I must rise again.' He tried to sit up, flopped back on the dried grass piled up at the foot of the rock. 'Let's go for three stones – for the Trinity: Father, Son and Holy Spirit.' He was chewing a carrot. 'I should be higher. Nearer heaven. At this height they still reach me. I must rise up, to serve the Lord. Oh Lord.'

'I'm not sure about the height.' Theodoretus looked doubtful. 'And three layers? Difficult, as it had been at Ephesus, quarrelling over the Trinity. 'You look lofty enough when you're on the one stone. A splendid symbol. Higher might be ostentatious? And food? And water? And – excuse me – washing?'

'Isn't that the point? They need to see me. I'm their symbol, their intercessor with the Lord. It's no good squatting on this dumpy thing.' Simeon nodded in the direction of the rock, stretching his arms to the sun. 'I must rise, closer to the Lord, further from earthly ties. Three stones, yea – for that Trinity!' Theodoretus winced. 'The locals will do anything I ask.' He paused. 'Remove me far from my vanity and lies; give me neither poverty nor riches; feed me with simple food.'

Theodoretus was on his way home from a most contentious second Christian council at Ephesus. It was a tricky time in the Church. In 428 the devout, scholarly and dynamic Patriarch of Antioch, Nestorius, had been selected by Emperor Theodosius to become Patriarch of the capital of the Eastern Empire, Constantinople, seat of the Emperor, who saw his city at the head of the empire. 'Let the Pope in Rome have his say. I shall have mine.' So Nestorius should be seen as the prime Patriarch in the Eastern Empire. Nestorius was now in place to impose his views on the rest of the Empire. And his most contentious view was on the position of the Virgin Mary. As Mother of God? As Mother of a tripartite God? No! Mother of Jesus, Mother of Christ! He argued that references to Christ should clearly distinguish his godly from his human form. The great achievement of Nicaea a century earlier had been to establish the Trinity of the Godhead: Father, Son and Holy Spirit. For Nestorius, however, the human aspect of Christ must be more clearly distinguished from Christ as an indivisible part of the Godhead. Put very simply, said Patriarch Nestorius, Jesus Christ the man must be distinguished from God. Mary fell on the human side of the equation.

This was a contentious argument throughout both Western and Eastern Empires, whose populations were particularly devoted to the Virgin Mary in a more exalted, holy position as would reflect her status as Mother of God. This position was passionately supported by Patriarch Cyril of Alexandria, who maintained that Nestorius arguing for Mary as merely the mother of Christ (the man), was undermining the sacred agreement reached at Nicaea, by denying the foundation of the faith. Anguish, dismay, anger, distrust flowed back and forth in the Eastern Empire.

So in Theodosius chose Ephesus to be the site of the great church council to decide the issue in the summer of 431. Ephesus had once been the shrine of the great Greek goddess Artemis and the Roman goddess Diana. But had already been devoted to Mary, mother of God or Mother of Christ. Theodosius himself was occupied building massive walls against nomadic marauders from the plains of the north and east, disliked the distraction of church arguments. He had after all been responsible for the appointment of Patriarch Nestorius to that of Constantinople. He was unyielding in selecting Ephesus. Alexandria, Constantinople, Rome must share the core of the divine message.

Simeon had little respect for such niceties as the mother of Jesus, but he respected this man on his way home from the Ephesus Council. Drawn by the antics of this remarkable young man, he came down from his rock. He was cold and had lost his companions. The hoopoe had sensibly flown south and the chameleon was safe underground and warm. Even the Arabians had gone south to their winter grazing. 'I must rise nearer the warmth of angels' wings.'

Jacob groaned. 'Don't talk to me about rising. How do you know the angels have warm wings?'

'I don't *know*. But I am *sure* they do. Oh yes, I have risen, and must go on rising. Up, up, my friend. To the shelter of those warm angelic wings. Above you all. I have sat in holes, lain in caves, roasted on rocks. Still I sin.' He suddenly shouted – 'Three stones – the blessed Trinity. That's what I need, what all these people should see.'

Theodoretus had a certain respect for the young man but was worried about his motives. Arriving that autumn, weary from his journey, he was greeted by Bassos, who also had his doubts about three stones. Theodoretus now had a thought, nudged by current disputes within the Church. Simeon greatly respected the Patriarch's integrity. 'The Church is divided by dissension,' he told Simeon, who grunted a reluctant agreement. 'Let your rock be a symbol of its unity.'

Later he spent the night talking with Simeon now huddling in his cave (O Heavens, the stink!). Next morning, back to the enclosure. 'So now you want three stones – God the father, God the Son, God the Holy Spirit. That's what the bishop of Alexandria, Patriarch Cyril, says. We may have to go along with it. But a bit pretentious don't you think?'

Simeon chewed an onion. 'You are right. But I should be higher. Nearer heaven. Three stones. The Trinity – just as that man in Alexandria says.

We must rise up, to serve the Lord. And you, bound to the earth, must tell the village, I cannot help. The locals will do anything you ask. Ask them. After all, I bring them prosperity'. He paused. 'Remove far from me vanity and lies; give me neither poverty nor riches; feed me with food for the soul. And the wings of angels will warm my nights.'

'Quite.' Theodoretus had his doubts but discussed it with the brethren below. Ostentatious yes, they all agreed. 'But maybe these people need it?' suggested Superior Bassos, generous soul. 'Let us build a chapel nearby, serve the sacraments, maintain orthodoxy. Three stones do help after all.' As for the Trinity, they agreed, 'not easy – even as a symbol. But if that's what he wants.' Theodoretus, knowing the vulnerability of that orthodoxy, was reassured. 'I will exalt the Lord!' Simeon shouted to the villagers, to the Arabians heading south.

And so the order went out for three stones for that Trinity, to be assembled vertically – ah, three in one. One was already there, that Simeon sat on through spring, summer and autumn. A second stone would be raised on top of that. And maybe a third. Then a platform – wooden, from those old oak trees in the mountains – on which Simeon proposed to live, sleep (even die?). Each stone had to be carefully prepared. And of course, a ladder. Old Bassos put Joseph the ironmonger in charge.

'This really is crazy,' said the village. 'The man's mad.' But they loved him and he was a good asset, they agreed about that. They asked the village mason, Bar Abbas, for his advice. 'Find that old temple just up the hill, idiots! Roll them down!' The obvious solution. 'But do not ask for my help.' Bar Abbas was fed up with the whole business, people trampling over his olive grove up there, though one compensation was being asked to help build a hostel in the village for the better class of pilgrim. Theodoretus was more encouraging. 'You will find other masons,' he consoled Jacob. 'No problem – in these villages everyone is a mason of sorts.' And a whole crowd of villagers came to help and were sent up into the hills to fell trees for that platform – and the ladder. Telnessin was grateful to this provider of prosperity. 'It shall be worthy of the Lord,' they sang, revelling in the holy Simeon's magnetism. 'Yea, I sought the Lord, and he delivered me from all my fears,' Simeon sang back. 'Hosannah in the highest!'

At least they did not have to quarry the stones. At the old temple they found tall, finely turned columns supporting its portico, well leaded together so that the main problem was dismantling them, then rolling them down the hill to Simeon's enclosure and knocking down the wall of the old enclosure to get them in. At first Simeon refused to leave the enclosure, determined to oversee every moment but 'You are in the way,' said Bassos gently but so firmly that Simeon accepted and took to his cave. He spent the winter inside. The much-enlarged enclosure became a sacred space, a wall around it with a gate. 'And you will need a hut for a guardian,' Jacob shouted. 'Someone must keep out the mob.' He groaned, recognising his fate.

Winter with its wind, rain and snow. Simeon watched from the mouth of his cave, wrapped in his huge black blanket. An icicle hung from the mouth of the cave. Jacob's vegetables suffered. Down the hill the village celebrated the winter solstice and the birth of Jesus. The men staggered drunkenly up the hill to the cave, offering mugs of wine to Jacob. Simeon shouting at them all the while from inside, do this, do that, get on with it. Damn and blast him, some of the men were inclined to mutter, but the women kicked them into shape. 'Layabouts! Belly bulgers! Idle pricks! Damn the lot of you!' and in the quiet of their cottages 'Idiots! Can't tell a good thing when it's in front of your nose. Don't you see how this pillar business is in your own interest? Look at the crowds who come to worship him already. Three stones up, three times the crowd. We'll all be rich.' Villagers from far and wide came to help.

They were grateful to this provider of prosperity. 'It shall be worthy of the Lord,' they yelled as they panted up the hill, revelling in the holy Simeon's magnetism. 'Yea, I sought the Lord, and he delivered me from all my fears,' Simeon sang. 'Hosannah in the highest!'

The base came first; three shallow steps up to a flat stone with a hole in the middle for the actual pillar. A wooden structure was needed to raise the huge stones. The men were tired and cross. Bloody hell, said some. Not for me, nor me. Get someone else to work for you. Bar Abbas came at last. 'All right, you lot. Stop mucking around. Pick up those rollers.' He looked over the stones as they lay beside the platform – one on top of the existing stone where Simeon had sat all summer. A gantry to raise the stones. Just as the builders of ancient temples had done centuries earlier. The final stone – tricky; it was rolled into place, pulleys attached, and at a signal from Bar Abbas, was raised and ever so slowly lowered into place. A great cheer from the crowd. Then the scaffolding had to be heightened – that took several days. Then the third stone – the Trinity. Simeon was silent in his cave taking only water. No one was around to chivvy, to bully.

Bar Abbas and blacksmith Joseph had prepared molten lead to hold the stones in place. With considerable ceremony and bated breath,

Joseph climbed the gantry and poured the lead into the prepared grooves. A great shout went up. Bassos led the hymn: 'O all ye works of the Lord, bless ye the Lord!' Everyone joined in. 'Praise him and magnify him for ever!' Simeon's horn sounded across the hill.

Bar Abbas now ordered Jacob off to find someone to make a wooden platform for the top. 'The holy Simeon plans to live up there!'

'I do indeed.' shouted Simen. 'I must have room to move FOR LIFE, man, FOR LIFE!'

'A rope. And bars aroind so he doesn't fall off.'

Who's going to get him up there? Hmm.

Jacob slogged up through the woods to the temple again, humming a Manichaean hymn, only returning at dusk when everyone was packing up, to be greeted with another blast of abuse from Bar Abbas through which he was just able to explain that, yes, he had found a suitable tree for the platform. But he could not bring it back on his own. Bloody hopeless, these Mespots, swore Bar Abbas; only good for mud in their part of the world. Give me good Syrian wood any day.

'But I am giving you Syrian wood' protested Jacob and next morning he led a grumbling group of youths up the hill to collect stones to cap the column and to support the platform on which Simeon proposed to live. Joseph blacksmith was summoned to make a low railing and fix it round the square platform to prevent the holy one falling off. 'I shall need a new chain,' Simeon shouted across to them. 'I may feel giddy at first.' Quite an admission.

'Come now,' said Bassos. 'Are you so scared of movement, Simeon? That's chain's expensive. Think of others, young man, who need support,' he cautioned. 'The weakness of all ascetics,' he murmured to Theodoretus, who had decided to spend the season in Telnessin.

Lent again. 'I'm off,' said Simeon, massaging his legs as he left the enclosure. 'I'm going up at Pentecost,' he yelled. Bassos patiently installed him in the cave with the regulation loaves and water; Jacob walled him up. 'We'd better move fast,' said Bassos. Forty days' peace and quiet. 'No fasting for the likes of us this year – we need our energy.'

In the cave Simeon plunged his fingers into the earthen floor, buried his face in the soil they excavated, inhaled the ancient aromas. He ran his hands over the walls of the cave, every vagary of the mountainside, every whim of the Great Creator, revealed in their contours. Anguish filled his soul; he sobbed dry tears. 'Let me lie on your earth, leave me low, let me suffer as the lowest suffer. Do not make me rise', he cried. He fought against the darkness: 'Give me your eternal light,' he called out so loudly that even Jacob awoke from his own vigil and saw the angels pass through the mud and stone wall blocking the mouth of the cave, which they then filled with music and song. He blew the horn. Awash with their glory, Simeon sank to the floor. Time was running short. They were into the thirtieth day of the fast. Jacob worked on the wall of the enclosure. Friends helped him with his hut. He planted extra veg. Villagers came to guard the pillar: 'Can't have anyone climbing that to speak to the holy one,' said mason Joseph. Then the platform, smoothed and adorned with a railing to prevent Simeon from falling, had to be raised. Finally, the scaffolding was dismantled.

Villagers plaited a rope.

Forty days fast and all was ready

They fetched Simeon from his cave. Too weak to walk, Jacob carried him on his back across the hill. On the way Simeon spotted the pillar. 'O my!' he shrieked in Jacob's ear. 'What have you done! My pillar! Lord has mercy!' and a few minutes later Jacob deposited him on the steps carved into the platform in which the pillar was set. 'O Heavens above!' he croaked to the crow who was pecking at last year's crumbs.

He proclaimed that the feast of Pentecost would see him on top. Fifty days! And look at him now after the Lenten fast. 'Best feed him up,' Bassos muttered.

The news of the intended climb spread. Everyone wanted to be there. 'Of course, we do our best to make you comfortable,' said the villagers, greedily eyeing the crowds. Local farmers gave armfuls of new wheat to Jacob to present to Simeon. Also Persian merchants from the Sasanian capital of Ctesiphon near the River Tigris came with bags of tea. A camel train from the great city of Edessa. And a pigeon seller from Antioch with a donkey-load of carrier pigeons on his way to Aleppo. 'Fastest birds you'll ever use,' he shouted as he came up the hill. 'From here to the Emperor in a week!' Jacob bought several.

'Liars and swindlers,' groaned their grander visitors looking for a reasonably pleasant pilgrimage, as they made their way between the beehive hovels of the overgrown village to latrine pits crudely hacked out of the ground outside the village. And the whores from Aleppo in makeshift tents all over the place. At least in the city they kept to their patch.

'You don't have to come,' shrugged their hosts withdrawing behind black walls with their chickens and their dogs, leaving the visitors to pitch tents, light fires, yell for lost children – bang, clatter, bark and shout in a sea of mud that turned to dust as the weather warmed up.

Sergius, a well-heeled merchant from Aleppo with caravans passing by Telnessin heading to and from Antioch along that Road, had an eye for opportunity as well as comfort; that was how he had made his fortune after all. With plans for a decent hostel, he had become a regular visitor at Bassos' little monastery and had watched the young Simeon's austere antics from afar. The roots of superstition extended deep beneath his faith; he needed some luck in his trading in these unsettled times and therefore propitiated all gods, including Simeon's.

Sergius had also observed the swelling crowds. So a hostel was commissioned. When he heard the pillar was ready Sergius decided on a spring outing for the family – with all necessary comforts of course: no need to emulate Simeon. His wife Faustina would only come if he provided those, for her friends as well as herself. 'Just some of my friends,' said Faustina, choosing among the ladies of the city's haute monde, those who had expressed interest in stories of Simeon's austerities. Messengers were sent to Bar Abbas. 'Get on with it,' ordered Sergius. Bar Abbas sent a messenger to say the hostel was nearly finished.

For the ladies it was a long journey from Aleppo. They were at least two weeks on the road, staying at monasteries on the way. 'Not quite what we expected,' sniffed the ladies. 'You might at least have warned me about the way,' frowned Faustina after a whole day being carried over that well-worn road. 'I would never have come if I had known, especially encouraging my friends.' The caravan also included a string of camels laden with oriental goods, which Sergius proposed to send on to Antioch. Donkeys, mules, servants, above all, provisions. They reached Telnessin just before dark with hardly any light left for the slaves to set up the menage: a flurry of servants, a circle of tents and beds, privies, fresh water from the village wells. And meat grilling – that's the best. Sergius had brought quite a party with him, four sons including Bacchus the youngest, due for baptism, wife's parents, brother and family and a host of loosely connected cousins. And Faustina's friends! 'We may feel like holy starvation when we get there,' Faustina had told a friend over a glass of wine in Aleppo, 'but it's best to take precautions.' On arrival her complaints were long and loud. In one tent Sergius and sons, in another the stout Faustina and her friends. 'Hardly an inch to move.'

Ha! muttered Sergius as he slipped through the night to find Bar Abbas. All set, he was assured.

The party felt moderately refreshed next morning. The ladies had washed their faces in asses' milk to maintain their exquisite complexions, eaten their curds and honey, and were now relaxing on silken cushions, sipping mint tea lightly laced with special Syrian spirit.

'Rather a relief not to have to sit at his feet all day,' one murmured to another.

'Isn't that what we've come for?'

'So dull, waiting for him to climb up that pillar!'

'A long way to bring such comforts. But thank God for them, Faustina dear.'

'Absolutely!'

'I do think, Sergius,' said Faustina to her husband, who had ventured to visit their tent that morning, 'that some kind of hostel is essential.' He had been discreet about his investment; better to show off when it was finished. He rubbed his hands together.

'You may well be right, my dear,' her husband smugly consoled her.

Many of those who came to see Simeon ascend his pillar wanted to be baptised, among them the usual crowd of Arabs who were there for the summer. With Simeon ready for his climb and rightly anticipating a mammoth partaking of the sacraments to mark the occasion, on Saturday Theodoretus, Ezra and his deacons, Malek and Mark, led a procession to the nearby river for a mass baptism.

Many people were baptised that day, emerging cleansed, purified, sins all washed away they hoped, and praying that the same fate would befall all enemies: wash them away! 'Great is your mercy, O Lord!' they shouted at each other as they headed back to houses, camps, tents, nostrils twitching with the thought of food. Bacchus was the hungriest.

Δ

'Secret, Sergius?' Suspiciously Faustina climbed into the chair. Their camp was set a short way from the village, away from its squalor. In a few minutes they were standing beside a newly erected wall. Bar Abbas was waiting for them. 'This way, good lady,' and he led her through a gap in the wall. 'Lo and behold!' Sergius helped her from the chair. 'The hostel you were asking for! For the better sort of pilgrim of course. Like yourself, dearest.' He bowed obsequiously. Faustina was astonished. 'Not much to see, is there?' she commented sharply. 'You wait,' Sergius was not at all discouraged. 'Now they've finished with the pillar, I'll have the best masons in town at work on it.'

'Quite an investment!' she conceded. Real praise. Sergius glowed.

Presbyter Ezra had spotted them and came over to the building site. Merchant and priest had plotted the hostel together, occasionally consulting Bassos to ensure not only his approval but maybe also the holy Simeon's. 'The holy Simeon is not concerned,' was Bassos' only comment, 'but I do beg you to give it at least the appearance of austerity.'

Sergius sent a slave up the hill to find son Bacchus and bring him to the camp. 'Come, the ladies have organised a bacchanalian feast for the new Christian.' He chivvied the boy to the tents outside the village. Faustina was waiting to present him with a magnificent platter of barbecued sheep.

Sergius rejoiced that night in the thought of the pillar and how it would bring guests to his hostel.

Pentecost. Jacob and his friends cleared a path from cave to pillar. The ladder was finished. Jacob tested it. It connected with the edge of the finely made platform. Bassos appointed the deacons to restrain the crowd of pilgrims and sightseers clustered round the sacred enclosure for this unique celebration of Pentecost. Then Simeon had to be fetched. The crowd craned its collective neck. There was no movement from the cave. Dead! Dead! The holy Simeon has died! The word spread through the crowd; women began ululating. But 'Fools,' muttered Bassos. 'Of course he lives. Thank God you live, young Simeon,' he shouted into the cave.

Simeon crawled out of the cave. He relieved himself. The crowd cheered. Looking across the hill Simeon caught sight of the finger pointing to that eternal heaven he wished to approach. 'Oh Lord,' he yelled. 'Set me up upon the rock that is higher than I, than all those crowds, for you have been my hope, and a strong tower for me against the enemy.' He stayed by the cave for the day, then slept in Jacob's hut. The salukis lay beside him and growled at anyone who came too close.

Bassos and Jacob, Ezra, Malek and Mark came to him at daybreak to pray and eat together. They were sombre: Simeon made it clear they wouldn't eat together again. 'Only room for me up there,' he said.

'You're bound to come down,' said Jacob.

Simeon: 'Never.'

Theodoretus: 'It's not in the power of man to say never. And visitors. I might want to visit.'

Simeon: 'You're right. But the Lord does not intend me to descend. My penance, if I'm to reach everlasting life. And with that goal be as a guide to others. I don't expect to come down. Help me with my toe nails, friend Jacob. A real sign of friendship to cut them. They are too long. It hurts to walk. After today it won't matter. Hee! Hee!' He giggled. Jacob reluctantly obliged. Bassos handed him a new tunic and pulled it over Simeon's stiff shoulders.

He was empty-handed; he had no possessions.

Leaning on Jacob's arm, Simeon walked, as cautiously as an old man, slowly across the hill to the pillar. The crowd was vast, everyone was there waiting. Women abandoned kitchens; men gave up planting; nomads penned their flocks. Children were washed and dressed in their best. So great already was Simeon's fame that there was even a band from Aleppo: singers, drummers, lutists, flautists, playing for everlasting life.

'God, he looks awful!' whispered Faustina. 'What do you expect?' They sipped syrup of figs, concocted in the village.

'They might at least have cut his hair, given him a wash.'

He certainly stank, a holy aroma. The incense helped, smouldering at the foot of the pillar. 'We offer you this incense,' sang the deacons, 'we beseech you, Lord,' eyes raised appropriately to a cloudless sky, 'receive this savour of spices.'

Arabians who had been watching from outside the enclosure let out another great gust of Hallelujah, startling birds.

'Our Father which art in heaven,' chanted Presbyter Ezra and everyone with him, their zest energising Simeon as he stood looking up at the monstrous pillar he had chosen to sit on and – worse – climb up.

Presbyter Ezra went on with his prayers. The deacons swung their censors but Simeon grew impatient. Cramp crept up his thighs. Theodoretus sensed his impatience and laid a hand on his head. 'Blessed are they who climb pillars in the name of the Lord,' he murmured so only Simeon heard, his strength returning through the hand on his head.

The body of Christ – crumbs on his tongue he could barely swallow. The blood of Christ – he spluttered on the wine. Then his voice came back. 'Glory be to God on high!' He stood straight turning to the crowd and shouted: 'We praise thee! We bless thee! We glorify thee!' All around him a thousand voices joined his shout, giving him strength. He was uplifted, flung his arms most lovingly round old Superior Bassos who held him tightly, sadly. Bar Abbas the mason and Joseph the blacksmith stood proudly at the base; Simeon bowed to them and they, speechless, to him. Gazing up, shading his eyes against the sun, now high in the sky, he noticed every mark on the stone, stone on which his life, his penance, would depend. He vowed he would never see those marks again.

Stumbling he put two hands on one rung, a foot on a lower one and tried to get the other foot up but such weakness in arm and leg that all he could do was beckon feebly to Jacob who was longing to help. Young deacon Malek also came to the rescue, hoisting Simeon on to Jacob's back.

Thus, Simeon left the ground.

Now it was all very well for Jacob on his own to go up and down the ladder. He'd done it at speed, conscious that time was precious. Jacob's Ladder, the villagers had teased him. But the load slowed him down, the weight caused the ladder to sway in the middle and that seriously upset Jacob. He paused on the twentieth step, the ladder jumping beneath him. The ground was swaying. 'What's the matter?' demanded the load on his back. 'No good leaving me half way.'

Jacob did not answer; it was taking all his energy to keep down the flimsy contents of his stomach.

'Are you sick or something?' Simeon's voice in his ear.

'Yes, holy one,' whispered Jacob, resting his head on the ladder.

'I had better carry on myself,' said Simeon and all at once Jacob felt his load leave him, transferring itself to the ladder, and there he was, staring at Simeon's scraggy shins as ever so slowly they swavyed on the rungs above him. A vast collective sigh went up from the anxious crowd.

Simeon breathed fast but shallow as he climbed, filling his veins with the energy to take him up. You pointed the way to this pillar, Lord, the least You can do is make sure I get to the top. His arms and legs suddenly filled with blood. He stared through the rungs at the acanthus capital – where had they got that from? – and at the underside of the platform it supported. Then he was at the edge of the platform, reaching for Joseph's little railing, pulling himself up and over. Lord God Almighty. A roar from the crowd far below. Thanks to the Lord God! Saviour of the world! Hosannah in the highest!

O worship the Lord in the beauty of holiness! Let the whole world stand in awe of him!

On his own, finally alone, while Jacob stood on the ladder in shame, Simeon's spittle on his shoulder. He raised his arms to the sky. A thousand voices acclaimed his ascent.

Δ

Simeon mounted his pillar around the year 431 or 432. Word spread to the furthest bounds of empire, carried by pigeons despatched north, south, east and west. In the year spent erecting the pillar there had been all sorts of movement on the frontiers of the empire: Attila and his Huns, Athaulf and the Visigoths, Khusraw and his Persian cohorts. Not surprisingly the pillar and its aspiring occupant were seen as the symbol of a stability for which so many yearned. Emperor Theodosius sent an emissary, so did his Empress Eudocia, and the Emperor's virginal sister Pulcheria, each instructing his or her representative to deliver detailed reports on the state of the empire as viewed from the foot of the holy man's pillar. 'He certainly hasn't chosen to hide himself away,' Emperor muttered to Empress. 'I must ask him what he thinks of the world today.'

The Bishop of Rome took an interest. So did monks from Egypt, from Palestine, from Cappadocia, most of them disapproving, following the founders' convictions that man must discipline himself in the eyes of God by hard manual labour and obedience as well as prayer – none of this exhibitionism. Bad enough men shutting themselves away in caves but pillars! And at a crossroads no less. Who does he think he's saving, himself or the world? And who is the crowd worshipping?

News of the crowds caused consternation when a few weeks later it finally reached Antioch. Some of the churchmen thought he was not behaving as an orthodox Christian, as a member of the universal community, humble and praying to the Almighty, should behave. Orthodox versus unorthodox: a treacherous battlefield. Climbing a forty-foot pillar was sinfully ostentatious. Showing off – that terrible sin. 'Lord has mercy,' sang Simeon from on high. 'Lord has mercy but...,' muttered the clergy of Antioch, 'we cannot allow this to happen.' And out they bustled.

The churchmen eventually pushed their way into the enclosure. Jacob was so distracted that he had carelessly left the ladder tied up against the pillar and one of the younger clerics seized it and began to climb up. Jacob grabbed his tunic, tore it away. The man continued to climb. Malek began to shake it: useless. It was too heavy. Even Bassos added his feeble muscle. Simeon was standing at the railing adding his voice to those on the ground. 'The Lord God put me up here! Heathen, pagan, puffed up men of the church: who do you think you are? I am Simeon, sent to be a torch to men, a signpost to the Lord! Look around you! Why do these people come? Not to worship me. But I show them the way of the Lord. And I do not argue back and forth about the nature of the Lord. I KNOW who he is, I SHOW who he is. Now GET DOWN YOURSELVES! Go back to your churches and preach to your congregations – if you have any – how the holy Simeon points the way to the Lord. And he will not bother their heads about the nature of the Lord!'

'Oh Lord give me courage!' cried the cleric swaying on the ladder. Simeon, suddenly at his eyelevel, hoisting a filthy loin cloth and thrusting testicles in his face.

'Get off my pillar!'

At that, the poor man could take no more. He took a flying leap from the ladder, fell to the ground and broke his ankle, swearing vain imprecations.

Simeon's soul soared, like the hoopoe that took off from the railing as his head popped up above the platform. He felt a surge of ecstasy; he trembled from head to toe. A chameleon biding his time, stays hidden.

After a while he began to explore the platform carefully, gingerly even, not entirely convinced it will not wobble. The ignominy of any fall, not that he'd be alive to suffer if he did fall. He was proud of the workmanship. He noticed the precautions taken to prevent accidents: the little knee-high railing – not very adequate – but, more important, the chain with its fetter at the loose end. That must have been Joseph's work. A leather sock beside it to protect the ankle. He pulled it on. A key was in the lock of the fetter; he unlocked it, opened it, fitted it round his ankle and slammed it shut. Then he threw the key to the ground, saw Jacob pick it up and waved to him. Jacob waved back. Now he felt safe.

He eyed the pile of nourishment which Jacob had left. A jar of water, a pot of vegetables. Dates from Arabian friends. Some dried apricots. More than enough. A rope was fastened to the railing and peering over the edge he saw the basket hanging from it on the ground. There was Jacob's garden; as if to celebrate his arrival, he pulled up his tunic, squatted down and aimed for it with his thin trickle of urine. Not easy from that height: the breeze caught the feeble stream and blew it to one side. He squeezed tight to hold it in, tried again; this time it splashed against the pillar half way down. Damn. He leant right out next, risking the dizziness, and this time the few remaining drops spattered on the freshly turned soil.

Plenty of time to practise.

All he needed is that basket for food, dangling on its rope. 'My soul shall be satisfied, even as it were with marrow and fatness' – hysterical laughter – 'when my mouth praises You with joyful lips.' And water.

He knelt again on the finely smoothed patterns engraved in the wood by the millennia, repeating the patterns of the ground below, the distant fields, the eddies of the distant silvery river, all God's creation. 'There's no mystery nor misery that can't be resolved if you put your faith in the Lord. Man and God, divine and human, never mind about the mixture, that's for others to fuss about. And they certainly fuss. Some people like to make a mystery of life, fill the blanks with devils and demons (I know them well enough), strange gods and goddesses, essences divine and human. I fill life with love, that's what I shall tell them. Keep it simple. Of course it's easier from up here.

'Listen! Wind that cools and desiccates, air that feeds and suffocates, sun that warms and burns, frost that revives and bites, rain that cleanses and drowns. Blessed are the elements of Heaven, the many hands of the Lord that caress and chastise me day and night. O all ye ending of sorrow, I tell them but do they listen? Do they understand? I listen to them, listen to their woes as they come to my column.'

An owl alighted on the railing, a mouse dangling from its beak. It blinked at the scrawny human, twisting its neck as only owls can, dropping the mouse to the platform, picking it up to toss it from side to side to complete the killing, swallowed it and hopped back on to the railing, lowering its eyelids once more to squint at the man. The man grinned back as he tucked himself under the old black blanket, arranged the chain, succumbed swiftly to the sleep of the devout, of the truly holy. The owl watched over him, astonished, leaving from time to time but returning to its perch and only leaving as dawn once more prises open the heavens and men's eyes.

9.

INTERLUDE

Mid seventies. Distress in the 'Middle' East, between rival faiths, rival tensions. In Lebanon civil war between rival 'tribes', rival faiths. In 1979 the Shah of Iran was deposed. He was replaced as head of state by a fervently Shia Ayatollah Ali Khomeini, much to the excitement of the Syrian Alawi regime. However, the rise of the Ayatollah led to the re-opening of the ancient schism between Sunni and Shia in Islam increasing hostility between the conflicting persecution of Shia Muslims in Iraq by the Sunni regime of Saddam Husain. This was accentuated by territorial challenges. Syria offered a haven for Shia Muslims from Iraq. Hence the popularity of the Jinn. Providing consolation to the suffering multitudes of this world.

Off stage a powerful Israel, stirring the pot of tensions.

The resurgence of Shia Islam was more than matched by the growth in fervour of the Sunni Muslim Brotherhood. The Brotherhood had developed in Egypt over many years but was inspired to spread to Syria to combat the rise there of the Shia Assad regime. It took root in the traditional Sunni stronghold of Hama, a beautiful medieval town in central Syria famous for its huge grinding water wheels but also for its severe dedication to Sunni Islam. Dogma versus dogma deep in the heart of Syria. Attacks on government offices in Damascus soon spread to Aleppo.

Patrick Seale, author of a superb biography of Assad, memorably described the situation in Aleppo as it was in 1979. Armed fighters burst into buildings, closed shops, whipped up anti-government demonstrations and murdered notable members of Assad's government, especially Alawis. In June 1979 terrorists massacred over sixty cadets at the Artillery School in Aleppo, assumed mainly to be Alawis but also some Christian. The gunmen were assumed to be Sunni Muslims. The event marked the onset of full-scale urban religious warfare. In June 1980 Assad just missed being assassinated, it was assumed by members of the Brotherhood. The next day Hafiz' younger brother Rifa'at despatched army units to Palmyra (known to Syrians as Tadmor), location of a notorious military prison. His orders were obeyed: the majority Sunni prisoners were slaughtered.

Thus began a decade of misery and violence throughout Syria. It included the punishment of

Hama, probably on the orders of the President's brother Rifa'at.

In 1980 I was staying once again at Baron's where Armand greeted me with his usual *sang-froid* as we sat over our sugary coffee. We had been discussing the effects of the horrendous Iran-Iraq war in the east and the floods of refugees in Aleppo's streets. Suddenly the bartender came over holding a telephone. 'For you,' he said, and then I heard Ibrahim's voice, stammering at the other end.

'Our son!' I heard him cry. 'Our Said! Killed in the *suq*, ya Sara. Guarding the khan! Come if you can, ya Sara. Maryam needs you!'

I could see that Armand had caught the gist of the cry. He tossed back the remains of his coffee, stood up and ordered, 'Go to them. You must comfort them. Maryam especially. Now come with me. Today is the Feast of the Assumption of the Virgin Mary. To many Muslims she is as important as to Christians – a whole chapter in the Quran devoted to Maryam. Hence Maryam Mazrui. Come and I will show you something. Then tomorrow you will go to Qalaat Simaan and the Mazruis. You've told me something of the issues of the early Christians in this part of the world. I shall now introduce you to the grandest of Aleppo's Armenian churches – dedicated to that complicated divinity in the Church of the Holy

Mother of God. There will be a huge congregation this evening – everyone praying to her for peace and tranquillity.

We set off. 'The church is brand new, only just consecrated,' Armand explained as we made our way across the city. 'Money from Armenians from all over – from Aleppo of course, from Armenia itself, from America – the wealthy diaspora. It will be packed – everyone worried by the political situation. And as always turning to the holy mother for support. There will be some heavily shrouded women in the crowd. Muslim probably – impossible to tell.'

I spotted the building. It was huge – a testimony to the wealth of those Armenian communities, many of which bonded as a result of terrible persecution but others from the traditional trading between east and west. There was a crowd of well dressed Armenians pushing its way inside. There were indeed some women invisible under their wraps, only shoes revealing their sex. We followed, through a large forecourt or narthex into the body of the church. Also in the crowd were small groups of much less well-dressed families, rather nervously slightly hanging back from the main crowd. 'Iraqi Christians,' Armand muttered. 'They're as much persecuted by the Iraqi villain Saddam as the Shia from southern Iraq. And no doubt they also look to the Virgin Mary for compassion.' Persecuted also, I muttered, by the Ayatollah. Many were weeping. Not surprising to see perhaps but soldiers guarded both church and crowd.

The body of the church was lit by thousands of candles. 'We Armenians usually light candles as soon as we enter a church.' Armand offered one to me. I noticed him putting some coins in a slot machine and picking up a tiny statue of the Virgin Mary. My eye was also caught by a group around a much larger icon of Mary; it was so popular, so kissed by the devout that she was in fact covered with glass with a bottle of 'windowlene' and a roll of kitchen towelling on a ledge beside her to ensure hygiene – 'we hope,' whispered Armand beside me, 'they hope.' I noticed again the Iraqis (if Armand was right) kissing the icon with even greater fervour, many of them in tears.

I was reminded of the controversy that led to the downfall of Patriarch Nestorius – the argument over the sanctity of the Virgin Mary as to whether she was the mother of God or had dual personality as the Mother of Jesus and the mother of God. The dispute came to a head at that Council of Ephesus in 431. A strange place for Emperor Theodosius to choose for a council of churches to settle the problem of the Virgin Mary. For over a thousand years Ephesus had been a sacred spot – home of the Greek goddess Artemis and the

Roman goddess Diana the huntress. I wondered how the fierce Patriarch Cyril of Alexandria reacted to the choice, haunted surely by the spirit of the great mother goddess Artemis. Ephesus the home of goddess protectors for millennia?

When we got back to the hotel Armand gave me a tiny package. 'This is for Maryam,' he said, 'a mini Mary. Don't let Ibrahim see it. He'd be furious that we should give her such an image. And here for the night is an English Koran. Have a look at the chapter on Maryam, mother of Jesus. A whole chapter to herself. Much more than we get in the Gospels.' I unwrapped the little package and found inside a miniature statue of the Virgin Mary. Upstairs I did as I was told and spent much of the night reading the *Surah* (chapter) Maryam.

And discovered how revered Mary is in the Quran. The only woman mentioned by name in the Koran and how venerated she is by all Muslims both Sunni and Shia – 'friend of God, Virgin, Mother' according to subtitle of a recent book on the subject. Not surprising that Maryam Mazrui was named after her. And not surprising, despite the apparent 'masculinity' of Islam, that the female in all of us is as crucial in Islam as in Christianity, as it was in the ancient world.

Next day on the way to Qalaat Simaan I spotted my piece of ancient road beside the village of Tel Aqibrin but no triumphal arch this time;

I wondered if the villagers kept it hidden away somewhere, to be brought out at the right tactical/political moment. Difficult in the current situation to know when. Given the current upheavals in the region any intermediary between man and God was to be sought and I wasn't surprised to find the space below the Jinn's hill packed with cars and buses including the old bus from Aleppo but many cars with Lebanese number plates. The Jinn was much needed. That was full of heavily shrouded women. Every so often I heard bursts of extravagant sobs. Children were all over the place with trays of sweets hung round their necks. Water! Water! they were waving their plastic bottles. Lots of pushing and shoving as each tried to outdo companions. Sweet papers littered the ground. I sat down on the rough wall where I had first met my ghostly friend. What myths one can discover in such ancient stones. Ibrahim was waiting for me in the car park. I was so glad to see him. When I tried to commiserate over the death of Said, he silenced me. 'The hand of God,' he said briefly. 'Come, Sara,' and we walked slowly through the village. Ruined churches and houses were occupied by the latest exiles – from Iraq, from Jordan. 'You should see the families in the cave below the church,' Ibrahim commented as we paused by the ruined arch of a little chapel. 'Not so many Iranians these days. The Ayatollah likes our President – for the moment. Iraqis come instead, driven from their holy shrines. I wonder what they think of our holy Simeon.' I wondered too.

Maryam was sitting with some neighbours when we came round the corner. 'Oh Sara!' she cried out and was soon wrapping me in the warmest but saddest of hugs.

Later I described the scene in the great Armenian church in Aleppo and the kissing of the images of the Virgin Mary. 'Did you know' – she almost grabbed my arm to reinforce her words – 'did you know that Maryam's mother of Jesus is the most holy woman in the Quran? Has a whole *surah* (chapter) in the blessed Quran dedicated to her? More than the Christian Maryam in your holy book? And she is a virgin when she gives birth to a son, Jesus. Just like your Mary. Our Maryam gave birth in the desert, beside a date palm. It showered dates around her when she clung to it when pushing the baby out.' And Maryam leapt to her feet, rushed indoors and re-emerged seconds later with a copy of the Quran. She held it out to me pointing to the relevant passage, the pages well thumbed.

Ibrahim read the passage aloud, then slowly began trying to translate. My thoughts ran again to Ephesus and that bitter battle between Cyril and Nestorius watched over – I was sure – by the spirits of those fierce goddesses, Artemis and Diana. I later learned of a long history of virgin births – the Egyptian god Horus, son of the virgin Isis, the Roman god Attis, the son of the virgin Nana; he even went on to be resurrected. Maryam, mother of Jesus, though, of course, in the Quran, her son never becomes the Son of God.

The sun was setting. Maryam went indoors to pray. I followed her and sat in the corner of the main room. When she had finished, I handed her Armand's little package. 'Don't let Ibrahim see,' I warned as the content was revealed. She gave a little shriek as the Madonna appeared. 'Oh!' she was clearly slightly scared, nervously revolved the miniature figure in her hands, looked at me very hard and gave me one of her great hugs. Tears poured down her face. 'Maybe one day I will go to that big church in Aleppo' – she was shaking again with sobs as she tucked the tiny figure in her voluminous dress.

Next morning Maryam walked me through the town overflowing with temporary inhabitants. 'I want to show you something,' she said and took the overgrown path that led round the side of Simeon's hill. I knew it led to the cavern beneath the great western arm of the basilica. After a couple of hundred metres, she paused to part the jungle of acanthus that almost overwhelmed the path and pointed. And there, almost completely hidden, was the tiny ceramic statue of the Christian Mary. Shhh! 'I put her there today after dawn prayers' she said.

I continued along the little path that led round the base of the hall. And there was the Jinn, wispy as ever. He beckoned me round the side of the hill into the great cavern. Poppies everywhere, purple irises emerging and acanthus bursting with new green leaves, where I spotted the remains of various camp sites. He led me to the narrow stairs at the rear. Up we scrambled, to emerge at the western arm of the basilica. The crowd had arranged themselves around the rock assumed to be the remains of the pillar, their leader facing them on the ground with his back to the pillar. They shooed away the sweetie sellers, the water hawkers.

See how they come – whatever their god, whatever their prophet. Comfort them I say and I felt the Jinn open his arms wide as if to embrace the whole world. Looking westward into a sun already dropping down over well-tilled fields I had the sense that just for a moment the sorrowing world behind me was indeed finding comfort in the Jinn and his survival in the battlefield that had wrecked their lives. We all need our go-betweens, intercessors between us and the Almighty before whom we can pour out our heart's sorrows. Hence all over the Muslim world Muslims seek consolation at the tombs of those regarded as worthy of that role, who may alleviate the troubles of this world and intercede with the Almighty for a place in Paradise. In the Salihiyyah district of Damascus above the city are the tombs of revered 'saints' that are always crowded with weeping men as well as women. The tomb of Prophet Muhammad in Medina, Saudi Arabia, is hugely revered by Muslims of all persuasions. And no wonder Mary mother of Jesus was worshipped equally by Muslims and Christians. A whole chapter in the Quran dedicated to her.

And Simeon, my Jinn, surviving in the hearts and minds of the Syrians also attracts the bereaved, the bewildered, the angry. Faith versus fanaticism: Mother Maryam, Mary Mother of Jesus, Mother of God! No wonder Spaniards parade her through the streets of cities up and down the country. No wonder she crops up at shrines all over France. And most especially at Lourdes. No wonder she has such pride of place in the Quran. No wonder Armenians worship her so fervently, given their history in this part of the world. Successful merchants over the centuries maybe, but also long-suffering victims of persecution.

The next time I was in Aleppo was in 1983 during the Iran-Iraq war. The market was full of heavily shrouded women, many of them dragging a long line of weary, hungry children. The stalls were strangely dark and silent. No one was selling sticky tea. No Chinese scarves, no heady perfumes. The Great Mosque was full and in the courtyard an elderly cleric was leading a crowd of dishevelled men into the prayer hall. They looked exhausted. In the Mazrui compound there were only a couple of bales to sit on. 'What can you expect?' – Muhammad handed me a coke – 'thugs everywhere. And now war. Your Jinn must be busy. No one is safe. And no trucks on that road of yours.' Later I noticed some men on crutches squatting at the entrance to the Great Mosque – from the Land of Two Rivers I murmured thinking of Saddam Husain's Iraq. Aleppo's citizens entered the mosque courtyard, including some well-shrouded women. The women shuffled off to a side entrance while the men went through a ritual washing before entering the prayer hall.

Baron's hotel was beckoning and I slowly walked back to the hotel. It was virtually empty except for the usual group of dour Russians tossing back the vodka.

10.

TRIALS

Simeon's pillar stands at a crossroads where geography, history, politics, above all the nature of God have for ever been disputed. In 323 the Nicene creed had solved the problem of the 'trinity' for some but in the further reaches of the empire and beyond it conflicted with the concept of an Almighty God, one and only. Oh dear, sighed Theodoretus, the great conciliator, tramping between the northern and eastern corners of his domain, pausing at Telnessin and Simeon's pillar to catch his breath. Squabbling Patriarchs – Cyril in Alexandria and Nestorius in Constantinople – led in 431 the Emperor Theodosius to summon another Council of the Church, this time at Ephesus. This was the site for the veneration of Mary (as in earlier times of Artemis and Diana – a strange choice). Not a particularly easy place to get to and inevitably the patriarchs and their entourages of bishops arrived in considerable disorder and presumably stayed in discomfort – hundreds of them. And it was early spring – cool and wet. No wonder they squabbled. The proceedings pleased nobody, least of all the obstinate chief Patriarch

Nestorius. His principal opponent was the fiery Patriarch Cyril of Alexandria.

Political turmoil was matched by the rampaging of Huns from the wide-open spaces of Asia attracted by the riches of the settled world. It was more than matched by confusion in faith, especially the concept of Christ as man versus Christ as God. That 431 Council of Church Fathers had still not solved the problem. 'The devil, full of envy and wickedness, unable to bear the sight of the Church sailing on with favourable winds, stirred up plans of evil counsel, eager to sink the vessel steered by the Creator and Lord of the universe,' wrote the anxious Patriarch Theodoretus. Was Christ man? Or was he God?

'What does it matter?' sighed Simeon, addressing his favourite visitor who was one of the few visitors allowed up the pillar when he was on his way home from Ephesus. If a man believes with love and compassion towards his fellow men, what need of definition? Patriarch Theodoretus, was based in Cirrhus, a city that claimed to be one of the earliest to convert to Christianity but was also a long-established centre for all sorts of beliefs: Zoroastrian, Manichaean, Judaic, as well as many versions of Christianity. No wonder the Patriarch tried his best to be harmonies to all.

How did these men get around? On foot (surely too slow), horseback or donkey (dependent on well-organised changes of mount), or by galley. Messages carried by a series of horsemen. Or a succession of couriers on foot braving warring tribes. Or pigeon (quickest of all). Or the stormy sea. Dearly beloved Theodoretus, traipsing from his see of Cyrrhus at the north-east end of the eastern empire, had chosen boat then ten bumpy horse days from Antioch to Telnessin where he now slept, in the little hut built for old Bassos. Worn to the ravelling by his travels from a Council of some five hundred bishops at Chalcedon just opposite Constantinople. Luckily Telnessin was in his domain.

Meanwhile the Huns of the grassy plains were threatening the walls of Constantinople as well as the north end east of the Syrian plain, keeping people on the move. Along that Road of course: who knows what comfort might be found at the feet of the crazy man of God on his pillar.

That morning the pillar hero has risen to standing. Simeon's stiff days – should go up and down more. Waves his arms round and round, hugs himself tightly for warmth, bloody minded, on one leg, oblivious of the crowds, the brightening dawn, the hoopoe on his head. A bulbul sang on the railing. But the hoopoe flew off, irritated by a new disturbance, a new creature on the platform. He urinates over the railing on to Jacob's vegetables. An Arab woman was approaching the enclosure with a bucket of water. She waved to Simeon.

Then 'Move, man, move!' Someone was shouting at him from the ladder.

Why should he? Who is that shouting? Trouble was, bird shit got in the way. Who cares? Neither me nor the Lord God Almighty. It was everywhere. 'Bloody mess.' The holy one cast an eye on the new arrival. Hideous creature – must be a savage.

The dwarf was indeed not much to look at, not the best of nature's products: deformed, wart-covered, mane of hair scraped into bunch at the back. Shaggy chin. Clothes in tatters. Short bowed legs, enormous hump on back. Waddling. Miracle it had even got up the ladder. Who'd let him up? Where by the Holy Virgin ('mother of God?' – who cares) was Jacob? 'Jacob!'

'You won't get much joy out of that man.' The hunchback was perching precariously on the railing. 'Likes my brew too much. I know a drunken snore when I hears it.' He was already climbing over the railing. 'Don't think you're rid of me in a pig sty,' and the creature vanished the way he'd come. 'I am Zerco!' the creature announced as he headed down the ladder.

Simeon lowered a leg and pondered. Another dawn breaking, hillside stirring. Sun in the east – he turned his face to it, blessed sun, warmth even in the first ray to stir the blood. It'd be hot later on. A crow landed from scavenging on the hillside, scraping its beak on the railing. It went on and on – something sticky on its beak. Simeon watched it, envious of its agility. Oh God, he was stiff. Slowly he began his prostrations, interrupted by bladder, pissed a meagre stream over side, couldn't see old Jacob's patch these days, tried to stand up but head spun. There we go. He got himself upright. Scratched his balls, removed a tick or two. The crow watched, its head tilted with disdain. Simeon spat in its direction, looked for water but the jug was empty. Curse Jacob, and he leaned over the edge to haul up new supply. There was that creature, down the ladder, filling the jar on the rope at the bottom. 'Not too full!' he croaked, as loud as he could, and began hauling on the rope. Then he saw Zerco the newcomer on the ladder again, the vat on his back. He'd no right coming up like this. Simeon tried shaking the ladder, the usual way to discourage any intruder who got that far. But he didn't have a lot of strength today, and in no time at all the savage face was grinning up at him and the wretched deformed body was heaving the vat over the railing. Poured a cup and drank it, re-filled it and passed it to Simeon.

'Me first after the trouble I've gone ter. Drink up.' He'd tied a bundle of twigs and some rags to his belt. 'I'm going to give this place a scrub. They call yer holy down there. Holy! They've no idea the state ye live in. Yuck!' The holy one wasn't used to protest – he'd forgotten how after twenty years above it all. He was in a stupor. Shrank into a corner, muttered a prayer.

The dwarf doused the platform, scrubbed away. Crows watched, several of them on the railing now the sun was up. Pigeons too, waiting for a message. They'd never seen anything like it. Dirt of ages, bird shit, old hair, cabbage stalk; you wouldn't think the holy one's lifestyle would leave much in the way of muck but twenty years more or less was quite a span. He had to scrub hard, dirt ingrained in the stone. Eventually he was satisfied, the sodden platform gleaming in the sun, getting hotter by the minute.

The hillside had woken up. There was the usual babble, din even, a few voices raised in song. There was still no sign of Jacob but a posse of half-naked self-appointed guardians were at the gate, noisily blocking it to intruders. Simeon rested his head in his hands. They'd leave soon; roasting summer was coming in. Dimly he saw the Arabians taking their animals up the hill.

'Your turn now.' The dwarf had hold of his arm. 'Time for a scrub.' His loin cloth was wrenched off, water poured over him. He was being skinned. No part spared. The creature's fingers preyed round his crutch. 'By all the gods I've ever known, you're lucky not to be crawling. Eggs everywhere! Ah that's got ye' – and he held up a squashed louse. 'Bloody lice eating into your body. No wonder they tell tales about miraculous ulcers. This isn't holiness. Didn't your mum teach you to keep clean?' More water. Simeon spluttered. 'Now sit,' and the dwarf put a heavy hand on his shoulder. 'Let's have a go at those nails' – the dwarf had pulled a knife out of his belt, grabbed one of Simeon's feet and rested it in his lap. 'Worse than a goat kept on grass. This'll be a job.' And he began sawing. The occasional visitor who was prepared to risk the climb reported that his finger nails were long and his toe nails curved right under to enter the ball of his feet. 'No wonder you stand on one leg.' Simeon winced as the dwarf worked, grunting. Ouch! Then the other foot. 'Let's have your fingers.' Simeon handed them over, limp as the rags he'd been washed with. 'Bit better. You've been biting them. Ye should try the toes too.'

'All very well for you.' Simeon was coming alive. 'You're closer to your toes. By all the gods!' The dwarf was having a tough time with the thumb. Stop calling on all these gods of yours. For Christ's sake.' He was getting nettled; his blood was circulating.

'Ouch! Aren't you a Christian?'

The dwarf looked up. 'Christian? Bloody hell. I tell ye, I've been everything in my time.'

'In your time!' Simeon looked his assailant over. 'Fickle, are you? That's no way to salvation. Who are you?'

'Let's get some o' that 'air off ye first.' The visitor stood up, shuffled behind the holy one and grabbed the thin grey congealed locks straggling down his back. 'Then we'll talk gods.' He pulled a knife from his belt. 'Snip. Yuck. Full o' bird shit. You should tell those crows to offload somewhere else.' The hairdresser waved a handful of hair at the crow on the railing. It took no notice. 'God, it's crawling.' He threw a handful over the railing. 'I'll need more water. Don't think I'm letting you off – I ain't,' the last heavily emphasised as the dwarf wiped his hands on the skirt of his tunic and squatted again in front of Simeon.

'Who am I?' he asked, thrusting his face against Simeon's. 'I am Zerco, devoted slave of best, best beloved Bleda,' he shouted, rocking his heavy head from side to side. 'Bleda, brother of Attila, murdered, oh God, murdered by Attila.' And huge tears wound their way down the dwarf's furrowed cheeks. 'I loved him, holy one,' he sobbed. 'Lord and master, how I loved you.'

'Who is this man, Attila, who killed your master, Bleda?' Simeon asked after another scrub. He'd heard the name only the day before when a bunch of unfortunates had arrived from the north, moaning about their misfortunes at Attila's hands, hoping to find consolation courtesy of Simeon.

The hunchback scowled. "Who is Attila?" this man asks. By the Holy Mother, virgin or no, how can a man not know? How? By sitting on a pillar for half a lifetime. Ignorant of virgins, no doubt, as well as Attila the Hun.' Zerco dropped his heavy head in disgust. Simeon let him be. After a moment Zerco fumbled in a pouch hanging off his belt and held up between his fingers a blood-red jewel set in a gold ring. He stood and pushed it in front of Simeon's face.

'See this, holy one? It comes from two thousand, three thousand miles away, a distance only the warriors ride. My master Bleda wore it, as he and Attila rode across the ice-cold plains of Asia, faster than any Roman horseman, faster as the wind itself. I took it from his finger as the blood spurted from his throat, as his life was borne away. On the bitter winds of the Hungarian plain.' The dwarf waved a hand towards the town below. 'Some down there can tell you about Attila, how he ravaged their women, cut the throats of their children, spilled the blood of their cattle, torched their homes. That's why they're here, for God's sake, looking to you for comfort. And he slaughtered my beloved master. Bleda.' And the dwarf yelled an anguished howl, arousing the crowd below.

Simeon took the jewel. The stone gleamed at him like an evil eye. The gold setting was carved with strange dragons; he felt their hot breath on the palm of his hand, the movement between his legs of the horse that was carrying him over mountain, across plain, he who had never ridden a horse but still yearned for that life of movement that he had forsworn. He thrust the jewel back to Zerco with utter revulsion, terrified of the impulses it imparted. 'Why do you stay?' he demanded.

The hunchback tipped his head back to release a thunderous groan. Then he heaved himself over the railing on to the ladder. 'God alone knows, old man. But I love you.'

Sometimes Simeon can't see for staring so long at the sun. Zerco becomes his eyes. The sun glares down, gathering strength as it moves past the summer solstice: the man on the pillar stares back, sightless. Oh God I am forsaken, help me for I am lost. Hot black world. Oh Christ where am I? (Must pray, pray, pray, to the Lord, pray for my eyes). Don't move. Head for heights? Sure when you can see the height. Oh God let it pass for I'm dead with this blindness. Should I rejoice to be dead? Surely yes, to be reunited with the Lord. Yet how to rejoice when I leave so many blind below? Give me my sight, Zerco!

It's stupid to stare at the sun but it confounds those (like the heathen Zerco when he first came) who said the sun was god, a god to make their blasphemy worse. I'll defy the pagans, I will stare at the sun. But my eyes are sore and I'm blind, the world is hot as midday and black as midnight.

I don't want to fall. Oh God this giddiness.

He shares the giddiness with Jacob; they have much in common.

The column is fenced off from the crowd by the stockade. Jacob and now also Zerco guard the entrance. No one may enter the enclosure without their permission and never any woman. He can't stand women. 'Demons, demons!' he shrieks if any come too close. You've heard how he treated his mother? He is attached to the world by a ladder, a basket on a rope, bread, lentils and water. Not an attractive figure though better than he was thanks to Zerco. Even the hairy ascetics in the crowd are cleaner than Simeon, though they try to ape his dirt while Zerco tries to curb it. More animal than human. Especially bad after Lent; despite Zerco's efforts a rank smell of excrement pervades the platform on top of the column now that summer approached. He'd been too weak to relieve himself over the edge. Thank God for the spring clean that Zerco insisted on for Pentecost. That platform needs a good scrub – bird shit everywhere despite Zerco's efforts. Jacob's garden thrives thanks to the dwarf, with a good crop of onions, lettuces, radishes.

Simeon's day was punctuated by prayer, meditation and lofty but nearly inaudible addresses to the crowd. Sometimes he sings but he's too weak to blow the horn. On special occasions Zerco blows it for him.

The days, the weeks, the months pass by. Crowds come and go depending on all sorts of things. The Huns for one thing, forcing refugees on to that Road that led for some to seek security at Simeon's feet. Spring storms, summer torpor, autumn gales, winter snow, keep most people at home, though not the perennially itinerant merchants, military men, nomads – they're always passing by, maintaining the economy of Telnessin (as well as the wider empire, don't forget), keeping Jacob alert at the enclosure. And the displaced, the refugees – never without some of them: invaded, unhoused, brutalised, defeated. Pilgrims come of course – pilgrimage is all the rage. To Simeon, north-east to Edessa, above all via Simeon to Jerusalem and Jerome, especially the women, following in the footsteps of the mother, Empress Helena, of the great Constantine, he who exalted Christianity as the empire's true religion. And unfortunately, the dreadful hand of orthodoxy, following that exaltation; its representatives try (and fail) to persuade Simeon not to exalt himself up on that pillar. And their victims, they also pass by, seeking consolation.

Down the hill, in the multiplying dwellings and hostels of Telnessin, visitors question Sergius, corpulent, old, owner of the best hotel. His son Bacchus is in charge now so that Sergius can rest on his cushions and entertain the clients. The clients are a different class of pilgrim from those camped on the hills: state and ecclesiastical officials oscillating from one imperial corner to another along the highways of imperial order, an order bruised but not bowed by barbarian assaults. They are intrigued by the holy Simeon, some even interested.

Sergius feels duty-bound to advertise Telnessin's principal attraction. 'Whatever hour it may be you'll always find him awake,' he tells them, 'at least his eyes open though they say he has a way of switching off: if you stuck a pin in him he probably wouldn't notice. Not that you'd have much chance to stick pins in him because they'd never let you up. Standing all night, often with his hands above his head. Then it's prostrations – forever down up. Makes me tired to watch.

'Go on up and see him,' Sergius directs his audience. 'Bacchus'll lead the way,' which the young man does, thankful to get away from the repetitious story-telling of old age. He is followed by a crowd in holiday clothes, ridden out from

Aleppo. They puff past tall acanthus, daisies, irises ready to burst. 'Look at the old boy!' At the top Bacchus points to Simeon bending up and down. 'Like a pendulum. We counted up to a thousand once. Keeps the bowels moving too!' The ladies titter as they are supposed to. 'You wouldn't think he'd have much in his bowels living on the starvation diet they send up to him every day.' Bacchus puts an arm round the waist of a comely Antiochene wench. 'Feeding time at the zoo we call it, quite a quaint ceremony if you wait around. But you watch, regular as clockwork he moves to the edge of that platform, squats and out it comes on to that little veg patch you can see below.'

When they reach the enclosure stiff old Jacob drops in a story. 'You've probably heard how when he went up he chained himself to the railing you see round the edge of the platform to stop himself falling off. Anyway, the venerable Patriarch of Antioch, Patriarch Meletius, told him, "No need of chains, Simeon. You trained your mind to the chain of doctrine. Get the blacksmith to undo it." Holy Simeon refused at first but later relented. Up went Joseph blacksmith, knocked off the fetter, then had to undo the leather gauntlet protecting his shin from the iron. And lo! the leather had been protecting two dozen huge BUGS! Holy Simeon knew they were there and could easily have killed them but for his extreme respect for God's creatures.'

Patriarch Theodoretus arrived from Ephesus, a long journey by road, by boat, by land again. He laboured up the hill. With Zerco's help, Jacob steadied the ladder against the pillar. 'I'll take a carrot if I may,' and Jacob pulled one up. Theodoretus slowly climbed the ladder painfully, clambered with difficulty over the railing. He kicked a space free of seed shells and squatted down. Simeon watched him unmoving; Theodoretus took Simeon's hand as if to control his own emotions, tears were in his eyes. 'I was seen as one of his supporters,' he wept. Simeon wrapped the Patriarch's hands in his own, bent his head and kissed them.

Theodoretus handed half the carrot to Simeon. 'It's all a question once again of defining the Ineffable God. The transcendent God's been around forever in these parts, even those noisy Arabians you get on with so well. You can see that in the way men flock even to you.'

Simeon offered the fronds to the hoopoe who tossed them away in disgust. 'They don't much care about who's or why's or wherefores.'

'I wouldn't be sure. Men need intercessors. Christ was both God and intercessor, God and man. But I blame it all on the Greeks. They'll argue the legs off a donkey and in language no one understands.'

‘Keep it simple, I always say. All I can do is show them the path to the Lord, one in three, three in one. Who cares anyway? Not these people’ and he waved an arm vaguely over the hill.

‘Easier said than done, holy one. That’s why I’m in trouble. The Patriarch Nestorius was even more so. But then word came that he had died unconsoled in the Egyptian desert. His books were once more burned in the streets of Constantinople.

At Ephesus the Emperor was persuaded to dismiss Patriarch Nestorius from Constantinople. The fierce Patriarch of Alexandria, Cyril, had the old man packed off by boat to Egypt and the desert.’ The Emperor may have envied Simeon his pillar given the political and religious squabbles that still beset him. ‘Give me Huns any day,’ he complained to his wife, the saintly Greek Eudocia, finding himself walled in by church and state advisers, most of them failing to meet his own high standards of rectitude. Meanwhile Huns were outside his walls. Thank God he’d had the time to build them; these theologians were within.

But there was Simeon, a man commanding the respect of thousands and free of that sin of quarrelsome pedantry, which so infected the clergy. Simple faith, thought the emperor, wilting beneath the trappings of office (Oh for a mere loin cloth.) and the bitter blasts of contention in the patriarchal hierarchies. What an immobile contrast to the heroic athletes of the faith, hurrying from one council to the next. 'Come to Constantinople,' he ordered. Simeon refused. 'A monk out of the wilderness is like a fish out of water,' he sent a pigeon back. 'These divisions are the work of the devil. Beware, most high majesty; humble thyself in the eyes of the world. Bring peace!'

With so much unrest on the imperial borders there was little point in shuffling luxurious silks, incenses, spices from market to market. So the merchant Sergius had become a full-time host.

The road to Jerusalem was a hazardous journey. In the mid 450s Arabian raids in the south had overwhelmed even the imperial general Ardaburius, finally promoted from his remote Euphrates garrison. 'You can't pin them down,' he complained to Sergius, passing by the hostel, 'they're as bad as Attila.' Fast, elusive horsemen, like Zerco's old friends, the Huns. Many fled before the Arabians to Telnessin. They disregarded the town at the foot of the hill, despite the titillations of the ladies by the hot bread stall, riding straight to the enclosure. They would have forced their way in had it not been blocked by so hideous a creature at the gate that the horses reared up and backed away. The leader of the Arabians tried to scare the creature – hunchbacked, bow-legged, frog-like – by rearing his horse in his face. Whereupon the hunchback stabbed at the horse's genitals and sent the animal and its rider screaming on their backs. 'Turn about!' he screamed at them and with surprising good humour they did, only to return a few days later with their households: wives, children, herds, tents, one of which they presented to Zerco.

In fact Simeon did a far better job of controlling the Arabians than the people of Telnessin or indeed General Ardaburius. Simeon converted them. Vast numbers went away with Simeon's blessing and the Presbyter's baptism, to the consternation of the town and the delight of Simeon and the imperial authorities.

'Hear them when they call, Oh God of righteousness! Hear them when they call. See how they stare up at me, mouths open, shouting their miseries, as if I didn't have enough of my own. They moon and moan, homeless and moneyless. Down up, down up – circulation through prostration. Hear me when I call, Lord!'

Thanks to the protection of the Arabians, the Augusta Eudocia was finally able to make her way to Jerusalem. Surprisingly courteous and careful, they ensured her safety. Unwanted, unloved, she persisted in her goal, ending her days in another cave, not too far from that of the deceased Jerome, but infinitely more comfortable.

Then – terrible day – Simeon fell ill.

With the cooler weather of the autumn equinox, pilgrims came from miles around to light bonfires, dance and sing and revel – old bacchanalian pleasures at the foot of the monument to austerity. They celebrated a successful harvest and threw flowers to the foot of the pillar. Nut sellers, water sellers, fruit sellers – ripe, golden, refreshing apricots for sale! HONEY! The hungry, the thirsty, the greedy reach eagerly for their purses. Simeon couldn't see them from that distance. Many of them were Persians from the Land of Two Rivers on their way to Antioch maybe, even Constantinople. Accord between the two emperors encouraged communication – political and of course commercial. Not faiths of course but freedom at least to recognise differences. The equinox was for all passers-by at Telnessin. Hurrah! Alleluyah! Simeon shouts to the hoopoe on the railing. Alleluyah!

A party of elderly villagers, shepherded by their deacon, shuffled apprehensively up the path from Telnessin, eyes darting from one stranger to another. The harvest is in, they have brought fruits of the earth to give to Simeon and they plan to spend the equinox at the pillar. A woman disguised as a soldier flings herself into the enclosure and throws a fit when turned away by Jacob; too many loonies, he scowls. An old man with a beard sweeping the ground shouts to Simeon to remove the demons who have possessed his young wife, sent her off with another man. 'Not much I can do from up here,' shouts Simeon. 'Find another wife! Make her eat rhubarb! That'll cure her lust!'

This was the equinox after all, a major feast in the old calendar and now sacred to – what did you say? Oh yes, Mary, Mother of God, did you say? Hmm – not too sure but good for a festival. And even people from distant Antioch; a multi-faith lot in that city that can lead to street brawls but not here, not now. They had come a long way and were pleased to find acquaintances, exchange news. 'Have you heard the latest?' Some more disrespectful than others, pushing and shoving, knocking Jacob out of the way with guffaws and titters. Girls ran into the enclosure, joining hands to dance round the pillar, singing sexy songs, until they caught Simeon about to urinate on them. He screamed at them to get out, out, out, OUT! and abashed they skipped back giggling, to picnics laid out by indulgent mothers.

In the occasional lull in the celebrations Simeon could be heard singing loudly on top of the column. 'Sing praises to the Lord!' He had that harp and now plucked it skilfully thanks to instruction from Malek. 'Upon an instrument of ten strings, upon a harp with a solemn sound. For you, Lord, have made me glad.' How they stared up at him, mouths open, shouting their miseries, as if he didn't have enough of his own. They mooned and moaned, homeless and moneyless.

A donkey was coming up the hill led by Bar Abbas, the grumpy mason who didn't want to be bothered with the column but now thought differently. Yesterday he ordered his wife to cook a bean stew; this morning he went off to fetch water from a distant spring (the best around, strictly out of bounds to local flocks). Bar Abbas and his donkey disdain the crowd, push their way through the tents, the rugs, the litter to the enclosure. 'Welcome,' said Jacob; the mason was one of the few privileged to enter the enclosure. Bar Abbas growled back.

Simeon heard the growl, even from his height. 'Blessings, good Bar Abbas,' he shouted down.

The mason shouted back. 'I've brought food. Should satisfy your appetite, holy one.' Jacob grinned at the uncharacteristic respect. Bar Abbas unloaded the donkey, left beans and water at the foot of the pillar and headed back down to the village.

'I'll throw in an onion, brother,' old Jacob called up to Simeon. Zerco uprooted one and added it to the pot which he placed, with the water, in the basket that Simeon had lowered. Simeon pulled it up quite slowly; it was heavy and he was weak. 'Thanks,' he shouted down.

At the end of each day Superior Bassos and Jacob knelt at the foot of the pillar. Bassos was stiff and arthritic these days. They prayed with Simeon. 'Lord now let your servant depart in peace. For my eyes have seen your salvation, which you have prepared before the face of all people.' Bassos prayed with deep feeling. The night sky was peopled by stars: pagan gods ranged on the side of his God, the one God, three in One. Animals penned for the night; families fed. Jacob had lain down in his hut. Bassos, old and weary, retired to the hermitage adjoining Bar Abbas' chapel outside the enclosure; he was too tired to climb up and down the hill every day. He too lay down after sharing Jacob's meal.

The owl had replaced the hoopoe, dropped a mouse at Simeon's feet. Avoiding the still twitching creature, Simeon knelt on his platform, quiet now, listening carefully, to catch laughter on the breeze. Not just laughter of course. 'Lord God Almighty, have mercy on my soul. Lord have mercy. Jesus Christus have mercy. I pray for myself; I'm no intercessor, whatever they may think, Mary mother of God is our intercessor. But there's power in that repetition. Lord God Almighty, have mercy, mercy, mercy, mercy. I can go on for ever. Hear me, O Lord, for till you hear me I know not what to say.' *Listen, Simeon, and soon you'll hear,*

hear the voice of the Lord in the stillness of the night. The bats caught the habit and squeaked it out in the shadow of my shaft. Look how the owl listened, wide awake.

Down in Telnessin in Sergius' smart new lodgings the conversation was more on military matters since the principal guest lying on the cushions was General Ardaburius on his way from guarding the empire's eastern borders against the Persians. He was mightily relieved to have a break from watching out for Persians. A wealthy and stately Spanish widow, on her way to Jerusalem, simpered on his every word. 'So, what news from the north?' asked the garrison commander. 'How is his Majesty the Emperor? Is there war or peace in the north?'

'War, war, and more war.' Sergius was disgruntled. 'My mules ...'

'Power politics, that's all it is,' pronounced the widow, stretched in Persian silk on a sofa. 'Where is the faith of these men? What would the Empress Helena have said? Or the holy Jerome?' Sergius, pouring more wine, was cross; he could sniff a threat to the town's prosperity if these trifling divisions were allowed to fester. 'Couldn't agree more. Why is this mob up there on the hilltop, moping around a holy man on a pillar? It's faith, isn't it? I've great respect for that man up there. He does an excellent job, relieving our anxieties. Mother Mary does the same. Who cares whether or not she's mother of God? Faith and doctrine two quite different things. Give me faith any day, wouldn't you agree, dear lady?' and with a conspiratorial smile he passed the widow a sweetmeat from a pile on the table. She chewed it with evident pleasure. 'Speciality of the house!' he murmured, passing another to Ardaburius.

Patriarch Theodoretus, traipsing from his see at one eastern end of the empire to Antioch at the other end, came again and again to Telnessin, taking refuge from patriarchal crises at the foot of the pillar, scribbling away all day long – history of the church, stories of its saints, legends, miracles, hearsay – tucking copious notes into his saddle bag. The interest, even admiration, was mutual, and Theodoretus was the one person to humble the man on the pillar.

'A simple man of great goodness,' Theodoretus wrote, 'whose goodness irradiated all sorts and conditions of men.' He described Simeon's childhood, his shepherding, his call (hiding the divine word in the deepest furrows of his soul). 'Among those who came to see him, were not only those who live in our region but also the Israelites, and Persians, and Armenians, and men who are further inland than they; and there also came men who inhabit the furthest parts of the west. Spaniards, I say, and Britons, and Gauls. It is unnecessary to speak about Italy, for they say that at Rome he was so celebrated that they set up small images in all the forecourts and parishes to provide protection and security.'

Theodoretus also recorded the latest miracles around the pillar. Among these miracles was the conversion of the Arabians, previously slaves to the darkness of irreligion. Simeon on his pillar, wrote Theodoretus, was like a lamp on a lamp-stand, sending out rays like the sun, in particular to the Arabians. His success with these unenlightened barbarians may have been partly due to their Queen, barren and longing for sons, sending to Simeon, praying that she should become a mother. Lo and behold, she did conceive, gave birth to a son and her husband even accepted the child as his (a miracle in itself, some would say). Upon this achievement the queen set out for Telnessin and since women were not allowed to approach Simeon, she handed the baby boy to a disconcerted Bassos with instructions to carry him up to Simeon for a blessing.

'For it was you,' she declared, 'who drew upon me the rain of divine grace,' a suitable analogy for a queen of the desert.

'I cannot take him up to the holy Simeon myself,' apologised Bassos, suddenly inspired. 'However I will put him in the holy one's food basket.' Which he did, shouting instructions to the man above who did exactly as asked, hauled up the basket, blessed and spat on the infant and lowered him back to the Superior. 'Blessings on you all.'

So then the Arabians flocked in even greater numbers, two to three hundred at a time, smashing images which they had worshipped before they saw Simeon's lamp, giving up their orgies, learning the laws of their new faith from Simeon's tongue. Even, marvelled Theodoretus, renouncing their habit of eating donkeys and camels. The conversion of the Arabians was just one illustration of the value of the man on his column, sending out so great a ray of the knowledge of God as to lighten the minds even of barbarians.

Another miracle – the greatest perhaps – was in persuading the Persians not to invade the Empire. According to Theodoretus the Persians, long-standing rivals of the Romans for control of Mesopotamia – the Land of Two Rivers – were all set for attack. Even the Scythians were ready to join them. But when Simeon heard of their preparations for war from the thousands who had fled from villages in the east, indeed from Sergius whose caravans could not get through, he sent pigeons warning the Persians that the Divine Will was against them, they would be annihilated, their lands overrun. What was more surprising, wrote Theodoretus, was that the Persians listened, took heed, were discouraged and were finally prevented by internal discord, no doubt also the product of Divine Grace.

'Indeed, these matters suffice to show the spiritual contemplation of the holy Simeon's mind. But for how long shall I try to measure the depth of the Atlantic Sea? For just as men cannot measure that, so the things which were done by Simeon each day exceed the telling.

'Above all I admire his endurance. By night and by day Simeon stood so that all could see him and marvel, from time to time bending, kneeling to offer worship to the Lord.' A man counting such obeisances to the Lord reached the figure of twelve hundred when he himself collapsed with the effort of counting. He ate only two or three times a week, nourishing himself on the divine sacraments.

Many of those who came, reported Theodoretus, having seen the true light, required to be baptised.

'There's no water on the hill,' Zerco pointed out. 'Not enough rain last winter.'

'They certainly drenched me. Once I was even turned to ice. Find a new spring.'

Zerco grabbed the bucket.

'He has no idea where to go,' growled Jacob, weeding his plot. 'God go with you,' he added squinting up at the top of the pillar where Simeon could just be glimpsed standing with arms raised to the sky, 'but I daren't leave the enclosure.'

So Zerco went off into the hills with a boy from the village who frisked from rock to rock, restless as a goat. Several hours later, worn out with the search, resting under an ancient olive tree, eyes only half open, he found himself staring at a clump of irises coming into bloom. Transfixed by the beauty of the deep purple-black flowers he suddenly sniffed success: the mud around their rhizomes was damp with seeping moisture. He kicked the snoozing Barnabas to life, told him to memorise the location of the spring and hurried back to Telnessin.

Alleluyah Alleluyah! sang the hillside. Ezra was delighted. 'Did he not say to Nicodemus, "Verily, verily I say unto you, except a man be born of water and of the spirit, he cannot enter the kingdom of God"?'

Simeon's voice crackled across the hill. 'The wind blows where it lists, and we hear the sound thereof; but we cannot tell whence it comes and whither it goes. So is everyone that is born of the spirit.'

'Alleluyah!' shouted Gregory with the crowd.

Jacob washed outside his hut. 'I have known my soul and the body that lies upon it,' he sang, recalling the Manichaeans, 'that they have been enemies since the creation of the world.' Sometimes Simeon's behaviour filled him with the old foreboding. Here was the holy one ordering him to dig the ground, grow vegetables that wept when about to be cut; apricot and olive trees howled when about to be pruned. Jacob had fled one persecution, trudging fearfully over the Syrian desert in the footsteps of cosmopolitan caravans and imperial battalions, only to find another in the dominance of the holy Simeon on the pillar Jacob had helped to build, helped the holy one to climb. He never forgot that vertigo.

He did as he was told but sometimes with a heavy heart that only partly, slowly lightened as he saw his vegetables sprout, watered and soiled by Simeon from above. Painstakingly, before it dried, he scraped the faeces off the pillar. Theodoretus had tried to cheer him, noting the glum face that let him into the enclosure. 'You should read the great Patriarch Augustine,' he told Jacob.

'Can't read,' moped Jacob.

'The holy Augustine has some good advice. When all is said and done, he told his congregation over in North Africa, is there any more marvellous sight, any occasion when human reason is nearer to some sort of converse with the nature of things, than the sowing of seeds, the planting of cuttings. It's as though you can see the vital force in each root and bud.'

Jacob shrugged, only a little encouraged.

'Augustine too was a follower of Mani once,' Theodoretus tried to reassure him again, 'until he saw the Light; you too shall see that Light. Let us find Bassos and I will give you your first lesson.'

But that day there was no sign of Bassos. Bassos was dying. Theodoretus found him lying on a couch in the room beside Bar Abbas' chapel. From there he could just hear Simeon chanting consolations to the crowd. Presbyter Ezra was trying to feed him sips of sugary water but the old man pushed him away. 'I turn to the Lord,' he whispered. 'I've no need of other substance. Read to me, Ezra.' Ezra could hardly hear; he bent right over the bed. 'What the holy Paul told the Corinthians.'

'Not yet, father,' Ezra protested, holding Bassos' hand tightly. 'O Lord save your servant who puts his trust in you.'

'Send him help from your holy place –'

'– And ever more mightily defend him.'

Darkness came, the hill slept. Zerco trudged up the ladder with a report on Bassos for Simeon.

'I'm coming down,' said Simeon eventually.

Zerco: 'You won't be able to.'

'I can, with your help.'

'Oh Lord, save your servant,' sighed the dwarf as the ladder began to shake under Simeon's weight, slight as it was. What a descent, almost as bad as the original ascent. In the midst of life, we are in death. The descending Simeon trod on his hand. That cleared his head and he scrambled rapidly down, offering a hand to Simeon as he touched the ground. The man staggered against him. 'You'll have to carry me', and Zerco felt all of Simeon's weight against him. 'I can't walk,' Simeon moaned. He climbed on the dwarf's back and they left the enclosure, sensing the snoring world, and made their way to the chapel.

'I am here, holy father,' said Simeon, hobbling into the little room on painful feet; he knelt beside Bassos.

'Bless you too,' whispered Bassos putting a wasted hand on Simeon's head. Simeon wept and asked for forgiveness. 'I forgive you,' whispered Bassos, 'for the sin of arrogance,' and a faint smile passed his lips. He stirred slightly. 'Now is the time for the holy Paul's letter to the Corinthians.' His voice rattled slightly, a sort of laugh. 'O death where is your sting?'

'Oh death, where is your sting? O grave, where is your victory?' Simeon was whispering too. 'The sting of death is sin, and the strength of sin is the law. But thanks be to God, who gives us the victory through our Lord Jesus Christ.' The two men spoke in unison, Bassos' voice getting fainter. His hand slipped from Simeon's head. Simeon went on alone. 'Man that is born of woman has but a short time to live, and is full of misery. He comes up and is cut down, like a flower, he flees as it were a shadow.' His tears fell on his old friend.

There was no sound from Bassos; softly, quietly, he had become that shadow.

Ezra whispered: 'Remember the holy Paul who taught us not to weep, not to be sorry, as men without hope, for them that sleep in the Lord.' But Simeon did weep, as did the others; they were bereft.

'Give him rest with the devout and the just,' they prayed next day beside Bassos' grave, 'in the place of the pasture of rest and of refreshment, of waters in the paradise of delight, whence grief and pain and sighing have fled away.' But Simeon, with Jacob's help, had already climbed back up the pillar. No one saw him passing by in the night.

And no chains for Bassos now. Was it the Prophet Job who said: 'I cast away clothes, I threw away food, I discarded family and friends. I spat out lust and thirst and hunger. God filled the void.' As the stars filled the sky, so God indeed filled Simeon's void. As he very slowly climbed the ladder once again.

That year also, 450, The Emperor Theodosius fell off his horse and died a few days later. He was succeeded by Marcian, the soldierly husband of Theodosius' bossy elder sister, Pulcheria, who was vowed to virginity. At least Marcian was able to keep imperial enemies at bay – Persians in the east, Huns all over the place. The Road was crowded. So was Simeon's hill.

11.

INTERLUDE

In the old city in 1990 I sat with Muhammad Mazrui in the family khan. We talked about the Iranian revolution, the Iran-Iraq war and now the latest horror of that Iraqi villain Saddam Husain, his invasion of Kuwait. And the death of that family defender of the faith – the young Said Mazrui, shot dead by Islamic thugs before the eyes of his uncle.

There were very few sacks or crates or general clutter around. 'See for yourself,' he replied when I cautiously asked about the state of the market. He was sitting on a small pile of bales and drew on his *nargileh*. 'A lot has happened since you were last here. Most people hardly dare to come into the *Madinah* these days. No sellers, no buyers. And now the invasion of Kuwait. And no doubt you saw in Damascus the Iranians who come to pray at the head of the great Shia martyr Husain killed at the battle of Kerbela in 680 in southern Iraq. They'll certainly be there at the feet of your saint. Not too many Shia in Aleppo but I dare say you'll find them at the feet of your favourite.'

I wondered what life had been like for members of the English Levant Company which had set up in Aleppo in 1608. The Company had been established in 1586 to secure trading privileges in the Ottoman world, including in due course Aleppo. In that warren of Aleppo's old city was an intoxicating mixture of Turks, Syrians, Greeks, Armenians. In a 'healthy' year, hazards included bubonic plague and the horrible disfiguring 'Aleppo boil,' superbly studied by a Scottish doctor (and merchant) Alexander Russell in the 18th century. Lockdown is now familiar to much of the world; not much fun anywhere and certainly not in Aleppo. But what compensations these foreigners enjoyed when released: fabulous New Year festivities, cricket, duck shooting and the most superb banquets. And of course, the latest delicacy – coffee! Brought direct from Yemen.

Next morning, with that foreign community on my mind, I took myself to the citadel, figuratively to call on the Ottoman Sultan's representative. I crossed the great causeway to the entrance, flanked by two dragons and in due course came to the heart of the building, the magnificent reception hall commissioned by Sultan Suleyman, known appropriately as the Magnificent by Europeans after comparing his lifestyle with that of their own rulers. This would be where foreign merchants – Venetians the first but soon also

French and British – might have been received by whoever was representing the Sultan in Aleppo at the time.

What did they think of the Jinn as they tramped along what became known as the Silk Road, riding between the Mediterranean and the celebrated market place of Aleppo? Almost certainly passed by Qalaat Simaan to or from the coast, though the main port on the Mediterranean was now Alexandretta (later renamed Iskenderun) rather than Antioch, admiring ruins of the superb basilica, perhaps even pausing to discuss the holy Simeon with earlier generations of the Mazrui family. Maybe even having drunk from the same well that had refreshed me at Tel Aqibrin from time to time.

And hunting expeditions out of town – why not to the remains of that pillar beside the great east-west Road whither I now headed myself. Off to Simeon.

A bus was parked at the foot of his hill and a few cars; seeking reassurance no doubt. The driver also parked there and to my surprise set off up the hill. 'We need these holy men,' he shouted over his shoulder. Then I spotted a much older-looking Ibrahim Mazrui squatting beside the proscenium arch, a large bag beside him. 'Welcome! Welcome, sit Sara,' he called. 'Come,' and he led me up a side path, the bag on his back.

He took me round the side of the hill first. We came to the cave under the western arm of the basilica; a large family was camping inside. 'Looks almost comfortable,' I commented. 'The best refuge around, it's always full these days,' Ibrahim nodded. 'My family and Maryam's often used it in the past. I hope not again.' And he handed over the bag. 'They're Kurds from beyond the river. Maryam has cooked some food for them.'

A crowd was clustered round the remnant of the pillar itself. Men as well as women were weeping loudly and one woman seemed to be tearing her many shawls to ribbons. 'Iranian Shia Muslims – refugees maybe – mourning the loss of relatives in the war,' Ibrahim muttered. 'Horrible fighting in Iraq. Why should we Syrians be involved?' Was the wispy old goat watching from behind a column? Ibrahim greeted some of the visitors, one family group in particular he clearly knew well judging by the hugging and hand shaking that went on. 'I know them from Aleppo,' he told me. 'I give them milk and meat – they had a goat three days ago,' and he pointed to the head of the gift. 'They have lost sons in the fighting. Like Said, our great loss.' They insisted we join them, at least for tea. We settled down amongst the spread of monastic ruins on the east side of the basilica; I leaned back against the warm remains of a wall. Monastic life had clearly had great appeal in pre-Islamic times, indeed for some while thereafter. And a much-used camp site for invaders and invaded since. And maybe parties of European merchants, loaded with merchandise from east or west. I was brought a tiny cup of ultra strong coffee and recalled the craze for the drink when it reached London.

Where was the Jinn that day? I thought I glimpsed him, squatting on the ruined southern arcade and I even fancied a wave. He wasn't usually embarrassed by the crowd but maybe there were too many children.

I dreamt that night of the English merchants in Aleppo writing about their experiences – trade, plague, much as I was doing. At dawn, when I felt Maryam rise to pray, I also rose and picked my way through the apricot orchard, past the shabby tents of the visitors, the gawdy blankets of the Kurds, the pots and pans of the Palestinians, to perch beside the oldest looking tree to remind me of later passing Europeans chasing along my Road after a quick route to or from India, post Napoleon's invasion of Egypt. In the early 1800s a British general battling against the French in India complained that he had no idea what was going on in Europe; news only arrived after three months at sea. How to get the news there and back faster, was the mood of the moment in the early years of the British occupation of parts of India.

And in the early 1830s an ambitious and dogged army officer, Francis Chesney, came up with the idea of launching steam boats on the Euphrates and thus halving the time taken by the mail to travel between Britain and India.

I suddenly sensed the Jinn had joined me. He was wrapped in an old blanket (*'Present from the people of the desert,'* he whispered, *'left it by the pillar. Knew I'd find a use for it.'* Ah! I pulled a little book out of my pocket. 'Come,' I beckoned to the Jinn. 'Something for you to listen to.' Surprisingly he did as I asked, and settled at my feet.

Chesney offloaded his little steamers at Seleucia, ancient port of Antioch, and headed for the upper Euphrates omitting Qalaat Simaan and the pillar. But other foreigners met the Jinn and surely reported on him. And that inspired a long and mournful poem by the English poet, Alfred Tennyson, who had never been near Qalaat Simaan but thought he understood the Jinn.

In 1833 Tennyson was a most unhappy young man; his father had died a year earlier and Alfred was obliged to leave a moderately successful life in Cambridge and return to his deceased father's Lincolnshire rectory. In the summer of that year, he invited his much-adored friend and inspiration Arthur Hallam to join the family. In the course of that blissful season Hallam became engaged to Tennyson's sister Emily. That autumn, however, came the terrible news that Hallam had died in Vienna of a cerebral haemorrhage. Tennyson's poem Simeon Stylites was written that same year. His imaginings of Simeon's moods – as he saw it – must reflect his own anguish. I began reading. It's an interminable poem; I knew the Jinn wouldn't tolerate all of it.

Although I be the basest of mankind,
From scalp to sole one slough and crust of sin,
(rubbish – I wasn't that bad)
Unfit for earth, unfit for heaven, scarce meet
For troops of devils, mad with blasphemy
I will not cease to grasp the hope I hold
Of saintdom, and to clamour, mourn and sob
Battering the gates of heaven with
storms of prayer,
Have mercy, Lord, and take away my sin.

Let this avail, just, dreadful, mighty God,
This not be all in vain, that thrice ten years,
Thrice multiplied by superhuman pangs,
In hungers and in thirsts, fevers and cold,
In coughs, aches, stitches,
ulcerous throes and cramps,
A sign betwixt the meadow and the cloud,
[*hmm NOT THAT BAD*]
Patient on this tall pillar I have borne

Rain, wind, frost, heat, hail, damp,
and sleet, and snow;
And I had hoped that ere this period closed
Thou wouldst have caught me up into thy rest,
Denying not these weather-beaten limbs
The meed of saints, the white robe and the palm.

O take the meaning, Lord: I do not breathe,
Not whisper, any murmur of complaint.
Pain heaped ten-hundred-fold to this, were still
Less burthen, by ten-hundred-fold, to bear,
Than were those lead-like tons of sin that crushed
My spirit flat before thee. (*that's so*)

O Lord, Lord,
Thou knowest I bore this better at the first,
For I was strong and hale of body then;
And though my teeth, which
now are dropped away,
Would chatter with the cold, and all my beard
Was tagged with icy fringes in the moon,
I drowned the whoopings of the owl with sound
Of pious hymns and psalms,
[*they all liked that & joined in*]

Suddenly I felt the Jinn scramble to his feet. *'That's enough!'* I sensed him shout. *'Load of rubbish! He's no idea what he's talking about. Shut that book! He's never sat on a pillar – no idea what it's like. No wonder his boyfriend died.'*

So that I scarce can hear the people hum
About the column's base, and almost blind,
And scarce can recognize the fields I know;
And both my thighs are rotted with the dew;
Yet cease I not to clamour and to cry,
While my stiff spine can hold my weary head,
Till all my limbs drop piecemeal from the stone,
Have mercy, mercy: take away my sin.

O Jesus, if thou wilt not save my soul,
Who may be saved? who is it may be saved?
Who may be made a saint, if I fail here?
Show me the man hath suffered more than I.
For did not all thy martyrs die one death?
For either they were stoned, or crucified,
Or burned in fire, or boiled in oil, or sawn
In twain beneath the ribs; but I die here
Today, and whole years long, a life of death.
Bear witness, if I could have found a way
(And heedfully I sifted all my thought)
More slowly-painful to subdue this home
Of sin, my flesh, which I despise and hate,
I had not stinted practice, O my God.

[IT WASN'T THAT BAD! I ALWAYS HAVE FRIENDS TO LOOK AFTER ME]

The Jinn was shouting: *'Not that bad!'* he yelled. *'Ye heavens. I wouldn't have stayed if it had been that bad!'* Now the Jinn was wispier than ever but in full voice. *'That countryman of yours! He should have taken the trouble to see for himself – enough of his countrymen trekked past with their spices and silks. And guns too!'* I felt him put an arm round my shoulder.

'He was an unhappy man,' I tried to sympathise with Tennyson. 'You at least had your hoopoe to moan to when you felt miserable.' I cast an eye up the hill where a crowd encircled the remains of his pillar. 'Look at them,' I pointed out. 'Howling their hearts out – just like poor Alfred.'

Ah, this is *middle* east – where anything might happen including a crazy man on a pillar for thirty years or thereabouts. And here is Syria, forced into a wider world now penetrating this 'fertile crescent'. Along 'my' Road that ran past Qalaat Simaan, home of my friend, European incursions became more intrusive, more aggressive as the century wore on. One wonders if Tennyson ever considered how his Simeon would have surveyed the world of this later 'middle east'. I heard him shout up the hill. *'Got it all wrong!!! All wrong!'*

I'm not so sure and decided to continue with more of Tennyson's gloom:

> Then, that I might be more alone with thee,
> Three years I lived upon a pillar, high

Six cubits, and three years on one of twelve;
And twice three years I crouched on one that rose
Twenty by measure; last of all, I grew
Twice ten long weary weary years to this,
That numbers forty cubits from the soil...
A flash of light. Is that the angel there
That holds a crown? Come, blessed brother, come.
I know thy glittering face. I waited long;
My brows are ready. What! deny it now?
Nay, draw, draw, draw nigh. So I clutch it. Christ!
'Tis gone: 'tis here again; the crown! the crown!
So now 'tis fitted on and grows to me,
And from it melt the dews of Paradise,
Sweet! sweet! spikenard, and balm,
and frankincense.
Ah! let me not be fooled, sweet saints: I trust
That I am whole, and clean, and meet for Heaven.

I prophesy that I shall die tonight,
A quarter before twelve. But thou, O Lord,
Aid all this foolish people; let them take
Example, pattern: lead them to thy light.

I imagined those European traders tramping between east and west like so many before, pausing to calculate the ancient height of the pillar. But the Jinn waited a little while longer before he was led to that light.

12.

REGIME CHANGE

The 450s.

A year after that divisive Council of Robbers at Ephesus, the Emperor Marcian was urged by his virginal wife Pulcheria to organise another Council, at Chalcedon this time, nearer the capital, near enough for his powerful wife to bang a few heads together. Over five hundred bishops came, though not Theodoretus, still confined to his see in northern Syria, too old and ill to move even if he had been allowed to do so. Now it was the Pope's turn to dictate the truth, to define an acceptable Divinity. Christ, said Pope Leo, was perfect God and perfect Man, of the same substance as us, as a man, as God in his Godhead. The permanent distinction of the two natures in – that was the operative word – the incarnate Lord. Clear?

At least Telnessin was part of Theodoretus' see. 'It's a mess,' Simeon shouted to him from his pillar, despatching another pigeon. (Maybe to Jerusalem? Or Antioch? Aleppo – he sent them all over the place.) 'Don't pay any attention. Worship the One God, the Lord God, thank God for his

Son, his sacrifice, find your consolation in that divine Love.'

The daily routine began. Unlike Jacob, Zerco had a good head for heights, climbing most days to sweep the platform, to bathe the holy Simeon's sore eyes. He had acquired a small tent from the Arabians which he erected beside the enclosure. Inside it was stifling and stank of the skins of the creatures he hunted on the hillside: rabbits, rats, hedgehogs. As for the enclosure Zerco loathed intruders, bitter against their avarice for his master's saintliness (which he only dimly and gradually grasped). The hunchback had always been single-minded in his devotion, now pandering to Simeon as he had once to the beloved Bleda, whose slave he had once been.

The pillar hero was standing as usual, bloody minded, on one leg, oblivious of the crowds, the brightening dawn, the hoopoe on his head. A bulbul sang on the railing. The hoopoe flew off, irritated by the disturbance, the dwarf on his platform.

Theodoretus, much loved Patriarch of Cyrrhus, famous for his wisdom and generosity, a much travelled man, felt sadly abused. He was a man who went through life with a raised eyebrow, neither censorious nor sceptical, perhaps too accommodating to the foibles of his fellow men even when such foibles were to his detriment. As a friend of Nestorius, though not in total agreement with Nestorius' resolute humanisation of the Virgin Mary, he too was punished.

In winter came frost and snow. Simeon's Arab friends had packed up their tents and gone home, not before putting a heavy sheepskin in Simeon's basket. The villagers were keeping their animals indoors. The water froze in Simeon's jar and in the baptismal cistern. No baptisms in winter. He doubled his prostrations, flung his arms open to the Lord, prayed for the fire of the Lord to descend. Some nights he curled up beneath the sheepskin, smelling the lamb of God. And sometimes the owls covered him with their wings, blanketing him from the winter.

A messenger from the Council of Chalcedon galloped by Telnessin bringing news of his punishment to Theodoretus. 'I'm on the way to Cyrrhus,' he shouted up. Simeon had been standing on one leg – that Mesopotamian madness – but now lost his balance. 'What?' His voice was loud and clear.

'Confine the Patriarch to his see,' said the messenger sitting on the step.

'Patriarch Theodoretus? Who thinks he can do that?'

'That Council of Patriarchs – in Chalcedon.'

'They've no right! The holy Patriarch is nearer to God than any of them.'

'Ah, but nearer to what God?' The messenger spoke with trepidation.

'What does it matter? If a man believes with love and compassion towards his fellow men, what need does he have of definition?' A waste of time.

'But a man must know what he believes,' protested the messenger. He spat out a stone from a basin of beans Jacob had passed him. 'This is a time of great confusion.' He looked around the hillside, barely visible in the night: camp fires dwindling, voices fading.

Jacob sighed. 'Why do you think this mob is here on this hilltop, moping round an old man on a pillar? All argument and ritual. These people have had enough of warfare. We pray for the one-ness of the divine world, its unity.' There was a pause. 'Watch out, friend below!' And the messenger was just in time to jump out of the way of a trickle of urine from above. Simeon cackled in the darkness. 'That's how Jacob keeps me fed. He plants the seeds, I water them. By the by, get him to send me a pigeon on your way out.'

'These divisions are the work of the devil,' the deacon wrote for him and ensured it was mailed via the pigeon to Emperor Marcian. 'Beware, most high majesty; humble yourself in the eyes of the world. Bring peace!' Innocuous stuff but people liked to think he was in touch with the world.

Patriarch Theodoretus laboured up the hill. 'You wouldn't believe it, brother Simeon. You'd never believe the gossip in the guest houses. As if we didn't have enemies enough without God's Church being torn apart by wolves. Can I come up, holy one?' he finally asked.

'If it will help,' said Simeon.

So Theodoretus began his spell of confinement. Luckily Telnessin was in his patriarchate; he could continue his account of the saints. 'Consider how the Lord God has thought up such antics for the benefit of the slothful. Isaiah was ordered to walk naked; Jeremiah was told to tie up his genitals, others to wear wooden or iron collars. Why, Hosea was ordered to take a prostitute as a wife. Did you know all this?' he called up to the creature above him. 'The novelty of the sight of the holy Simeon should be sufficient proof of belief – surely why these crowds come here.'

'I shall sit on the shoulders of the Lord,' sang the creature on the pillar. 'He shall bear me aloft, a witness to his might. One stone for the Father, one for the Son, one for the Holy Ghost, three stones in one pillar, one pillar in three stones – most marvellous and equal trinity!'

Simeon sang to the stars, to the angels of the Lord. 'O wind that cools and desiccates, air that feeds and suffocates, sun that warms and burns, frost that revives and bites, rain that cleanses and drowns, blessed are the elements of heaven, the many hands of the Lord that caress and chastise me day and night.

'Lord have mercy. Mercy, mercy, mercy. "I show you sorrow and the ending of sorrow" Will they never listen? Can they understand? Listen to them, listen to their woes as they come to the column, sighing and groaning for all they're worth, yes, even as I sighed and groaned. My mother came among them: I sent her away on your instructions, Lord. You're a hard task master. I wept and wept the night of her death. If I were still down amidst all that sorrow, soaked in those tears, I would doubt your love myself. Brawls break out in the night; someone treads on someone else's face. I hate the squabbling. I no longer know women, scarlet, brazen, seeking my unwary body and soul.

'Have mercy, Lord, have mercy, mercy, mercy.

'Only my friends of the desert behave as if they were free.

But are they free? Ha!'

Word came that the Patriarch Nestorius had indeed died, alone and unconsoled in the desert. His books were once more burned in the streets of Constantinople.

There were upheavals in palace as well as church. Not only were there Huns on the Empire's northern borders and Arabians in the south, much much worse were the quarrels in the Emperor's palace, in the private quarters of his own house, where his virginal wife, Pulcheria, sister of Theodosius, scrapped with his widow, Eudocia.

This masterful lady had selected Theodosius' successor, the sturdy soldier Marcian, and married him despite longstanding vows of virginity (which most maintained she never broke). She now despatched her rival, her widowed sister-in-law Eudocia from palace to pilgrimage. 'How about Jerusalem?' she murmured during a palace banquet. The messenger galloped in with the news just as darkness was falling. Theodoretus, resting at the foot of the pillar, read the message.

A couple of months later the Augusta Eudocia was on her way to Jerusalem. 'A pilgrimage to holy Jerusalem. City of God, dear sister,' ordered the Empress Pulcheria and the bereaved ex-Empress took the hint. 'You can drop in on my brother's favourite saint on your way,' mocked the new Empress.

By storm-tossed boat to Seleucia, Eudocia reached Antioch, thin from her voyage, homesick for Constantinople. Eudocia felt she could do with some consolation among the good lady Faustina (she who several years earlier had fondled Simeon). Faustina and her cronies rose magnificently to the occasion; they massaged her in the city's baths, fed her on Antioch's renowned sweetmeats, soothed her with music, and also provided worthy fathers of the church to stimulate her appetite for philosophy. This was a great city, famous for its schools and universities, its shrines and its churches. Its wrangling. Notorious, some would say, for its heretics. A passionate pagan heritage, which the Athenian-educated Eudocia was keen to investigate. The governor, a modest poet and philosopher, lent her a villa on the slopes of Mount Silpius, its gardens overlooking Antioch sparkling in the spring sun, while escorting her on daily outings to the city sights: the Great Church, countless other churches, palaces, even temples.

With her entourage she rode out to Daphne, paid homage to the nymph among the laurels and cypresses shading the celebrated cascades, visited the temple of Apollo, ruined by devout Christians, its walls and pillars festooned with funereal trails of ivy. Nymphs enticed them into temples and brought them plates of delicacies: grilled goose livers and sea urchins, pickled dormice, snails fed on milk so fat they split their shells, figs and dates cooked in honey. On cushions they sipped the sweet white wine of the region. With like-minded friends she discussed the waywardness of the bishops, the new Emperor Marcian in Constantinople. 'I have no objection to my husband Theodosius' successor,' she said, lying beneath a silken canopy beside the cascade. 'The Emperor is a worthy soldier who served my husband well. But oh dear, such manners! Uncouth. Illiterate. You should hear him pray!' Young men, philosophers from the schools of Antioch, nodded in serious sympathy, they deplored incivility, the inharmonious conspiracies of courtly life. Here, where they lay on their cushions and mused on the meaning of life, the harmonies of nature, here by the nymph-haunted woods and cascades of Daphne, here man could not fail to be civilised.

Eudocia set off for Telnessin with Faustina and friends. It was early summer. 'A marvellous time to visit the holy Simeon,' they declared, 'especially wondrous since he will have been resurrected from Lent. There'll be lots of people; we shall have great fun.' Feasts were commandeered, slaves sent ahead to prepare the camps on the way and ensure that Eudocia should be spared all discomfort. 'Let's leave that to the holy Simeon,' they laughed. 'Thank goodness for Sergius' hotel.'

Each night the procession paused at the gates of the many monasteries along the road where the Augusta Eudocia requested lullabying psalms from the monks as she took shelter with them. One night she found lodgings in the Telada monastery which Simeon had entered as a boy. Lepers thronged the tiny courtyard, scrabbling over food with fingerless hands. A blind man stroked her cloak as she walked past. 'Careful, careful, my lady,' her squeamish chamberlain protested. That evening she sat in the room of the ancient abbot, dutifully sipping herb tea. 'The Arabs bring this to me every year,' his hand shaking as he drank. 'They gather it in the desert and tell me it will ease the aches and pains. I tell them there is only one way to ease aches and pains and that is to pass on to the next life, to unity with the One True God.' Insects flew into the flickering light of the oil lamp, consumed with a morbid splutter.

'The holy Simeon sits on his pillar at a difficult time for the faith,' he sternly told Eudocia. 'A great force for unity, though not easy to live with. The holy Theodoretus and I have discussed this often.' He pointed an arthritic finger at the lamp. 'Look,' he said. 'As my lamp attracts all the moths of Syria, so the holy Simeon draws the faithful to his column and reassures them.'

'I hope they don't frizzle in his shadow,' said Eudocia with an amused tone. 'Self immolation?'

'Indeed no.' The abbot was shocked, death too much on his mind.

'And the Patriarch?'

'A case of mutual admiration. The holy Simeon, the holy Theodoretus.'

Antioch to Telnessin was many miles. Spring festooned the hillsides, pilgrims festooned the road, many of them in a celebratory mood, so much so it was sometimes all they could do to force their procession through. Some in a holiday mood with music, singing. Some travelled in groups, other singly, among the latter a scattering of dirty, ill-kempt ascetics in ash-smeared nakedness.

Eudocia closed the curtains of her litter in passing such brazen sanctity. Occasionally she directed her physician, Isaac the Jew, to tend to some wretched specimen by the roadside. 'Don't drop too far behind,' she warned, 'I may need you at any moment myself.'

Most pilgrims walked, some rode, a few were carried in cramped litters, bounced for days on the shoulders of porters who competed for giving the roughest ride. Not the Augusta. Thanks to the governor of Antioch, her sumptuous litter was smoothly carried by his slaves (pilgrimage yes, parsimony no). Make way, make way, yelled the attendants as they pushed a way through the crowds.

At Telnessin, despite warnings from Faustina, she insisted on being carried up to the enclosure, demanding entrance from its guardians who turned their backs on Zerco's instructions, muttering loudly against disgusting displays of material extravagance. Zerco himself was in a foul mood, lips pulled back in a leonine grin that spewed bad breath. He and Jacob barred the way. 'Go back where you belong,' Zerco spat at the newcomers. 'Where alas is that?' wept Eudocia. Simeon saw them and, halting his prostrations, reminded her hoarsely that it was easier for that camel to pass through the eye of the needle than for a rich Empress or flabby eunuch to enter either the enclosure or the kingdom of heaven. Women! O Lord, preserve us.

'I insist on being allowed in,' she addressed herself to Jacob with a tear on her cheek. 'I am the Empress. No women inside your enclosure, did you say? No women? Is the holy Simeon so scared of us?'

'The Lord God shall root out all deceitful lips, and the tongue that speaks proud things,' Simeon called down to her. 'The Empire is nothing to me. Look inward, to yourselves, not outward, fearfully, to empires. Oh woman, get out of my sight, take your wiles and whinnying with you!' Suddenly seeing one of the Augusta's African eunuchs climbing with great difficulty over the wall, 'Jacob!' he shouted, 'get that capon out!'

Her chamberlain, a resplendent castrated gentleman, murmured consolation in her ear while Faustina hustled her to Sergius' hostelry. Simeon croaked after them to renounce their licentious ways, jewels, slaves, castrati, and ordered them to get on the road to Jerusalem as fast as their legs could carry them. And use your own legs, harridans! His audience enjoyed it greatly, reducing these high and mighty rulers to their level; dirty ascetic upbraiding golden empress. Even Eudocia felt edified by the vitriol, stinging her eyes to tears like a raw onion.

The merchant-turned-host Sergius made his hostelry the most sumptuous on the pilgrim route. Old Bar Abbas had grown rich on its construction. Pretence to austerity had been banished. Slaves lounged outside the great wooden gates, waiting for a summons. You entered through the gates into a wide courtyard shaded by fruit trees laden with blossom. A small fountain sent cooling ripples across the surface of a pool into which a peacock drooped its tail. Sergius, forewarned by Faustina, portly and rheumatic and leaning on the arm of a slave, emerged from a shady cloister. 'Welcome, welcome, Augusta!' Eudocia felt courage and strength swell her bosom.

'Kind friend' – Eudocia was effusive with relief – 'your dear wife told me I should find a haven here.'

'Haven from hell, haven from war, whatever haven you may need, mighty Augusta! Our task is to console. Too much unhappiness around these days. Sergius, madam, Sergius Vacillus from the city of Antioch. And my son, madam' – beckoning to a younger man hovering – 'Bacchus, madam.'

It was a practiced routine that had served them well in the past.

'Bacchus?'

'Sergius and Bacchus, madam, two notable martyrs, madam. My father, honoured be his name, gave me the name of Sergius, a noble Roman name. While I, mindful of two most honoured Syrian martyrs who died together in pagan times, named my son Bacchus. Every spring we pay our respects to our namesakes in the great city of Resafa, on the way to the great river Euphrates. Not so easy in these turbulent days. Thus we came to hear of the holy Simeon. The Lord be praised for such witnesses to his holiness. But welcome, welcome and enter!' And the old gentleman ushered the Augusta from the courtyard into a salon filled with enticing cushions, windows along one wall open not only to the breeze but also to a view up the hill to the old ascetic on his pillar.

'Yes, ma'am,' repeated the merchant when he as well as the Augusta had subsided. 'Sergius and Bacchus, martyred well over a hundred years ago, martyred for refusing to sacrifice to Jupiter.'

'Really?' said Eudocia, sceptical of such motivation. 'I feel it hardly matters these days to whom one sacrifices, after my wretched friend

Nestorius was sent into exile for upholding the One True God. "God a baby?" he used to say, quite rightly in my opinion. Now we are told to worship three gods in one. I despair.'

'Sergius was deeply shocked. 'My lady!'

'In Athens, where I come from' – she spoke with a certain haughtiness – 'we were even-handed in our worship. The pagan gods sometimes respond to pleas, sometimes punish for transgressions. So does God the father, son and holy ghost. I suspect my philosophical friends in Antioch would also have some thoughts on the matter. After all, my friend, you've had problems enough sorting out the nature of God. I gave my support to your countryman, the Patriarch Nestorius, though it did him little good.'

'Blessings on you, good lady!' Sergius was obsequious. He turned to the small group.

'I'm no saint myself,' he held forth to the assembled company, 'a conversion of convenience, you might say. But I know a good opportunity. Take note. This is where the future lies. Don't fret about Jerusalem. Or Rome. Or Constantinople. Even those uncouth Arabians the holy Simeon seems so keen on. Everything will be all right in the end. With faith like this around' – he waved an arm out of the window – 'there's nothing to fear. Cities come and go. God goes on forever.'

And he laughed jovially. 'Mind you, a lot of

those you see around here have obviously never done a good day's work in their lives.' Not for them the merchant's generosity.

She smiled a little with the handsome young Bacchus. 'Bring wine!' she commanded from her hovering chamberlain. 'Wine for Sergius and Bacchus! I do hope you make the most of your name, young Bacchus.' Simpering beneath the cowl of widow and pilgrim.

'Of course I do!' He took the flask from the chamberlain and filled her glass. 'There are few places better than Antioch in which to be named Bacchus.'

The younger man had taken a tray of sherbet from the slave and was bending over the Augusta. 'Thank you, thank you,' she smiled most graciously.

'A most useful son, a fine merchant, best bargainer in the market place.' Bacchus scowled at his old father.

'Don't scowl, useful Bacchus.' The Augusta was relaxing; she could tease. 'So Bacchus, Syrian pilgrim, merchant of the wider world.' She beckoned. 'I don't suppose you mind too much about the nature of God?'

He sat back on his heels and laughed. 'Why should I care? My concern is for the business. And of course your comfort, Augusta. I'll leave the nature of God to those who know best.'

That night and for several thereafter Bacchus consoled the Augusta, strengthening her for the journey to Jerusalem, ending her days in another cave, not too far from that of the deceased Jerome, but infinitely more comfortable.

Meanwhile Attila the Hun, having been turned from the gates of Rome by a brave Pope Leo (who may have found the Hunnish foe easier to deal with than warring churchmen), was found dead, in mid-coitus with his new wife, Ildica. The Romans were not the only ones to breathe a sigh of relief when they heard of the vast burial given to the Huns' leader – such a sigh that they never bothered even to discover where that burial took place.

Then – terrible day – Simeon fell ill

You cannot keep standing still for nine, ten hours a day, sometimes more (despite prostrations) without discovering from time to time that on the whole man is incapable of such fortitude. Simeon's system of prostrations kept his circulation going remarkably well and his body adapted to its regime in the same way that other animals adjust to unfamiliar environments. The danger came at equinoxes, when the weather changes, giving his body little time to adjust especially given the rigours of the Lenten starvation that always left him semi-conscious on his platform. He developed an ulcer on his leg.

The despair at Telnessin was terrible, so many dependent on Simeon's proximity to the Almighty, so many travelling so far to benefit by it, now finding their go-between stricken. Jacob (no longer in his first youth, any more than Simeon) struggled giddily up the ladder with daily poultices which the holy Simeon ignored. He grew weaker and weaker, finally ordered Jacob to stay on the ground. 'You'll know when I'm better.'

In my leg I see a hole, Lord, golden like that sun, searing as the sun, glowing with Life! Marvel at that shin of mine, Lord, that it should contain such a hole. Rich, teeming with life that winds, twines, slimes in and out of the bone, sinuous bodies of sin. Look – one falls out, twists and crawls to the edge. Gone! – that should be me. If I stare at that hole too much it'll close up and I'll lose my glimpse of paradise. I sink into that paradise now – down, down, never again up. Oh how soft it is, enchanting as a woman's temptations. No. NO! No, Lord, I take it back, I'm sitting up. I'll stand if you like. I'll not lie back again. My eyes are on the hole – close it up, I say, before I dream again of hell. Close to the end of the day. The night over my eyes is shifting but it's only dusk they see in its place.

With relief Jacob and Zerco let him be: the smell from the ulcer had become overpowering. No food, no drink. No movement from the platform, though they could see he was lying down, his ulcerous leg stretched out in the sun. A terrible time for him though there were blessings for others. An Arabian chief for instance found a worm from the suppurating wound fallen on the ground; he picked it up and placed it on his blind eye and it was instantly cured – a precious stone with a precious light.

Distraught messages came from the capital. The ailing Theodoretus sent a pigeon with a prayer. The Patriarch in Antioch sent a representative. Funereal vultures anticipating his demise, muttered Jacob.

But Simeon recovered. One morning, as the anxious crowds were struggling out of sleep and into the harsh light of another day, someone suddenly noticed the basket descending and the small figure on the pillar standing upright in conversation with the Almighty. Those nearest could even hear his voice. 'Blessed, blessed, blessed day!' they cried.

Slowly he rose and began again. Down up, down up. Or up down – I muddle – I'm too old. That's what old Theodoretus muttered last time he came up. Halfway between heaven and earth, half alive, half dead. And look at them all, pouring in from miles away to squat around me, nourishing their woes, weeping and wailing, weighed down with self-pity, determined I can make things easier for them. The Emperor as well. At least he doesn't come here himself. I can't do anything about their problems myself; all I can do is show them how to help themselves – show them the path.

But my torch is getting dim.

So also was Theodoretus'. His light in this world finally extinguished in the year 457, to the great sadness of all those living within his see of Cyrrhus, to all those who had known him in Telnessin, above all to the man on the pillar to whom he had brought guidance and consolation for many, many years.

'For we needs must die,' Simeon sang softly, almost to himself, 'and are as water spilt on the ground, which cannot be gathered up again; neither does God respect any person.'

13.

INTERLUDE

Tennyson shocked me with his thoughts on Simeon, written in 1833 as if he actually had been to see the pillar and its occupant, but in fact written by a poet who had never been anywhere near Syria, let alone the Middle East, or even left the shores of his country. The poem revived the pillar and its occupant as symbolic of Syria's position in the *middle* east, often referred to in the mid-nineteenth century as the *near* east. Poor Syria. Poor Simeon.

Some seventy years after Tennyson wrote his poem, Simeon received a fresh horde of unfortunates. They were Armenians from what had once been the medieval kingdom of Armenia, an offshoot of Greater Armenia in far north-east Anatolia. This new medieval kingdom gave them access to the Mediterranean world, as well as to Syria and the Land of Two Rivers. They flourished on those Cilician shores where Simeon himself had briefly paddled on his way to Jerusalem. They built castles and palaces and welcomed the Frankish crusaders, who had struggled across the Taurus mountains to head for Jerusalem, and helped them on their crusading enterprises. But by the fifteenth century, Cilician Armenia was increasingly threatened by the Ottoman Turks and by the sixteenth century, it had been absorbed into the Ottoman Empire.

In the second half of the nineteenth century, relations between Christian Armenians and the Ottoman regime became increasingly unbearable. Turkish authorities began to dragoon Armenians to labour on an ambitious railway planned to link Constantinople primarily with Mecca and then also with Baghdad, one day to be named the Baghdad Railway. A section of the track ran through the Taurus Mountains, which rose above Simeon's village and whose tribal inhabitants had often threatened the Armenians. Churches were scorched, as were Armenian businesses.

There were already strong commercial links with the Armenian colony in Aleppo. 'Let us head to them and join their commercial world,' muttered community leaders. Slowly gathering portable possessions together, finding the mules and camels to carry them, the Cilician Armenians set off for Aleppo, mostly unfamiliar with the trials and tribulations of the journey ahead. Reaching Antioch, they were taken in and replenished by the considerable Armenian community there, warned about the problems that lay ahead and duly headed up the slopes of Mount Silpius, pausing perhaps at the various Christian shrines on the way up. Out into the open they trekked, along the same still-remaining road that Simeon had followed, as had the many armies of the past – Byzantine, Persian, Arab, Frank, Mongol, Turk et al. Villages along the way provided water but little in the way of provisions, and there were no longer monasteries to provide spiritual comfort. Frequently they were harried by Ottoman soldiery.

There must have been several hundred by the time they straggled into the village of Telnessin, now better known as Deir al-Simaan, house of Simeon. The town that had once flourished from Simeon's magnetism had dwindled now to a village. The refugees settled down for the night. Some had been told of the cavern beneath the western basilica and managed to push their way through the jungle of acanthus grasses. A few climbed the hill to see for themselves the wonderful basilica that had been built to shelter the diminished pillar.

'O my God! You should have seen them,' muttered the Jinn as we sat beside the baptistery, *'they were so wretched. Women, children, many of them shoeless, clothes in rags. I've seen many a crowd. They were exhausted when they stopped by. They knew all about my pillar.'*

When I asked him if he recognised visitors as

Armenian, he shrugged. *'No idea,'* he muttered. *'But they celebrated mass in the basilica, alongside my pillar – what was left of it. Put a picture of Mother Mary against it. And one of them hacked off a chip but they scolded him for that. Took good care of my house too.'* He circled the basilica with a ragged arm.

'A sad lot they were – men, women, children – and they stopped here, looking for food and water. I showed some the path to the cavern, and the locals brought a couple of goats and some wood so they could cook the beasts and warm the children. Of course, the children had to try to climb what was left of the pillar – not much then, though more than there is now. Oh yes, that ballad man should have noticed the comfort I gave to the sad and lost of the world.'

Strange to think Simeon himself had tramped along the same road, probably shod to begin with, then shoeless like the Armenians. Sore to begin with, then hardened by fervour.

The Mazloumians also came from Cilicia, reaching Antioch by sea and land, hiring the best horses and vehicles in the city, and also continuing past Simeon, pausing briefly to pay homage in the basilica but anxious to reach Aleppo as quickly as possible. In due course, the Mazloumians opened the celebrated Baron's Hotel. Armand told me how on one occasion they had had some eccentric English scholars staying there.

They had arrived filthy and explained that they had been digging pits in an ancient spot north of Aleppo – Carchemish they called it – at least as old as the oldest corner of Aleppo. No water there to spare for washing. 'My grandfather was a fanatic about washing! They say he almost didn't let them into the hotel. But business is business – you know what we Armenians are like. But those grubby Englishmen nearly drank us out of whisky.'

'Do you remember the names of the unwashed scholars?' I asked.

'One might have been a certain Professor Cottrell, instructor of his companion, the young man who became the famous Mr Lawrence. Mr Lawrence wrote a book about the Frankish castles that included the magnificent Sahyun. We used to have an ancient visitors book,' he muttered, 'but Lord knows where it's got to now. The younger of the two (Mr Lawrence) fought with the Arabs in the war and came back briefly after the war.' T.E. Lawrence, I realised, and probably the learned Leonard Cottrell were that grubby couple.

'*O yea,*' murmured the Jinn after some thought. '*I remember them sitting on the wall over there.*' He pointed to the battered end of the western basilica. '*They sat there for hours, pointing, scratching on the ground, rubbing out whatever it was. They wandered round the back – where the old temple had been – and off up the hill, noses on the ground all the time as if they could smell something. Then up to my pillar and called out for me. Well! I'd been watching them of course but unspotted. Then I decided to make myself known ...'*

They must have been a curious pair. I imagined them staring out over the fields and olive groves and setting sun, talking over the scratchings on the walls and the disturbed dirt.

Armenians were to endure an even greater calamity during World War I. Armand unemotionally told me the story. Relations between the Armenian community and the Ottoman regime had become increasingly difficult. In 1915 the regime became murderous. Village after village in eastern Anatolia was emptied by the Turks of their Armenian inhabitants. Most of the men, women and children were herded south into the Syrian desert. Mostly to their deaths.

'A terrible tragedy,' Armand said. 'We never forgave the Turks. We Armenians did our best to rescue those still alive and bring them back to Aleppo. But things were not easy for Christians in the city at that time. I'm glad to say the French drove the Turks out of the country after the war. Now once again with the present lot you never know what may happen. Look at the slaughter of the cadets. And the ransacking of the *suq*. That's why we adore the Virgin Mary. Just like those two

Englishmen or indeed you, my friend, pondering on such earlier passers-by.'

Δ

At the Treaty of Lausanne in 1923, Turkey regained the old province of Cilicia, once home to many of Aleppo's Armenians. The ancient arterial road between Mediterranean and Orient was thus severed by the new frontier. My precious Roman fragment of it became redundant.

How had Simeon regarded that? I wondered. Surely with dismay.

Then in 1938, the French government handed over the western province to Ataturk's regime. A harsh border was reinforced between the new Turkey republic and Syria, a sad change to that great road between east and west. Now did the Jinn have a bit of peace?

'After the Great War, there were hungry times for many Syrians,' Ibrahim Mazrui said, frowning over supper one evening. Everyone was addicted to fighting, as he put it. 'Even the Jinn would have been deprived of attention – too dangerous to visit him. That's when the town – our town – of Deir al-Simaan became a village – everyone left. So did we. My grandfather's brothers bought a small boat in Lattakia to trade up and down the coast – safer than by land. The family had a house in

Lattakia. Our fields were untilled. The land was devastated, worse than anything before.'

'In Aleppo we survived,' Armand recalled, 'just. Now what, I wonder?'

The Jinn recalled the famine that had prevailed over 'his' world. *'No one brought titbits for me. No children with sweeties in the village. No football. No one even in the cavern. It was as if I was dying again,'* he whispered amongst the tall rustling grasses. *'But plenty of them nowadays who are – no shortage of weeping.'*

Once again, I recalled my Armenian bus driver on that first visit to Simeon – not a very happy Syrian citizen. 'You never know where the next blow will come from,' he had said. I remembered the shadowy figures in the little Armenian church I visited on my return from that first visit to the Jinn. Dark and silent – so sad. In the war, many of the prisoners labouring on the railway line through the Taurus were British, captured by the Turks after their taking of Baghdad in 1915. Many others were Armenian.

'At least we have our own country now,' Armand added.

14.

PENTECOST

A messenger covered with dust and mud, on a horse dripping with sweat, on its last legs – literally – galloped up to the great gate of Aleppo's citadel and banged on the bronze doors. A head peered out of the wicket door. 'Tell the general the people of Telnessin say the old man is sick, maybe to the point of death,' he shouts to the face. 'And bring me some wine – NOW! And water for my horse. Take him with you.' The messenger jumps off and hands the bridle to the face, stretches to relieve the stiffness stealing up his legs and enters the citadel. He urinates in the bowl funnelled into the wall. Slaves attend him. Others run to wake the general.

Ardaburius, commander of the Eastern Imperial Army, former garrison commander on the godforsaken River Euphrates but based now in Aleppo, commended the messenger, conferred briefly on the threshold of the banqueting hall with his principal officers, and despatched a messenger to the city's Patriarch. The worthy father gathered his energy and set out to tour the city. He had no intention of following the crowd to

Telnessin but needed to find his clergy to go with the embalmer and their paraphernalia. Then he despatched a messenger to pass the news via relays to Antioch. The Patriarch there had already laid claim to the old man's cadaver. The city had been devastated the year before by an earthquake and needed a restorative holy body far more than Aleppo. Ardaburius collected his officers, sent them to organise the saddling of horses and slaves to fill barrels from cisterns and lash them to the mules. There would be quite a crowd once the news got about – couldn't trust people to think for themselves. With a small personal guard, he prepared to go ahead.

Pentecost – busiest time of year. Summer in the air. But Telnessin slept uneasily, disturbed by relays of messengers on horseback hurtling between Aleppo and Antioch. Antioch was a long way off, still weeping from the earthquake the year before. But the Patriarch there needed to be alerted to the imminence of death. In Telnessin Sergius' son Bacchus, who ran the town's best hostelry, made sure riders were fed and well-watered and especially well mounted.

Up the hill Simeon from under his blankets watched the grey shape of the dwarf out of the corner of his eye, his pesky broom propped up against the railing ready to sweep the dirt with the same daily dedication as the beggars below that he could no longer see but hear for ever whining for soup. Many were refugees from Antioch's quake.

Let me be, let me be. Zerco now sleeps on top, never listens to my moans, feeds me sodden bread for I have no strength to break it and no teeth to chew. Salt to keep my brain spinning with thoughts of the Lord, water to help me to speak. But I rarely speak. My soul feels stuffed with beans mashed with garlic, lots of garlic. I told the hunchback, you'll soon have no cleaning to do, you'd be out of a job. (He shits a tiny turd on the spot; a crow pecks dismissively at the result).

Jacob and Zerco were explanatory figures in Simeon's existence, both of them refugees from barbarian and religious upheavals. The empire had been repeatedly tossed in the air by internal and external wars, even earthquakes, forming new patterns, like a kaleidoscope given a good shake. Jacob and Zerco who had both tramped the bounds of that world, east and west, endured the tumult. They loved Simeon for his immobility in a time of restlessness, his closeness to the one true God. They too were old.

O God, care for us, care for us!

The two of them co-existed; no great friendliness there. They shared the guarding of the enclosure. They seldom spoke.

Jacob felt his age. Like Simeon he spent most

of the time deep in prayer. In winter he often stayed inside the little hut beside the enclosure gate. Now it was summer and he knelt outside. Faithful, useful. He still saw himself as the principal guardian but more and more he depended on a shifting relay of monks who took it on themselves to vet intruders, turning away the importunate, the harlots, the limbless. He was not averse to occasional blandishments – a pot of honey, basket of apricots, even a sheep – you can imagine the sort of thing. Zerco tried in vain to stop the practice. The self-appointed guardians would have liked to turn away the Arabians but without any success. They were Simeon's favourites.

As soon as there was light enough to see, Zerco was on the move: up at dawn, down the ladder, over the hillside returning with bundles of herbs, berries, the odd rabbit or rat which he would roast in the evening outside Jacob's hut. The aroma floated up to Simeon but he was indifferent, his nose no longer answering to smell, only his heart, faintly, to the companionship. He teased the dwarf for his greed. Marriage of opposites, grunted Zerco, offering a bone to Jacob. 'Your turn will come,' he shouted up to Simeon; 'one day you'll leave that pillar, take to the hills again. I've seen thistle down float as free as you'll do.' Simeon sighed, turned his concentration to stilling the remains of any such desire by standing on one desiccated leg until the sun rises between the dark breasts of the hills.

A hot grey day. Not like Pentecost should be. The Arabians lay listlessly smoking outside their tents. Even the goats were resting in what shade they could find.

Zerco had just climbed up with some scraps for the old man who needed the hunchback to feed him. The hoopoe stared disdainfully from the railing. Zerco scolded Simeon for not eating more; he was fed up with being a slave to birds.

The old man shrugged: Is it much longer, Lord? Soon to leave all this? Unshackled? Over there the Angel of Death is watching, mocking the drooling ancient. I see myself reflected in the mirror of his sword. Does he want the company of an old and toothless monster? Rotten I am, all man's rottenness heaped on me. I am stiff. Down up, down up – it is time to move on.

'Storms in the air,' said old Servius down in the village (now so heavy he can only be carried around by slaves) to a withered Faustina. In the pastures outside the town the Arabians lounged listlessly outside their black tents, their children snoozed in the shade of the apricot trees.

The news of the military mission gradually spread. The young men arrived first – they'd good legs. But soon others arrived, even families on camels. (Is that a box tied to the side of a camel?) A crowd was soon growing round the pillar fence, even some inside the enclosure, to Zerco's horror. The guardian monks stood by helpless. Jacob was sobbing at the foot of the pillar. Zerco clambered down to flap at them ineffectively with his broom, 'Speak to us, Father, that we may live. Speak to us!' Their cries reached even Simeon's ears but he stared down at them not seeing, the dim world of faces hungry as ever for reassurance. Not caring.

How tired he was of their pleas. He spat feebly. Groaning with their burden of misery. They sounded like sick camels.

A grey sky was crushing him; he was sinking into the mass of misery below. You speak to them, Father, not me.

'Water, Father, water! Send us water!' came the cry from parched throats. Simeon looked up at the leaden sky. 'Water, Father, send them water.' The plea hung in the air. Silence. He stared at the sky.

The storm broke quite suddenly. Rain in heavy drops, plopped on his bald head, warm and welcome. It felt good as another followed and ran down his back and another down his nose and life returned a little to his limbs. Oil in the joints – why, he even got to his feet as the sudden downpour engulfed him. Blessings from the Lord God Almighty!

Then he fell, slowly, creakily to his knees, peered over the railing, water pouring down, down the hollows of his face. A crack of thunder sounded over the hill. Calling on all his energy, 'Come back!' he shouts hoarsely. 'You asked for water. Now you have it and you run for shelter!' They stopped, even Zerco, amazed at the force of the voice which he heard so seldom nowadays.

Down below they were braked by Simeon's cry. Sidelong glances at neighbours; storm breaking around them with sharp reality. They knelt.

In the town the general Ardaburius had arrived and was savouring the comforts of Bacchus' hospitality. 'We hear the holy one is near death.'

Bacchus was terrified at the thought. 'Lord knows what will happen when he moves on,' he muttered.

And then Simeon did fall sick.

The village was aghast.

Ardaburius had already despatched messengers to Antioch. For the embalmers. Come quick, quick! 'Just in case,' he muttered to Bacchus. 'They want to have him in Antioch.'

Simeon lay above them all, hardly rising except to drink, maybe for an hour or two hunched over his knees in prayer.

He shrank from human touch. 'You must drink' – Zerco was anxious – 'Only the Lord knows when it's time to die. You've no right to force him.' Insistent.

But Simeon was dying.

As might be expected it was a prolonged affair. You don't live on the margin of this world for so many years without stiffening in limbo as it were, as well as in limb. 'Rigor mortis set in years ago,' moaned Bacchus when he heard of Simeon's state of health. 'He's been dying for the last forty years,' growled Sergius from his cushions. From the windows of the salon, he could just glimpse the pillar through rheumy eyes, waiting for its occupant to move on so that he too could leave. 'It's all very well for those who die but what about those who are left? My clients. My investment.' Bacchus felt he too deserved sympathy. He had just finished a new compound for visitors' animals, another extension would be ready next year

Zerco had never admitted to fear before. He hated the immobility of his master, lying now so prone. At night he hung around the fires of the Arabians, hoping their mobility would give him cheer. Whose rubbish would he sweep up? Precious little on top of the pillar these days; the crows did most of his work for him. But just enough to justify the climb, his own life and breath. No wonder he was scared. He loved Simeon. Simeon was a great tree that was slowly bending over before the winds of death. In a moment the tree would be blown down and its roots torn up, to reveal chaos. He felt about Simeon as he had felt about the death of Bleda when that beloved warrior was slain. A separation in the darkness, the emptiness. Sometimes he whispered to Simeon, 'O Father Simeon take me too', pleading for the first time in his life. When Attila died in mid-copulation the Huns buried him with all his favourite horses. The Lord of the Steppes could continue to ride over the lives and lands of the whole world. 'O Lord of the skies, let us too, ride away together. I shall take you. Away to my plains. On the fastest horse. Let me do the same with this old man – ride away, ride away.'

It made no difference: Zerco had both feet firmly in the world of the living. Simeon was well on the way to the world above. And therefore he, Zerco, not Simeon, walked in the shadow of death. 'I am the man,' said the Son of God, 'in whom whosoever abides, shall not see death.' Zerco could see death, all too clearly.

A faint cackle wheezed between the parched and toothless gums. 'Someone's calling. Can you hear?' Zerco deep in thought did not answer. 'He is calling me to a quiet place.' The old body rolled over to one side and peered down through the railing. '

'Afraid I'll escape?' he cackled feebly. 'So they should be. I shall escape all right from this world of shadows. I dreamed, hunchback, the fight was over, Lord God lowers a rope to me. But I didn't climb up, hunchback, I'm not climbing any rope once I leave this place.' Zerco could hardly hear.

'Know the writings of the evangelist John. The beloved Theodoretus often read them to me. "When you are old" – he sputtered – "another will bind you and take you and will carry you to where you will not want to go." Watch out, old friend, watch out. I do want to go and shall go.'

He sang to the clouds. 'My sins are many and my mistakes as numerous as the waves of the sea. But now I am pardoned.' Simeon had had seasons of difficulty and seasons of great faith; now at last, at the commencement of true life, he had no need to struggle to believe. 'I trust that I am clean and whole for heaven.'

'Still a little afraid of dying,' he admitted to the watchful hoopoe, waiting to lead him to the valley of comprehension as he had once led the mighty Solomon, but not afraid of being united with the Lord. '"For I felt his soul and mine to be one in two bodies," wrote the holy Augustine, "and so looked on life with horror because I did not wish to live as only half myself and so it may well be that I feared death, lest in dying I should bring about the total extinction of that man I loved so much."'

Zerco wept.

The column cast a shadow over the stone houses of Telnessin. It fell in the courtyards, climbed the dry-stone walls, quelled the squabbling hens and sternly forbade discussion among the anxious lanes. Zerco was halfway up the pillar to wash Simeon when he saw in the western distance a cloud of dust turned orange in the evening sun. Even Simeon hated dust storms. So it was a worried Zerco who clambered out round the capital and down the ladder. Simeon was bent in prayer, forehead on the ground. His neck could no longer support his head.

The dust came closer, too concentrated for a dust storm, and became a contingent of horsemen. Zerco assumed they were heading for the frontier. Wrong. They left the main road by the town wall and swung up the hill towards the pillar, as if there wasn't enough commotion there already. He hoped they wouldn't stay long. Simeon seemed oblivious. He lay so lifeless that Zerco attended first to the distraction, only now put his head to the skeletal chest to see if he were indeed quite lifeless. He still breathed. As the hunchback leaned over him, nearly blind eyes focused on him and Simeon grinned.

Zerco could see the commander of the horsemen talking to the deacons at the gate. He could recognise the man's importance by the glint of gold on his garments. He was clearly trying to enter the enclosure, the feeble Jacob trying to fend him off the gate. The pillar seemed in a state of siege. Was this a moment of death? Would that galvanise these people to action? How could he protect Simeon? What lies in store for me, Zerco?

Bacchus had followed the horsemen up the hill, wondering a little at their purpose. Seeing the commander trying to enter the enclosure, and his men standing by to see that he was able to do so, Bacchus hurried to offer hospitality and discourage the entrance. Ardaburius had also come up. 'We shall take his body in state to Antioch,' he announced. 'I summoned them. There is great sorrow in the city; the holy Simeon will give them hope after the quake.'

Bacchus was shocked, 'The holy Simeon yet lives!'

'Long ago the Augustus Marcian commanded me to protect the holy one in his dying hour. Maybe that has come. And afterwards' – Ardaburius lowered his voice sepulchurally – 'it was feared an attempt might be to remove him. There will be great rivalry for his bones ...'

'No! No! He is ours! He stays here!'

Ardaburius looked the innkeeper over. 'Not a welcome subject,' he consoled, frowning at the keening Arabians who smelled death and eyed the soldiers with suspicion and apprehension.

Bacchus was not consoled. 'Protect him by all means. But don't remove the holy one.' He was also worried for his future.

Ardaburius did not press the point, assured the hotelier he need not worry. He wished, he explained, to express the Emperor's concern to the holy Simeon himself. It might give the holy one more strength. 'I was hoping to persuade this faithful fellow to let me past,' pointing to the exhausted Jacob. Bacchus suddenly realised where his loyalties lay. 'They won't let you in. Collect your officers and come to relax.' Reluctantly but also tempted, they followed Bacchus back down into the town.

On top of the column two figures could be seen. Zerco and, slowly sitting upright as the hunchback raised him, Simeon. A sigh, now arose from the crowd.

Rheumy eyes stared at the failing sun, only faintly warming the bloodless rims.

'O all ye works of the Lord, bless the Lord, Sun and moon, showers and dew, mountains and hills. Frost and snow. Night and day. Lightning and clouds. All my days I have praised and magnified you before the eyes of thousands of your children. Hide me now, O Lord, under the shadow of your wings.

'Now, O God, let me depart in peace.'

The hoopoe flew into the gathering dusk.

Δ

Simeon died that night. He was as still in death as in life; only the vultures knew the time had come. They were discouraged by nightfall – a night as crowded by stars as Simeon's hilltop was with pilgrims waiting for him to die. Zerco had spent the night beside him and now covered him with his Arabian rug, before releasing a great howl that aroused Jacob huddled at the foot of the pillar. 'Woe! He is gone!' And slowly the hillside awoke. The canny vulture smelled death, tried to land on Simeon's head but Zerco waved angry arms at it. It flew off, expecting to return later. Jacob emerged from his hut to make his morning obeisance to the Lord, looked up at Simeon, saw Zerco covering him with his blanket, waved to the hunchback who stood up and opened his arms to the heavens. Jacob guessed what had happened, nudged the monk at the gate to let him through and ran across the enclosure and swallowing hard began his ascent of the ladder. The rungs were slippery with dew; Jacob's fear of falling joined hands with fear of death. He tried to hurry, his bare feet siding off the rungs. O Lord have mercy! He put his head over the top of the capital in time to see the vulture on the railing. Zerco waved an arm and it flew off, to be replaced by the hoopoe. That bird was allowed to stay. Jacob knelt beside the man in the blanket and wrapped him in his arms.

But wait! If Simeon is dead for Jacob and Zerco, for a few more precious hours he could live for the crows. Until they decided what to do. They propped the body against the railings. It collapsed; they propped it again. Jacob knelt down opposite and bent his head on his arms, unable to pray. He put his hands over his face and wept oh so bitterly, so hopelessly.

Those who were awake below saw the vulture fly away, saw Simeon against the railings and Zerco's arms around him. So he's still alive, thank God, and they turned away to stoke fires, fetch water, rummage for flour, milk the goats.

Zerco knelt up there till the sun was over the old eastern hills, wrapping the fleshless body in the blanket, whose soul had fled. He and Jacob knelt again by Simeon to pray, then stood to face the world and spread the news. Those nearby understood and shouted to those further away. The gathering emitted such sorrow and deprivation, at first silently but suddenly with a great outburst of sound, spreading the news beyond the enclosure to inform the village, the world. A storm of sorrow broke upon the pillar. Simeon floating above it, watching, amazed. Many dropped to their knees. Some wept for the loss, others for fear. Some for uncertainty – where now? Others because they were released from the bonds of suspense that had knotted up their feelings. And many were infected by weeping in company.

Zerco's own tears came to a halt. Beyond the noise of wailing he heard more vigorous shouts and yells and a few seconds later, trying to detect where a particular noise was coming from, he saw a group of Arabians galloping through the prostate crowd towards the enclosure. Then he saw a crowd of imperial soldiers, led by their general, riding from the other direction. He rushed down the ladder.

Holy Simeon! Ours!

No! Ours!

Stop them!

No! He's ours!

Whose? For heaven's sake, whose? Desert thieves whisking off to unholy wastes? Imperial soldiery bundling him to unholy cities? NEVER!

The two groups reached the enclosure at the same time.

The scimitar-waving. Arabians outnumbered. Women wailed. Children were running everywhere. Howling they started down the hill. 'Don't leave us!' yelled Zerco, who had climbed down from the pillar. The guardian monks cowered by the gate. Zerco was too late to keep it closed. A soldier imperiously pushed him from the gate and began climbing the pillar, then stopped when he was a third of the way up. 'I can't!' he wailed. He swayed. 'Fool!' yelled an officer. 'Get up there! Quick!' The officer came up behind him forcing him up. Together they swayed past the capital, climbed on to the platform. They pushed Jacob aside and gawping now at the figure propped against the railing they both fell on their knees, buried heads in hands.

Zerco popped up over the parapet. 'GET OFF!' he bawled. Terrified soldier and officer understood and scrambled back down the ladder. It swayed under their weight.

Zerco followed them and now came up again with a woollen cloak given to him by the Arabian women.

'It's so heavy,' he protested.

'You must cover him up with this,' they insisted.

Other Arabian women tore at their clothes but no good; their men had headed off. 'You loved him!' yelled Zerco, back at the top, but to little effect.

Now he and Jacob began the task of getting the inert and stiffened body off the railing to wrap him. Inert yes, but brittle with age. An arm snapped at them; fingers got in the way. The midday sun mocked them. They heaved the wrapped body to the head of the ladder. Bag of bones. 'Get it on my shoulder!' Zerco stepped on the top rung and helped Jacob push the bag on to his back. Very very slowly he climbed down, wondering with each step how so starved a body could be so heavy. A huddle of monks guarding the enclosure helped him lower his bundle to the ground.

Then there was Bacchus who had sweated up the hill. So had General Ardaburius. He thanked the soldier for trouncing the Arabians. 'A real menace – up to no good.'

'Not at all, my good man. Such sacrilege. Glad we were here. I knew we were right to come. Now we must get him down – it's a long way to Antioch and I don't want to be waylaid. Let's get that dwarf to help.' He put a reassuring arm round the hotelier's shoulder.

'Of course, of course.' Bacchus quite understood. 'We'll look after the holy Simeon,' he said. 'Don't worry about us.'

'Ah but we shall take the holy father with us.'

Zerco heard. So did Jacob. So did Bacchus. 'We must keep him here. You cannot take him to Antioch. He belongs to Telnessin! To us!' 'Bacchus was deeply shocked.

The general was surprised. 'What right have you to keep him here, in this backwater. Do you really think he belongs to Telnessin? Fools! He is the Empire's. We shall escort his body, well embalmed, first to Antioch, more embalming there, and for the people to say their farewells. Then we shall take him to the imperial city. Constantinople!'

O fools! Fools indeed! To imagine so small a spot on the surface of the world should keep so holy a body to themselves.

Now Ardaburius summoned a platoon of soldiers to take charge of the body. Despite the protestations of Zerco and Jacob and the howling crowds of pilgrims around the enclosure, the soldiery pushed them out of the way and marched into the enclosure. Simeon lay on the ground. He weighed nothing; his spirit had flown. Pushing aside the crowd of weeping, howling mourners they placed him in a cart they had brought up the hill; they pushed the weeping attendants aside, rolled the cart out of the enclosure and carefully descended to the village. Vultures flocked suspiciously overhead.

A fire had been lit in the middle of the town and a group of women embalmers was waiting, their tools on the ground beside them. Crowds of weeping howling mourners were growing, some descending from the hilltop with Simeon. The bearers laid Simeon on the ground and began unwrapping him quickly before rigor mortis set in. 'My God!' a soldier exclaimed. 'He's skin and bones!' 'He stinks!' said another. The crowd gasped, muttered, began to howl, in particular the women waiting for him, jars of ointment beside them. The soldiers laid Simeon beside them for them to unwrap him. Visiting Arabians produced balls of Arabian frankincense and aromas from a sack; the embalmers threw some on the fire and the aroma floated over the town on the breeze. A cauldron was suspended over the fire.

First the massage, the trickiest part because Simeon was so stiff even before death. How the women toiled. Zerco hung over them, passing more ointment from the Arabians for the women to knead those emaciated limbs. They straightened him, easing the bones. Jacob walked away, hid in the monastery nearby.

Once Simeon was straightened out, the embalmers got to work. Disembowelling Simeon was tricky – he was so shrunken. Under the direction of the Presbyter Emmanuel the innards were extracted and carefully wrapped in a cloth and sealed with wax – 'that should last the journey,' Ardaburius muttered to himself. No one noticed old Jacob waylay the young priest with the small bundle of Simeon's innards. 'Let me take care of those,' he pleaded. Willingly but with the token protest, the boy handed the soggy stinking packet to the old man. Jacob shuffled back towards the hill nudging Zerco to follow him. They headed up the slope. At the entrance to the enclosure, for once abandoned by the crowd, 'come – we'll plant these deep down in my veg patch. Simeon stays here.' They dug down and down through the soft well-tilled soil, placed the little bundle way down at the foot of Simeon's throne, replaced the soil and planted a row of onions on top.

'Thus he stays,' Jacob whispered to Zerco. 'Antioch may have his bones.'

'I will follow him,' Zerco whispered back and very slowly descended the hill.

Presbyter Emmanuel was given the honour of throwing some remaining guts on the fire. Visiting monks intoned a burial hymn. The body was laid on a winding sheet and tightly – very tightly (it was a long way to Antioch) – wrapped and roped. He was ready to go. A cart was produced, two donkeys harnessed to it. Two villagers were allowed on to the cart with bunches of herbs to discourage the flies. Other villagers were arriving with bundles of fresh hay, branches of olives, others with pomegranates, others with swatches of lavender. Soldiers on horseback stood guard front and back of the donkey cart. The procession set off on the long journey to Antioch.

How Telnessin howled that evening. Psalms in the church, in monastic yards, in the square around the funeral fire. How they all wept next morning as the catafalque slowly, so slowly moved off. Then the military – ahead, behind, alongside. A trail of village mourners followed.

The procession slowly moved off on the great road to Antioch.

Jacob and Zerco knelt beside his onion bed and prayed to the Jinn to never to leave the spot. He slept beside them through the night. In the morning Zerco climbed the rickety ladder to the top of the pillar and threw Simeon's blanket down to Jacob. 'I'm off,' he said. 'Ever the nomad. Keep the smelly blanket. The Arabians will give you another before they go home. Make sure the old man is warm.' (The Jinn, as he was becoming, nodded appreciatively as Zerco and Jacob embraced.) The gate of the enclosure was open and Zerco the nomad returned to the open road. The horses were tied up for the night at the edge of the town. Looking over them carefully, he slipped a rope over the head of his chosen beast, leapt on to its back and was away, away to rejoin a Hunnish band.

Jacob stood to urinate on his vegetable bed before rummaging in a pocket for some acanthus seeds. He sprinkled them at the foot of the pillar. He had a long road to follow to Cyrrhus and fellow Manichaeans.

'O Simeon, farewell.'

And the many who had served Simeon? Before they too died they tended his soul, whispered to him in the dark corners of the night, heard his cackle as they tended the vegetable patch below the pillar, heard that cackle where thorn bush scraped against stone.

As for Simeon – O Simeon, free as thistle-down, free as wind-blown acanthus, his spirit forever nurtured by those who came and went and came again. *Now O God, you've given me the peace I longed for atop that pillar. Let the world carry on with its troubles. I'll hang around, they will need me.*

But now I'll roam free as the hare on the hillside.

Let me keep my wise hoopoe.

I shall be safe with him.

So the Jinn made his way up to the pillar and with the hoopoe on his shoulder he patted the slumbering Joseph and slowly slowly climbed the ladder to the top.

Δ

In Antioch further tragedy: several years later the remains were taken to Constantinople for the gratification of the Emperor. The citizens sent a special plea to the emperor to be allowed to keep the cadaver as a talisman against the tribulations of the world. But Constantinople said it also needed the talisman. The bones of Simeon left his beloved Syria.

15.

OCTAGON

In the mid-fifth century, the Christian world both east and west was under attack. In addition to the threat of repeated invasions from the Asian plains, already imposing pressure in Simeon's day, there was also dissension in the imperial court in Constantinople. The death of Emperor Theodosius II in 450 was followed by a miserable time of unsettled government in Constantinople, ruled initially by his insistently virginal sister Pulcheria and her 'husband', the stalwart but docile soldier Marcian. Church problems had been settled at the Council of Chalcedon in 451, but barbarian incursions from the north were matched by Persian threats in the east. The eastern challenge fell to the lot of a new emperor – Zeno – in 477.

Zeno came from the Isaurian highlands above the towns and villages that were also Simeon's childhood surroundings. For several years until appointed governor of Antioch, he fought many battles – sometimes for, sometimes against Rome in the East, both in the palace and in the field. It was in the latter that he came across the much-adored Simeon, dead now some fifteen years but still worshipped throughout the province and especially in Antioch where his remains had been buried. Such a 'pilgrimage' was much to the disapproval of the orthodox hierarchy in Constantinople, concerned that argumentative Antioch was disputing that perennial issue: Christ as the son of Mary or the consubstantial son of God, an issue thought to have been resolved at the Councils of Ephesus and yet again at Chalcedon. Antioch was also the argumentative centre for pre-Christian schools of philosophy. Post-Chalcedon, such Christian discord could not be allowed, said the Constantinople Patriarch. It was surely on his authority that Simeon's remains were excavated in Antioch, transferred to the capital and re-interred.

Meanwhile, the pillar continued to attract pilgrims from all corners of the Empire as it had during his lifetime. Warriors. Traders. Bereaved. Inquisitive, Persian, Roman, Arab and Levantine feet trudged along that Road from east and west. Some came to pray, some to gawp, a few to dance at the pillar. Telnessin, at the foot of Simeon's pillar, flourished while scowling at the mess that accompanied the visitors.

So Zeno knew the holy Simeon from his time in Antioch as well as in his new abode in Constantinople.

And on his way along that well-trodden Road to inspect the garrisons guarding the eastern frontier against Persian incursions, the Emperor came to the great pillar, surrounded as ever by visitors, and noted the squalor of the hillside. 'Lord God almighty!' he was said to have called out to the ghost-like Jinn that stood astride the path leading up to the pillar. 'The saint deserves better than this. It's here, not in Constantinople, never in Antioch, that he should be adored.'

The Jinn took his hand. *'I certainly do deserve better and so do my pilgrims. They come, they come! Fall at my pillar. Chip away at the stone. I don't want to wobble when I pray up there.'* As they came to the crest of the hill, before the eyes of the astonished Emperor, the Jinn took a flying leap to the very top of his pillar.

The Emperor gazed up at the wispy figure. 'I will order a memorial to this holiest of men,' he shouted to his attendants who had panted up behind him. 'A basilica! Worthy of the saint!'

'But open to the heavens!' howled the Jinn, opening his arms to the heavens. *'No tomb! Open to the birds My hoopoe!'*

After a night in the much-enlarged hostel in Telnessin, and a chat with old Bacchus, grandson of the original owner, the Emperor continued eastward along that celebrated highway. 'No more chipping away,' he commanded (having the wherewithal to tip a group of nervous guards). 'If they want a chip, it's up to us to stop them. All the generations need the holy Simeon.' He was already contemplating an appropriate dwelling place for the skimpy figure who had addressed him. He also ordered Bacchus in Telnessin to send to Aleppo for an assembly of the finest architects in northern Syria. Reaching the city a few weeks later, he told the assembled craftsmen that he wanted the finest building in all Syria to commemorate the holy Simeon, one where all future generations might meet to revere and beg for the holy Simeon's compassion, his solicitude, his link with the Almighty.

'It must of course be open to the skies. He has insisted.' The architects grimaced among themselves but accepted the dictate.

Basilica-building had long been a skilled and revered profession in Syria, and the assembly represented the cream of the craft. A week later, after much debate, they duly presented the emperor with the outline of the proposed building ('Open of course to the skies,' they reassured him) and a rough estimate of the cost. 'We shall need some gold immediately,' they told him, 'to pay the quarriers.' The Emperor obliged and a team was assembled and despatched to Telnessin.

The complex that they designed commands the northern end of the hilltop. It is much ruined nowadays but until the 21st century, it was still so beautiful, so deserving of the reverence it has commanded across the centuries. I stood in the triple-arched entrance on my first visit in 1970, in awe. That entrance still stood, a magnificent triple archway through which to glimpse the pillar, the base of which was superbly decorated with 'windswept' acanthus leaves. Green-leaved acanthus grew along the path up the hill from the proscenium, stately flowers just emerging among the jagged edges of the leaves. They danced in the breeze so you can understand how the architects got the idea.

The basilica was commissioned by Zeno in 477, nearly twenty years after Simeon's death. The Emperor saw its construction as a gesture of legitimacy. ('See what a good Christian I am.') Hence this magnificent palace of God built for Simeon and all those who came to seek his comfort. His builders did him proud but sadly the Emperor never saw the result of his inspiration: he died in 479, after only three years on the uneasy imperial throne. But the Syrian craftsmen served him well.

A sturdy American antiquarian and admiring recorder of the site, Professor Howard Crosby Butler, observed in 1900 that 'the church was the most important and most beautiful existing monument of architecture of the period in Syria.' It is impossible to disagree. No other church could rival its size nor its splendour. And beauty. Agreed! Agreed! And somehow it survived despite the warfare of Syrian history. Maybe the Jinn was a good guardian.

Until the 21st century.

Despite adventures over the centuries, perhaps chiefly from earthquakes (the builders, familiar with that hazard, ensured the foundations were crucial to the survival of their building) the basilica was stunningly (literally) beautiful. I had admired the foundations' sturdiness on my various visits (good refuges too in its underpinnings). 'Basilica' because of the principal approach up the main southern arm; its wide, single aisle shaped after the form established by the pre-Christian Roman need for a place of secular assembly. Here it had to be wide enough to accommodate a vast crowd of pilgrims.

There were in fact four basilicas, for each point of the compass, centring on a magnificent octagon around the pillar. The octagon was already recognised as the supreme symbol of godliness, used even for the tomb of Emperor Constantine in Antioch. The octagon was also a symbol of security. Here's a big question: Was there ever a roof over the octagon? Of course not. After all Simeon had not needed one. The octagon had to be open to the heavens: how else could the Jinn talk to God? According to Crosby Butler, the three stones of the final pillar were most likely hacked out of the nearby hillside and rolled into place, ready for Simeon's momentous ascent.

The complex was huge. It needed to accommodate the crowds who came to worship even after its instigator had faded to an inspiration, a phantom comforting the distressed of an empire whose authority was challenged from the four points of the compass. The colossal scale and the lavish decoration signalled a desire by the architects to shelter, as demonstratively as possible, not just the congregation but more importantly the saint whose secular advice, to emperors no less, had been as much admired as his holy homilies. There was a suggestion that women were forbidden into the octagon area, as Simeon refused to allow them into the enclosure round his pillar. But my American professor was firmly in favour of their refusing to be spurned. '*Difficult to keep them out.*' I thought the Jinn murmured at my shoulder: '*No Zerco or Jacob.*'

'And they kept him well fed,' I murmured, noting a few onions growing at the foot of the pillar.

And clustering round the eastern arm of the basilica were the monastic buildings to house worthier (and wealthier?) pilgrims. I slept down there once myself when the Mazruis had retreated from the political mayhem of Syrian politics to the more peaceful coast.

The other part of the basilica where I had slept was right under the western arm, in the great cave where I have so often found other 'caretakers' of the basilica above. From the mouth, you gaze out on a prosperous landscape, covered with fields and orchards on my first visit in 1970 but frequently ravaged by invaders over the centuries. And increasingly likely to suffer again.

Syrian politics was about to enter a new phase of mayhem with the death, in June 2000, of President Hafiz al-Assad. A man with a reputation for caution, Hafiz had commissioned his mausoleum before he died; you never can be sure how your descendants will regard you. Such commemorative building was needed for his elder son Basil, who died speeding a car to the airport for a skiing holiday. It was reported that he was driving without a seatbelt at 240 kilometres an hour, hit a barrier, and died instantly. His chauffeur in the backseat was unhurt. His commemorative building is in his home village of Qurdaha. The architect was Japanese, Kenzo Tange.

And what could be more appropriate than basing this funereal design on that great religious symbol – the Octagon; sacred to Islam as to Christianity and, maybe relevant here given the nationality of the architect, to Zen Buddhism. The exterior of the building is white, also symbolic of purity and peace. There might be a few challengers of the relevance of those two symbols to the story of the Assad regime. Inside, the tombs of father and son are within another, inner, octagon. There is space left maybe for the second son, Bashar, now the president of Syria. Black-uniformed guards pace within and without the building.

Hafiz had died in his bed, allegedly in the old complex on top of Mount Kassioun overlooking Damascus. Gutted and perfumed and tightly wrapped in cotton cloths, he was laid in a prepared catafalque, carried to a waiting vehicle and sent on his last journey, accompanied by heavily armed guards. And followed by weeping men on foot or in black cars staggering in low gear. Noisily weeping women followed in the draped cars.

The chosen route to the family village of Qurdaha took them inland rather than along the more Christian coast road, through the towns of Homs and Hama, strongholds of the Muslim Brothers until their suppression by Assad's brother Rifaat. I boarded a service taxi to follow the procession as far as I was allowed. The car was full of weeping women. I passed round a box of tissues. Bypassing Aleppo, the procession joined my great east-west Road ('modernised' by the French in the 1920s during their occupation of Syria after WWI).

There was no perfumed arch over the road in the village of Tel Aqibrin and very few locals came to see him pass. I glimpsed the fragment of that ancient Road that had so often tantalised my imagination. Then Qalaat Simaan, Simeon's castle. And there, in the middle of the road, stood the Jinn, arms outstretched. And there beside him, Ibrahim and Maryam diplomatically bowing as the cortege drove past.

That decided me. Knowing I was unlikely to be allowed into Qurdaha by its Alawi guardians, I abandoned the taxi (leaving tissues with the women) and gently pulled the Jinn to one side. Ibrahim and Maryam took my hands.

We climbed the hill. I knew the ghosts were watching: Zerco, old Bassos, the ever-complaining Jacob. There in the octagon was the battered pillar. The Jinn hailed us from the top of the stump. I knew I was home.

And now?

From 2015, the news from Qalaat Siman was grim – as from elsewhere in Syia since the outbreak of civil war in 2013. The north-west of the country was particularly affected by the war as Bashir al-Assad's Russian-backed forces battled with those of Islamic *jihad.* Aleppo destroyed, Baron's roofless, Armand dying in that haven for so many passers-by. I kept up to date with the fate of QS as much as possible with reports from a well-informed Australian, Ross Burns, but even he couldn't help with the fate of Simeon and the family that had cared for me so often on my visits to the Jinn. He who had watched the prancing armies, their weeping victims, the happy picnickers such as those I met on that very first visit to the pillar and its Lord. And I feared for the family that had watered and sheltered me on so many visits. That has been my story.

With all these tragic upheavals I needed to know what had happened to the Mazruis and to their land, and of course to Simeon. I knew the family had mostly moved down to Lattakia on the coast, now virtually a Russian port – that warm water haven the Russians had sought for 150 years. So I made my way from a battered Beirut along the coast road that has seen so much history, and found the family packed into a tiny villa not far from the port. Maryam wrapped me in an enormous hug, tears pouring down her cheeks. 'Welcome! Welcome, Sitt Sara!'

Lattakia was a refugee camp, divided between Sunni and Shia. Crouched on street corners, holding out hands at traffic lights were the uprooted, the latest of generations of unfortunates turned out of their homes by the swings and roundabouts of history. And by faith. A sense of menace pervaded much of the city, generated by the young men lounging in doorways sharing a smoke – dirty, hungry, unshaven, maybe as Simeon might have looked. That night, a fight broke out below our window. There were shots. Men were racing down the street, pausing to fire at pursuers. Shutters rattled across shop widows. Then sudden silence. Broken by the wailing sirens of ambulances. A posse of soldiers hurtled past in a truck. More silence, maybe an invisible shrug. What else to expect. 'I am so scared for my family,' Maryam whispered. 'Sometimes I hold the little figure that you gave me and read that surah Maryam in the holy Quran.' I remembered the mini Madonna, the much-respected Maryam of the Quran I had given her.

First on his ancient Citroën motorbike and then on foot with their son Mahmud, we made it through hills and woods and nerve-wracking meetings with Shia militia guarding the approaches to the Assad burial spot of Qurdaha, via the great Frank castle of Sahyoun, dossing down in abandoned huts. One evening our route suddenly flattened out and I could smell that we were walking over land that had been scorched. 'Our fields!' Mahmud shouted. I remembered the fields of maize where the children played hide-

and-seek. The apricot orchards heavy with fruit. Now there was no apricot orchard. No apricot slab. No pistachios.

I heard a hoarse whisper from Mahmud as suddenly we crashed over a larger bump before the surface smoothed. 'Your Road!'

My Road – mine indeed. *The* Road tramped by so many thousands through the centuries. Voluntarily to visit Simeon, or on the warpath heading east or west. Even more crucial: where now was that pillar? And its owner?

The little town was seething with the uprooted.

'We go home,' Mahmud shouted in my ear, and then we were outside the steel gate that had so often opened to show me hospitality. Now it was barely hanging off its hinges. 'O my God!' Mahmud had pushed inside and fallen on his knees. Rats squeaked past. A hideous shamble. He gripped my hand. Grass sprouted in the courtyard. 'Tomorrow,' I said, 'we hunt for the Jinn.' We scrounged in the house for food but all had been taken. The house stank. Dogs were howling. Rats ran in and out.

No food – not surprising. We dozed and were up a dawn, making for the road through densely packed tents, vehicles, children, scraggy dogs. All scrounging for food.

I looked up the hill as the rising sun threw a smoky light on the ruins. The proscenium arch was completely overgrown by gigantic acanthus thistles, their spiky leaves still green, mirroring the famous wind-blown acanthus beautifying Simeon's temple. Mahmud suddenly stepped into their prickly jungle. 'This way,' he ordered and I followed. The acanthus jungle grew denser. 'It hides the path,' he said. The acanthus was over my head, certainly a good disguise.

Did I glimpse the old goat man dancing along the tips of the acanthus – was he following us? *Yes you did*, I heard that rasping whisper and looked up to glimpse a wisp, a whisper, indistinguishable from the sound of our sandals on the dry thistles. The Jinn. *Come*, he ordered, *this way*. And we followed. It led us along that well-worn path beneath the great arm of the western basilica. Was that his hand on my shoulder? I seem to think it was – digging into my flesh with his broken nails. *Come*, he ordered, *I am your guide. As always – as I am for all who come for consolation*. The thistle stems wove a prickly pattern round us – I suddenly recalled his chewing on them. We broke through. The vast mouth of the cave below the western basilica opened before us, I caught a whiff of smoke and there was Ibrahim, thinner and greyer, bursting out to welcome us. How we embraced. Tea, tea and 'moon of the gods' – apricot slab. No apricot trees last night but I remembered the many times I had shelled the ripe fruit with Maryam and drunk the sweet juice made from subsequent apricot slab – truly moon of the gods – or leaving a slab of dried apricots at the foot of the pillar. I chewed on what some describe as leather.

We watched the sun set over the burnt-out fields below Simeon's 'castle'. I've so often basked in this landscape of northern Syria: craggy hills, wild irises and roses in spring, orchards of ripe pomegranates and apricots in autumn. The cooing doves at dawn, an unforgettable aroma released from herbs. Now no birds. No people. We talked late into the night. Ibrahim told me how the great basilica had been occupied by soldiers, of which side he knew not. How they had aimed at people sheltering in the monastery ruins, and at the wild cats and dogs who'd chased the refugees away.

The next morning, we climbed up the tiny staircase that led up into the basilica. We gazed at the wreckage. Rocks and stones everywhere. A shattered crucifix was by my feet. Just beyond, an acanthus handsomely carved on a fallen stone. Pushed to one side and even more hacked about, the remains of the pillar, or rather its much-hacked stump. And there on top, arms raised to the heavens, the Jinn, Simeon, scraggy as ever. I hailed him, waved my arms. Happy to smell him. Hallelujah! Hallelujah!

He shouted back: *My mountain, my ruins, where I once lorded it over them all.* (Could I really understand a word he was saying? I seemed to think I did.) *Up there* (he pointed heavenward) *for forty years! Thanks be to God!* He shook his head from side to side. *I know it well, I've had the run of the place long enough. Run? Don't go away, wait a minute, wait.* He turned and seemed to be pleading. *I whisper to visitors: have you come far? They don't hear, they aren't listening yet. Grey-brown like the hills, between the stones. Plants in every cranny; the goats like them, tug them out. Yes, it blends well with God's handiwork, this handiwork of man, where once it attracted attention for miles around. Enemies will flounder. Syria shall survive. I SHALL SURVIVE! Praise be to God on high!*

Are you sure, Simeon? Are you so very sure? O Simeon, O Syria, much wounded Syria, you must survive.

∆

2023 CIVIL WAR. EARTHQUAKE.
Where are you now, Simeon, O Jinn?

ABOUT THE AUTHOR

Sarah Searight lived and worked intermittently in the Middle East for many years, writing about the modern and historical region. Among her non-fiction titles are *The British in the Middle East, Steaming East* and *Lapis Lazuli: a celestial stone. Simeon* is essentially fiction, inspired by events in the region during Simeon's 5th century life but also by events during the 'reign' of Hafiz al-Assad, Syrian president from 1970 to 2000.

ALSO BY SARAH SEARIGHT

The British in the Middle East

New Orleans: the City

Steaming East

(with Jane Taylor) Yemen Land & People

Lapis Lazuli: in pursuit of a celestial stone

Milton Keynes UK
Ingram Content Group UK Ltd.
UKHW040836011024
449095UK00004B/56